Blindsight

Bryan Lawson

A crime mystery in which time, place, and the characters all play a part.

Blindsight is the name given to an extraordinary phenomenon where blind people report seeing things.

About Blindsight   Bryan Lawson

Blindsight takes the reader from the historic city of Chester to the fascinating Dutch town of Delft and the magical island of Bali. Drake discovers that these charming places have a sinister side too.

The Centre for Industrial Design at Deva University in Chester combines creative design with AI. The Centre's Head, Professor Willem Kuiper, a Dutch national, has set up a unit called Blindsight.

There has been a break-in at The Centre. Someone has wrecked all the computers. Simultaneously, Professor Kuiper has mysteriously gone missing. Detective Chief Inspector Drake and his team soon uncover not one but three possible crimes. Are they related or purely coincidental?

BLINDSIGHT is the sixth of Bryan Lawson's Drake and Hepple mysteries series.

Other books by Bryan Lawson
A DEGREE of DEATH, 2017
WITHOUT TRACE, 2019
FATAL PRACTICE, 2019
THE FLAUTIST, 2021
DANGEROUS KNOWLEDGE, 2023

V1   © Bryan Lawson 2024

About BRYAN LAWSON

Bryan Lawson is an architect and psychologist. He studies the relationship between people and place. He has published over 300 books and articles and practised, taught and researched architecture for many years. He was Head of School and Dean of the Faculty of Architectural Studies at Sheffield University. He has worked on every continent except Antarctica. He draws on this experience to write about the places that form locations for his crime mysteries. Pictures of all the locations used in each book are available on his website (www.bryanlawson.org).

Details of all books by Bryan Lawson, together with news of forthcoming publications and a blog, may be found at: -
www.bryanlawson.org

My thanks to Rosie for her invaluable support and help.

Wherever possible, this book uses real locations. To see images of many of these, go to the website www.bryanlawson.org

Select" "novels"
Scroll down to "Blindsight"
Select "locations"

You can see the locations for each chapter. Try not to look at those for chapters not yet read, as this may confuse the plot.

There is no intention to suggest that any of the action in this book has anything to do with these locations in real life. It is a work of fiction.

Prologue

Frank Richards thought it was an ordinary Wednesday morning. He was wrong. This was when it all started. Frank liked to arrive early and get in before the mad rush of demand for his services that was inevitable on most days. The old Head of School, Walt Dickinson, would sometimes beat him to it, but not anymore. Since the "Big Change," Walt might arrive just in time for mid-morning coffee. So, Frank would have to open up. He delved in his trouser pocket for his keys. He looked up at the sign over the door. It was beautifully made with shiny stainless-steel letters on a polished black background. But it annoyed him every morning. It was now called The Centre for Industrial Design. As far as Frank was concerned, it had always been a School, and it still was. In Frank's opinion, too many things at Deva University were changing.

He let out a sigh as he put the key in the lock. It turned and withdrew the bolt with a satisfying clunk. Frank was an engineer at heart. He took pleasure in the way well-made things worked. These new front doors were a delight. They looked and felt substantial. They even sounded robust. They were not only secure but told you so. Frank thought you couldn't have a Centre for Industrial Design with a flimsy-looking pair of doors. You could open one, or you could open both to bring a trolley in. All was satisfactory. The old School never had a proper front door. Frank approved of that change. Given the secret nature of the work they were doing now, extra security was essential.

The front doors gave access to the studios, which were wide open spaces. There was just a waist-high wall separating them from the central walkway. Frank liked the way the architects had arranged everything. It was all simple and logical. He strode down the central walkway. To his left were the studios for first and second-year students. To his right were the degree year and postgraduate studios. The overall design was one of clarity and logic. However, the studios all looked like a complete mess. They always did. Drawings were scattered everywhere, as were half-constructed models. Frank knew that student designers at work almost always meant chaos. He marvelled at how they came up with such beautiful creations. One of the tutors, who he most respected, used a simple little phrase about design that he liked. Simplicity is on the far side of complexity. Frank knew he was not cut out to be a designer. He could not live with the chaotic mess that persisted for so long during the student design process. He was often in awe of their creativity. Secretly, he was fond of his students.

Some of the old-fashioned drawing boards were still around, but these days, every student place has a large screen for their computers. The students would arrive clutching their powerful laptops, plug in a screen and start work. Frank smiled to himself. This was a metaphor for the research for which the Centre had become famous. Computers were everywhere, and it had all happened in Frank's lifetime. The University only had one computer when he started as an apprentice technician. Now, students design everyday products that have more computing power in them.

Behind the studios on both sides, were the staff offices. Students always had easy access to tutors, and both liked that arrangement. Straight ahead was the computer lab and then the workshop. That was Frank's area. It also had a locked door, which was more for safety than security. Some of Frank's beloved power tools could remove the fingers, or worse, of careless students.

It was when he reached the computer lab that it hit him. For a moment, he stood, mouth open in amazement. It looked as if a tornado had swept through. There was broken glass everywhere. Computer screens were on their sides and smashed. The floor was littered with documents and half-smashed models. Then he saw the worst of it. All the expensive design workstations had been battered. Their cases were dented and scratched. It looked for all the world as if a madman had attacked them with a sledgehammer. In a moment of anxiety, he rushed to unlock the room where the main computer disc servers were kept. The door was already open. It was smashed, and the architrave was hanging off the wall. As he feared, the high-capacity computer server discs for the Centre network were in pieces. As Frank knew from setting them up, they had substantial cases. Someone had taken a hefty hammer to them. He tried to do a quick estimate of the cost of replacing them. Mental arithmetic had never been his strong suit. He gave up. It would be an awful lot of money. But how had the perpetrators of all this got in, and why had they done it?

A panic washed over him as he dashed over to his workshop. The door was ajar. Beyond, the outer doors to the delivery dock were wide open. Perhaps they had come in through the ground floor somehow, gone up in the service lift, through his materials store and then had free run of the whole place. His mind was in a whirl of confusion. He opened the doors to all his tool cupboards. His beloved tools were kept hanging on a pegboard screen. They were all exactly where they should be. Except! His heart sank. There was a gap where his heaviest and least used hammer hung. Had they used it to create all this havoc? Thank goodness, all his power tools were still there. The least important thing, he thought. He slumped down onto a nearby stool.

Frank was not given to emotional outbursts but felt tears filling his eyes. He sat shaking with his head in his hands. Feelings of fear and anger had taken over. He was paralysed. What on earth should he do?

Frank suddenly sensed the unseen presence of another person and turned round. It was Walt Dickinson, the previous Head of the School. Walt's face was twisted in an expression of horror.

'Whatever has happened?' he demanded.

'It looks like we've had a break-in overnight,' said Frank. 'Everything is damaged, probably beyond repair. It's years of work.'

'I'd better phone Willem,' said Walt. Frank admired his cool logic. Yes, of course, inform the Director of the Centre. That was the first thing to do. Walt pulled his phone out of his bag and pressed his most frequently used speed dial key. He stood impatiently, tapping his foot.

'He's not answering,' he said. Then his phone bleeped, and Frank could hear a voice.

'This is Professor Willem Kuiper. Please leave a message.'

'It's Walt. I'm at the Centre. It's been ransacked. Please get back to me ASAP.'

Frank began carefully picking up stools and chairs that had been knocked over and started to collect papers off the floor.'

'Perhaps you had better leave it,' said Walt Dickinson. The police will want to see what has happened. Put a notice on the front door saying the Centre is closed for the day and bolt the main door.'

Frank bustled around, complying with Walt's instruction. Why hadn't he thought of that? It was the right thing to do. Perhaps that's why Walt got to be Head of School, and I'm a technician, he thought.

For the next hour or so, Frank watched as Walt kept trying to call the Director of the Centre, Professor Willem Kuiper.

'I can't believe he isn't answering his phone,' he said as Frank came out of the workshop. He had made a small attempt to tidy up in the workshop on the pretext that this was for safety reasons. He knew well that this was the managerial equivalent of the ace of trumps. No one can argue about safety. He was about to put the kettle on when Walt let out a huge sigh.

'This break-in,' said Walt breathlessly as the reality of it all began to take over in his mind. 'All the main computers have been smashed, probably beyond repair. What on earth are we going to do?' Frank stood helpless, his arms outstretched, his shoulders shrugged. 'I've been trying to call Willem, but he doesn't answer. I've never known him not to answer a call. He spends his life on his phone. It's ringing and not engaged.'

'Something must be dreadfully wrong,' suggested Frank. 'Perhaps you should call Aletta. She will be furious at the damage to all her computers.'

'I think she's been at a conference the last few days,' replied Walt. 'OK, then. I need to take over again until Professor Kuiper arrives. No. Wait, why should I? I'll give the Vice-Chancellor's office a call. They get paid huge salaries over there. Let them earn their money and decide what to do.'

1

It was a quiet day at the office, so Detective Chief Inspector Drake had been finishing off a report he had to write for the "Super." That done, he turned again to a staffing matter. It had been troubling him for some time. Grace brought him a mug of coffee, and he idly picked up his pencil and made some progress with The Times crossword. It had been two weeks since they cleared up the previous big case, and Drake was getting itchy. It was more usual for him to have cases queuing up rather than having a gap. This gave him a chance to catch up with more administration. It was work that he detested, but it had to be done. His overactive brain searched for problems to solve and things to worry about.

At least he was getting home at a more reasonable time. This gave him time for flute practice in the evening. He now understood why his teacher had recommended daily practice. He felt he was improving. He knew he had a lot of work ahead of him and wished he had learned to play an instrument as a youngster.

Lying on the table by his chair was a volume of architectural history. He was gradually digesting it, but it was slow progress. These architects spoke a different language. He instinctively reached out and laid his hand on the book. When his architect wife, Cynthia, was terminally ill, he had promised her that he would study architecture to find out what she had been doing. The tragedy they simultaneously came to appreciate was that they had both been so busy with their careers that they had never understood what the other did.

At first, Drake found architecture strange and confusing, but now he was thoroughly absorbed by it. Every new building became like a crime he had to unravel. How had it become the way it was? How did it stand up? When was it built? What had happened to it since? These questions absorbed him. But each time he turned a page and studied a new building, his mind turned to his loss. He had assumed that grieving would be a time-limited experience, but he still mourned every day. In his mind, Cynthia would often "talk" to him about a building. He loved discovering things about architecture, but then he would think of her. His loss would frequently overwhelm him.

Detective Sergeant Grace Hepple came and stood by his chair and waited for him to look up. He patted the book, withdrew his arm and looked up at her.

'They've had a break-in at Deva University. It's in The Centre for Industrial Design. The Vice-Chancellor's office has called. They say the Director of the Centre cannot be contacted and they are a bit worried as it is so out of character. He is never "offline," as they put it.'

'Not sure it's a job for us,' grumbled Drake. 'It might turn out to be in due course, though.'

'Well, the Vice-Chancellor says you did such a wonderful job when their visiting professor was murdered. He specifically asked for you.' Grace grinned and waited for the response.

'Well, we're not doing anything else,' growled Drake. 'I suppose we'd better drive to that ghastly out-of-town campus and see what it's all about. Cynthia would have hated that place. It is soulless. Far from sharpening minds, it must dull them every day.'

'No,' said Grace. 'They've moved to new premises in town. In Nicholas Street, you know the road that crosses the bottom of Watergate Street. They told me the Vice-Chancellor's office is in that posh Georgian terrace. The Centre for Industrial Design is opposite at the corner of Weaver Street. The V-C wants you to go and look at the crime scene and then come to his office to tell him what you propose to do.' Grace grinned again.

'He's a real bossy so and so that one,' growled Drake.

'I suppose he's used to telling a whole university of people what to do.'

'And how to do it,' grunted Drake, levering himself gingerly out of his chair.

Grace soon had the Range Rover at the entrance to the Police Station. Drake performed his usual trick of sliding along the back seat, making room for his long legs behind the front seats.

'People always think you're lucky to be tall,' grumbled Drake. 'Mostly, it's good, but sometimes it's no fun being six and a half feet. The whole world is designed for people a foot shorter.' Grace set off with Constable Katie Lamb in the other front seat.

'Hello, Katie,' said Drake. 'They hadn't told me you were back from maternity leave.'

'Yes. It was wonderful having time with my new baby. But I'm glad to be back.'

'Ah, good,' said Drake. 'I feared we might have lost you. You have made a most promising start to your career. We particularly need policewomen like you.'

'Thank you. After a while at home, I knew I needed to get back. I can combine motherhood with my career.'

'And how is the little one doing?'

'She's fine, thank you and putting on weight nicely.'

'Who looks after her when you are on duty?'

'I'm so lucky that her Gran has come to stay with us for a while. Sadly, my father died just before she was born. So, it is good for Mum to have a new interest in life. But I'm so sad that Dad never got to see his first grandchild.'

'Life has these surprises for us,' said Drake. 'I think you probably know that I lost my wife a little while ago. I thought I would be over it by now, but it isn't that simple.'

'Here we are,' said Grace, bringing the Range Rover to a gentle halt outside the door. 'Katie, why don't you find somewhere to park it? I'll go in with the DCI.'

Drake looked up at the building. It occupied a street corner, stretching away in both directions. Drake thought there was little to commend it architecturally. He tried hard to admire it. The best he could think of was that he understood why the architect had placed the entrance on the street corner. The entrance section gave a vertical emphasis that punctuated and contrasted with the more horizontal blocks of accommodation. You looked at the building and immediately saw the way in, but it would not win any architectural awards.

Drake and Grace made their way up the steps leading from the pavement to the lobby. Drake pointed to the signboard. The Centre for Industrial Design was one floor up. Determined to get some exercise, Drake set off up the staircase but was puffing and holding his hip by the time they reached the Centre. Grace rang the bell, and the door opened almost immediately. Drake held out his ID.

'Police,' he said, in a why am I here sort of voice. 'The Vice-Chancellor called us.'

'Hello, thank you for coming. I'm Frank Richards, chief technician. Please come this way.' He led them down to the far end of the studios.

'Did the intruders make all this mess?' asked Drake.

'Oh. No, Sir. These spaces are always like this. Particularly, the undergrads tend to be highly creative but chaotic.'

'I see,' said Drake. 'My wife sometimes taught in a school of architecture. I remember her saying they often had trouble stopping the cleaners from throwing away important drawings and treasured bits of models.'

'That sounds familiar,' laughed Frank.

Drake was studying their guide. He estimated Frank was in his late sixties, average height and build, with a significantly receding hairline. What hair he had left was of the wispy ginger variety. He was wearing a long brown lab coat. Beneath this, Drake could see a pair of highly polished brown shoes. His study of Frank was interrupted by another man coming forward with an outstretched hand.

'Welcome,' he said. 'I'm sorry we are so untidy today. We seem to have had overnight intruders, and, as well as damaging expensive equipment, they have made a real mess. By the way, I'm Walt Dickinson. I was Head here previously. Since the "Big Change," I'm just another ordinary academic. In the absence of the missing Director, I suppose I'm now acting Head.' Drake and Grace picked up a slight grumpiness, perhaps almost sarcasm in his voice, and they looked briefly at each other as Walt turned to lead the way into the computer lab.

'It's bad enough that they should damage so much, but surely there's no need to make such a mess.'

'I'm afraid it's one of the things these people often do,' said Drake. 'They leave things turned over or lying sideways on purpose. This shows them where they have been. It's a perfectly normal thing for thieves to do. But I understand it feels like an invasion, which, of course, it is. We find that burglaries often create as much psychological harm as they do physically.'

'As far as we can see, it's not a burglary, more a case of extreme vandalism,' said Frank Richards, following Drake. He pointed to the computer room. Drake followed him in. The scene was even worse. There were cables and printers spread around everywhere.

'Our main servers have been hammered, literally,' said Frank. 'The heaviest hammer in my workshop is missing.'

2

Drake prowled around, taking in every detail of the scene. He took out his new iPhone, which his son and daughter had given him as a birthday present. He pivoted around, taking pictures from every angle.

'What has been taken?' asked Drake.

'Strangely,' replied Frank. 'I haven't noticed anything. It just seems to be pure willful damage.'

'Has anything like this happened before,' asked Drake.

'No. Never.'

'Do you know of anyone connected with the Centre who might have some sort of grudge?'

Frank looked at Walt. Walt's face took on a wistful expression. 'I think many of us have something of a grudge with the way we have been treated recently by the University, but I honestly don't think any of us would do this. After all, it provides our livelihood.'

'What about all the staff rooms?' asked Drake.

'They are normally all locked,' replied Frank. 'I'm afraid I haven't checked them all. Let's go and look.' Frank set off with Drake in tow. He checked each door. They were all still locked. 'Perhaps we should check Professor Kuiper's room. It's over here,' he said, pointing. Drake followed again. It was then that Frank stopped in his tracks. The door of the office was broken and half open. Drake went in and looked around.

'It all seems alright,' said Frank. 'No. Please wait a minute. His computer under the desk has been hammered. It looks in a bad way. I doubt that is going to work anymore.'

'What are you all doing in Willem's office,' demanded a woman's voice.

'Aletta, there's been a break-in,' said Frank. 'All the computers are smashed.'

'What! Surely not,' said the woman, looking first at her watch and then the smashed computer.

'We have the police in,' said Frank. 'This is Chief Inspector Drake.'

'How do you do? I'm Dr Aletta van Leyden. I'm a Senior Reader here. I manage all these computers, or I used to!' Drake shook her hand and pointed to the end wall.

'What about that?' he asked, walking over to the colossal whiteboard. It was covered in notes and diagrams with arrows and boxes. Some thinkers had been at work, thought Drake. A whiteboard is a sure sign of thinking. The central area had been wiped clean. A message had been written with a felt-tip pen that had dropped on the floor with its cap off. The message was all in capital letters. It read, "TAKE THAT."

Other members of The Centre had gathered in the room behind Drake. There was a collective intake of breath. Eventually, Drake turned and looked at the little group of his hosts.

'So, what do we think was the motivation behind all this? It does begin to look like someone with a grudge. He even had the time and nerve to send you all a message.'

'Vandalism, pure and simple,' said Frank Richards.

'I'm not so sure!' said Walt Dickinson. 'Maybe they were after our ideas.'

'Hardly,' said Aletta van Leyden. 'They would have taken the computers, not smashed them.'

'Is that your hammer there, Frank?' asked Drake, pointing under the desk. Lying on the floor was a substantial lump hammer.

'Yes, I think that's it,' replied Frank. 'Hang on, let me check.' He bent down to pick it up.

'Don't do that.' Drake raised his voice. He was suddenly in his I'm in charge mode. 'If that is what has been used to create all this damage, it might reveal the perpetrator's fingerprints.'

'Oh, sorry,' said Frank, bending down to examine the hammer. 'Yes, it certainly looks like mine.'

'Have you any idea how the intruder or intruders got in?'

'The front door was locked,' replied Frank. 'They may have come in through the service access and my workshop. Sometimes, people are not as careful about locking the service entrance. The trouble is there is no one person responsible for it.'

'Surely there must be some rules about locking it behind you,' grunted Drake.

'Rules and designers don't mix easily,' replied Frank. Drake was warming to this plain-speaking fellow.

'So, what is all this about the Director's disappearance?' he asked.

'Prof Kuiper has likely gone somewhere and not told us. He's probably forgotten to turn his phone on,' said Aletta.

'He doesn't forget to turn it on. Not that one. He's always on it,' grunted Walt.

'What do you think, Sir?' asked Frank, looking at Drake.

'Too early to say,' growled Drake. 'I'm going to be cautious. I'm declaring this whole Centre to be a crime scene. I'm afraid that you'll all have to leave. We will have a scene-of-crime team searching the place for clues. Can someone please tell me when Professor Kuiper was last seen?'

'He was still here when I left last evening,' said Aletta. 'I've been at a conference, and I came in on my way home to collect a book. That was quite late. I didn't look at my watch. It might have been around ten. We are all working late on an important project. He would have been the last to leave.'

'Where does he live?' asked Grace, her notebook at the ready.

'I don't know,' replied Walt. 'He's rather a private person. He never talks to me anyway.'

'Down on the canal somewhere,' said Frank. 'He told me about the view from his house. He said it made him feel quite at home. He comes from Holland. He was rather pleased to find somewhere close. He wanted to be able to walk or cycle to work. He said he would buy a bike to get about.'

'Does anyone else know where that is?' asked Grace. She scanned around the assembled bunch of members of the Centre. They were all shaking their heads.

'Grace, call Martin at the station,' said Drake. 'Get him to bring a scene-of-crime team here. It might be too early to designate Professor Kuiper as a missing person. We will review the situation again tomorrow. Now, Frank, will you see everyone off the premises for us? Will you remain here to receive Detective Inspector Martin Henshaw and the scene-of-crime team? They will need some time to work, so please give Detective Constable Katie Lamb a key. Katie, you remain on duty here to make sure nobody else comes in until the scene-of-crime team arrives.'

Grace made a call to the Vice-Chancellor's office. He had gone to a meeting expected to last for several hours. His assistant made an appointment for them on the following morning. Drake was functioning again. He had another case. But he suspected his daily flute practice was in danger.

Drake and Grace arrived back at the station. Grace got on the phone with Martin to brief him about the case so far. Drake studied her face. She was smiling. That made up his mind. He would speak to her. As soon as she put her phone away, Drake called her over.

'I'm not good at this sort of thing,' he said. 'I may do this rather clumsily, so forgive me in advance. You and Martin became quite close until he went to Hong Kong. Then, it all seemed to fall apart. I created an opportunity for you to go over and work with him, but you turned it down.'

'Yes,' said Grace. 'He had just expected me to follow him over there and hang around. I had my career to think of as well as him.'

'I understand,' said Drake. 'Since he returned, I have avoided asking you to work together. Should I carry on doing that?' Grace blushed. Drake didn't think he had ever seen her do that before.

'He has changed a lot. Perhaps it was a maturing process for him. I'm sure we could work together again.' Drake noticed a brief smile flick across her face. Her phone rang, and she dashed to pick it up. Drake could see her nodding her head repeatedly. He was briefly amused by the illogical human behaviour of gesturing to someone on the phone. He picked up his newspaper and opened it at the crossword. Grace knew this was his way of digesting facts about a case, and she would usually leave him alone, but she felt it necessary to interrupt him.

'I've got something for you to listen to,' said Grace. 'I think it is important. You will want to hear it. It's quite brief.'

'What's that?' asked Drake, looking up from his newspaper.

'The emergency 999 call service sent it to us. It is a call they received at 23:13 yesterday. They know the caller was somewhere in central Chester. They can usually only pin these things down to the particular mast that picked the call up. However, they hope eventually to find a location within thirty metres. They have initiated a search to discover who the owner of the phone is, but they say this might take a few days. I have checked the number that emergency say made the call. I rang Walt Dickinson at the Centre for Industrial Design. He confirmed that it was Professor Willem Kuiper's phone. Listen. It's very brief.'

Grace held her phone up on loudspeaker and tapped the play button.

'Help!'

'Sir, which service do you need?'

'Ambulance, police! I…'

'That's it,' said Grace. 'It was followed by a brief scrambled sound that has not been identified. Then the phone went dead.'

'Play it again,' said Drake. Constable Steve Redvers and Dave, the technician, had gathered around. Grace played the brief recording three times. The assembled group stood in a silence that Drake broke.

'There is a sense of distress in that voice,' he said. 'But that's not surprising when someone is calling 999.'

'Perhaps some people at the Centre might have other recordings of him that we can compare,' suggested Katie.

'Good idea,' said Drake. 'Grace, get onto the stand-in Head. What's his name?'

'Walt Dickinson.'

'Yes. That's the chap. We had better put out a call for a missing person. It looks as if we have a new case here. People don't usually make 999 calls like that and disappear unless there's been foul play.'

3

The following morning, there were still no reports of anyone discovering the whereabouts of Professor Willem Kuiper. Drake satisfied himself that the scene-of-crime team was still at work in The Centre for Industrial Design while Grace brought the Range Rover to the front door.

Drake performed his usual trick of clambering into the rear seat.

'Before we set off,' said Drake, puffing slightly. 'We don't have any definite facts about the disappearance of Professor Willem Kuiper, so please leave any comments about that to me.'

Grace spoke to Katie Lamb, who sat in the front.

'The Vice-Chancellor's office told me they have some highly valued parking spaces. They are at the back. I think I know roughly how to get there. Katie, can you direct me?'

'No problem,' said Katie. 'I know this part of town well. You go along Nicholas Street, and just before that row of Georgian terrace houses, you turn right onto the bottom part of Watergate Street. Then you take an immediate left onto Nicholas Street Mews. The car park is a little way down on the left.'

Sure enough, they were soon driving along Nicholas Street. Ahead on their right was an extensive terrace of fine Georgian houses.

'Aren't these delightful?' said Drake. 'It's such a surprise to see them in this city. Chester is mostly much earlier buildings. I can see exactly why the Vice-Chancellor wants to work in one of these. They also say something to visitors about the educated nature of the place. Those buildings on the out-of-town campus look ignorant by comparison.'

Grace smiled at this architectural analysis and turned right onto the bottom section of Watergate Street.

'I see where we are now,' said Drake. This is Watergate Street, which starts in the centre of town at The Cross. It is effectively the continuation of Eastgate Street.'

'Correct,' said Katie. 'Now, Grace, you need to turn left, and we drive along behind that terrace of houses. This is called Nicholas Street Mews.'

A little way along this back street, Katie pointed to the left.

'Look, there is the car parking area we were promised.'

They were soon easily parked, and there was even a posh-looking door with a bell that Katie rang. After a short pause, the door opened.

'You must be Detective Chief Inspector Drake,' said a youngish woman. Drake nodded his head as he studied their host. She was slight and with her hair tied back into a bun. She wore large, black-rimmed spectacles that took up most of her face. 'I'm Sally Wells, the Vice-Chancellor's PA. Follow me, please. The Vice-Chancellor is just on a group call. He won't be many minutes.'

They entered into a grand hallway resplendent with a large chandelier. The stairs opened into the space with two lower steps that swept around in a curve. Drake grasped the handrail, and the party climbed to the next floor. Drake's developing architectural brain informed him that they were now at ground level at the front of the house. People were meant to enter through the front door rather than from the car park. They sat on a neatly arranged group of seats, and their host opened a glazed door into her outer office.

Drake picked up a copy of Grand Designs and flipped through it. The Vice-Chancellor was interested in expensive property. Drake had not reached halfway through when the Vice-Chancellor's assistant opened her door and beckoned the police party in. An imposing figure stood in an open doorway. He wore the trousers from a pinstriped suit, held up by red braces over a light blue shirt. His cuffs were turned up once. They revealed an extravagant watch. His glasses were perched on the end of a substantial nose, and he had piercing blue eyes. His head was topped off by a shock of hair halfway between blond and ginger.

'I'm Professor Chambers,' he said, 'but everyone calls me Vice-Chancellor.' He laughed to suggest this was a joke, but Drake guessed it was an instruction. This was not a man to be messed with. The Vice-Chancellor turned on his heels and disappeared into his office. Across the room, in front of one of the well-mannered Georgian windows, was the grandest desk Drake had ever seen. It was set at an angle across the corner of the room. Drake remembered his architect wife, Cynthia, cautioning him to be wary of people who arrange their desks with the light behind them. Three chairs were placed about a metre and a half from the desk. Drake began to move toward one.

'No, we will sit over here,' came the booming voice. The Vice-Chancellor pointed to a large circular table in part of the room behind the door through which they had entered. It was a vast office. On the wall behind the table was a whiteboard. There were dozens of indecipherable squiggles, boxes, arrows, and comments. These were presumably from the meeting preventing their presence the previous afternoon.

The Vice-Chancellor took a seat directly opposite to those chosen by Drake and his team.

'These are new premises for you,' said Drake, following his general principle of beginning with some uninvited small talk.

'Yes indeed,' said the Vice-Chancellor. 'The University had commissioned the out-of-town campus before I was appointed. I have only recently been able to develop a better estate strategy. We need to be in the town centre. The buildings out on the campus were no more than sheds. There was no public transport out there. We must become a leading international university. Our new Director of Estates identified this area as having great potential. We expect to procure more accommodation around here as time goes by. We will move all our central administration here with those departments that prove they already have an international presence.' He glowered at his audience in a fashion that Drake thought many of his staff would find intimidating. Drake decided to lighten the tone a little by praising this bear of a man.

'Interestingly, you called the out-of-town campus buildings sheds,' he said. 'My wife told me that a famous American architect, Robert Venturi, once said that buildings could be ducks or decorated sheds.'

'That sounds too obscure for me,' grunted the Vice-Chancellor.

'No,' said Drake. 'It's a simple idea. Ducks explain to us how they work. We can see their feet and their wings. We can see the long beaks that they use to dip into the water to find food. Decorated sheds, by comparison, explain nothing and need signposts on them to tell us where to go and what they are.'

'That's very good,' said the Vice-Chancellor. I must remember to use that. What did he design, this Robert Venturi?'

'Well, the most famous building you would know is the extension to the National Gallery in London's Trafalgar Square. The previous design was referred to by the then Prince Charles as a carbuncle on the face of a much-loved friend.'

'Right, to work,' said the Vice-Chancellor. 'I need to impress upon you the importance of this matter to the University. The old School of Industrial Design was failing in almost every respect. They were not recruiting high-quality staff or attracting good students. There was virtually no research. I thought of closing it down. But this University should offer subjects like this. I gather Professor Kuiper has gone missing. Have you tracked him down yet?'

'I'm afraid not, so far,' replied Drake.

'Are you sure he is safe somewhere?'

'At the moment, I cannot say that.'

'Oh dear, that's awful,' said the Vice-Chancellor.

For a moment, Drake began to think this pompous man was showing some concern for Professor Kuiper. He was soon to be disabused of this assumption.

'My whole strategy for the new Centre is based around Kuiper. If we have lost him, it would be a major blow.'

'I can assure you, we are doing everything we can to find him,' said Drake.

'Good, good,' said the Vice-Chancellor. 'It was quite a feather in our cap when I recruited him. I was speaking at an international conference in The Hague in the Netherlands. He had asked to sit next to me at dinner. During the meal, he told me he did our innovative master's course in IT. I liked the idea of an industrial designer having expertise in IT. It's the way the world is going. There's IT in everything now. I told him he should come here and develop his ideas. I said we would support him, and I soon managed to net him. I'm no expert in his subject, but I've got some advisors in the field. They told me that he was a potential giant. His work can be exploited commercially across all advanced nations. I invited him to restructure the School. The previous Head is an ineffectual man. He does pretty drawings, but nothing ever comes of them. He cannot inspire the staff. The whole outfit was too comfortable. Kuiper is in a different class.' The Vice-Chancellor gave Drake another of those penetrating stares and continued.

'I was pretty clever, even if I say it myself. I let him set up his own company to exploit their work. The University has a minority shareholding. He calls his combined university group and company Blindsight. I've no idea what it means, but it's a catchy name. We allow them to use University space. If their work turns out to be as breakthrough as he says, we will get a substantial sum, but I have not had to take any financial risks. Clever, isn't it?'

Grace watched Drake's reaction. He smiled weakly and gave the tiniest nod of his head detectable. He looked uncomfortable. The Vice-Chancellor continued.

'He's a remarkable chap, Kuiper. He's done these amazing designs for exclusive watches. They only sell a small number of each model, but he gets one for his fee. He gave me this one. He said it would cost three hundred and fifty thousand pounds. He wears a watch worth one and a half million. Can you believe that? The silly fellow wears it every day. I told him not to. You can't be too careful now. There are plenty of muggers who would be prepared to knock him over. You don't think that's what has happened to him, do you?'

'At the moment, we have no idea,' replied Drake. 'But you are correct. It's a possibility we must consider. It would help enormously, Vice-Chancellor, to have Professor Kuiper's address. We have a rough estimate of where he might be, but there may be important clues in his house.'

The Vice-Chancellor went to his desk and hammered on one of the many telephones there. Drake thought they looked surprisingly old-fashioned.

'Sally, get Human Resources to give you Kuiper's address.'

'While Sally is here, Vice-Chancellor,' said Drake. 'Could I ask for as many photographs as you have of Professor Kuiper? They will help us enormously both in looking for him and showing to members of the public.' Sally made a note on her pad. 'Grace here will give you an email address to send them to.' Sally nodded, and Grace followed her to the outer office.

The Vice-Chancellor returned to the table and addressed his audience again.

'Kuiper has done an excellent job so far. He's rebranded the place as a centre, not a school. That sounded far too low-brow. They've taken over much better accommodation, and he's brought in a woman who is better material. She also came from the Netherlands, but like Kuiper, she speaks perfect English.'

Sally Wells came into the room looking a bit sheepish.

'I'm afraid HR say they only have his address in Delft. He gave an address in Commonhall Street at one time. Recently, mail to it has been returned with a note saying he's moved away. They have repeatedly tried to get his current address in Chester, but he never replies. They use his university address to communicate with him. He was chatting with me the other day while waiting to see you. I knew he came from Delft, of course. He said how flat it all is over there. Everybody goes around on bikes. He said he was going to get one here. He told me he walked to work every day. Maybe that might help a little?'

'Well done, Sally,' said the Vice-Chancellor. 'I hope that at least gives you a few clues, Drake. This is not good enough. Kuiper might be impressive, but he must respect HR. What's more, he should not have gone off wandering without letting me know where he was. I must have words when he reappears. Remind me, Sally.'

Drake decided he'd had enough, so he took the initiative.

'Vice-Chancellor, I can report we have a scene-of-crime team investigating the break-in at the Centre. These things must be done carefully. They must search everything without contaminating any evidence that might be used in a trial. It cannot be rushed. When we have any news, I will let you know. That applies both to the break-in and the whereabouts of Professor Kuiper. If you will excuse us. We have work to do.'

The three police officers left the building and climbed into various parts of the Range Rover. Drake let out a long sigh.

'Oh, dear,' he said. 'Was I too rude at the end? I had enough of the man. I've no idea how people can work for him.'

'I think it was fine,' said Grace. 'Shall we go back to the case room?' Drake grunted an acknowledgement.

'Right, we need a detailed map of Chester city centre,' said Drake to the team sitting around the central table.

'Tom Denson has one down in reception,' said Steve. 'I'll go and borrow it.'

'No, tell him to get another one,' said Drake. 'It is essential kit for us now.'

Constable Steve Redvers returned with an unfolded map flapping around as he walked. He laid it out on the table in the centre of the room and flattened out the creases.

Drake, Steve Redvers and Constable Katie Lamb stood looking at the map of Chester and its immediate environs.

'We know he has a house overlooking a canal,' said Drake. 'We've been told he lives close and walks home. Where are the most likely locations? Where does the canal come closest to The Centre for Industrial Design? Point to the Centre for me, Steve.'

Steve swivelled the map around to see things the "right" way up. He pointed to where The Centre for Industrial Design was. Katie Lamb spoke first.

'I've got some knowledge. As a kid, I went fishing and rode my bike along the canal towpaths. Look here. The canal runs under the A458 and joins the River Dee. There's a lock, of course, to adjust the water height. Tracing back, the canal goes as far as the Water Tower. There's a sharp bend to another lock with the other part of the canal system. From there, it runs for miles in both directions.'

'Yes,' said Steve Redvers. 'In one direction, it comes to the King Charles' Tower. There are some domestic-looking buildings there, I think. But nearer to the Centre, my best bet would be Whipcord Lane. There are quite a few smallish houses along there. Look, this part of the lane overlooks that section of the canal by the lock. I wouldn't mind living there.'

'OK,' said Drake. 'Could he walk to the Centre from there?'

'Oh, yes,' replied Katie. 'I guess it is maybe a quarter of an hour's walking time. You can see the route he would take. He would leave the Centre and walk down Nicholas Street to Watergate Street. Then go down as far as the city walls. Then it's a short distance up to that walkway over the railway and down the steps into the park.'

'OK,' said Drake. 'Let's try there. It looks like a limited area to search. You two go down there and knock on doors to see if anybody knows him.'

4

That afternoon, Steve and Katie arrived at Whipcord Lane. It seemed a charming little street. Down the right-hand side was the canal. Brightly painted narrow boats were moored alongside. To the left were solid-looking brick buildings. First, there were a couple of detached residences, then a terrace of smaller houses.

'This could be it,' said Steve. 'Professor Kuiper talked about seeing a canal from his window.' On the corner, at the beginning of the street, there was a large, isolated house.

'I doubt he would get anything this big just for himself,' said Steve. Next was a detached house. The owner was coming out and unlocking his car.

'Excuse us,' said Grace, holding out her ID. 'We're police officers. Do you know if Professor Willem Kuiper lives around here?' The man shook his head, got in his car, and drove off. Next came a larger building. There was an alleyway to its left. Steve jogged down it while Katie waited on the street.

'It's a whole cluster of student residences,' said Steve as he returned. 'The house on the street carries a notice. It is part of the student residences.'

'It looks like complete development,' said Katie. 'I think you'd have to be a student to live here.'

Next, there was a terrace of eight red-brick houses. They were in pairs with two adjacent front doors, set back under arched openings. Each had a bay window next to the front door. The bays continued through the first floor to meet a deep overhanging roof. The terrace was set back from the street by a tiny front garden. Right on the line of the pavement was a low wall made from bricks matching those used in the houses. Different types of gates occupied the openings in the wall opposite each house entrance. Cars were parked along the street in front of most of the houses.

The other side of the street was marked with a double yellow line. Beyond this was a line of railings. Almost immediately beyond that were narrow boats moored up along the canal bank. The bright reds and greens of the boats moored on the far side of the canal made picturesque reflections in the still water. Farther down, Steve and Katie could see a bridge and a lock across the canal. This led to a higher-level section of the canal. It doubled back alongside the section in Whipcord Lane. It was a charming scene. Katie stopped and listened. Only a faint hum of road noise was discernable. Katie thought a house here would be pleasant but within easy reach of the historic city centre.

Steve and Katie walked to the end of the housing terrace and found the road turned to the left, leaving the canal behind. More terraces stretched along this section but without a view of the canal.

'I doubt his house is down this far,' said Katie. 'Let's turn back.' As they returned, the two police officers took in more of their surroundings.

'Look,' said Steve. 'Beyond the two sections of the canal, I can see what looks like a large modern building. It seems to be trying to look like old industrial warehouses.'

'You're sounding like Drake with all that architectural analysis,' laughed Katie. 'I think they are probably flats. They look well-designed and have an excellent view of the canal. Kuiper could live over there. If so, we have a substantial search on our hands. Let's try these terrace houses. Somehow, they appear more likely, and there are only eight of them. Let's start at the beginning where we have parked.' Steve nodded his head.

They walked back to the first terrace house and began their search. After a little run of no responses, the next door opened. Immediately, there was a strong smell of cooking. Katie thought it was probably spicy. Eventually, a diminutive woman appeared round the open door. She was wearing an old-fashioned, flowery dress with an apron over. She had a scarf over her hair. She looked up at the two constables. Steve and Katie thought she had spoken to them in English, but they could not be sure. At best, it was

English with such a strong accent that neither Katie nor Steve could understand her. Katie held out her ID.

'We are looking for Professor Willem Kuiper,' she said. 'We think he might live along here.'

The woman nodded and spoke rapidly in what now seemed to be an oriental language. Katie and Steve looked at each other. The woman seemed a little exasperated and repeated the stream of incomprehensible words. Katie asked her to repeat it slowly. This made no difference. Steve beckoned to Katie, who spoke briefly.

'Thank you,' she said. Steve grabbed Katie by the elbow, and they started to walk away.

'Let's try the next door,' he said. 'We are not going to get anywhere here.'

They both turned, took a few paces back to the pavement and turned left to check the next house. The woman started yelling and came rushing after them. She grabbed Katie, pulled her around and pointed to the previous house. They had already knocked on that door and got no reply.

'I get it,' said Katie. 'She's trying to tell us he lives there.' She turned to the woman and thanked her. For some reason that she couldn't explain, she put her hands together as if praying and bowed her head. This seemed to work. The woman nodded her head repeatedly, laughed and returned to her house.

'Thank you,' shouted Steve as the little woman disappeared back into her house, slamming the door behind her.

'I think we've struck gold,' said Katie. Steve was already ahead of her, and the two went back out into the street and through the little gate in the low wall between the front gardens and the pavement. It was barely three paces to the front door. They rang the bell. Yet again, there was no response.

'Let's try once more with a long ring,' said Katie. Steve pressed his thumb onto the bellpush and held it there. 'I heard it ring inside,' said Katie. 'He can't be here.'

'Alternatively,' said Steve. 'He might be incapacitated or even dead.' He tried to look through the large bay window. 'There's a Venetian blind. I can hardly see anything.'

'What do we do?' asked Katie.

'OK,' said Steve. 'Let's take some pictures and go back to the station to get Drake's approval to enter forcibly,' said Steve. 'We probably need a search warrant anyway.'

Katie and Steve returned from their trip to Whipcord Lane. The case room was quiet. Drake was engrossed with his crossword.

'We think we've found the house where Professor Kuiper lives,' said Steve. 'We are getting no response, but the foreign woman who lives next door has repeatedly pointed to the house when we mentioned his name. It's a neat little place. It seems a shame to break in and cause damage.'

'The other problem is that I don't feel confident we have the right house,' said Katie. 'It was a rather confusing situation. We couldn't understand anything she said.'

'Do we need a search warrant?' asked Steve.

Drake scratched his chin and grunted. He spoke slowly and deliberately.

'We are trying to find a missing person who may be in urgent need of medical assistance. If we can show that there was reason to believe it is a matter of life and death, we can go in without a warrant. I'm prepared to do that and take any consequences. However, it would be better to try not to cause any damage. We have a locksmith, James Bull, we can call on.' Drake pointed to the photograph of the front door on Katie's phone. 'From this picture, I would think it is not a lock that would defeat him.' Drake picked up his phone while Katie and Steve made tea.

'That's sorted,' said Drake. 'He will meet us there. We need to go now.'

'Go and get the Range Rover, Katie,' said Steve. Everyone knew Drake insisted on a vehicle that did not cramp his long legs, but Steve just wanted to be sure Katie knew how important it was. They didn't need Drake to arrive in one of his grumpier moods.

5

The Range Rover was having the annual service, so they were stuck with an ordinary squad car. Inevitably, by the time they arrived at Whipcord Lane, Drake was complaining about being cramped inside "a tin can." They parked right outside the house thought to belong to Professor Kuiper. The locksmith, James Bull, was sitting on the garden wall waiting.

'It's this one,' said Steve, pointing.

'OK to go ahead then, Sir?' asked the locksmith.

'Yes,' said Drake, now looking bright and ready for action. The three police officers stood back. Steve was sufficiently fascinated to look over the locksmith's shoulder.

'You're making too much noise,' said James Bull. 'I need to listen to the tumblers.'

Steve stood back again to see Drake and Katie grinning at him.

'Never interrupt an artist at work,' said Drake. With that, the locksmith gave a little cheer. He pulled the handle down, and the door opened. All four went inside.

'Hang around, Jimmy, would you?' said Drake to the locksmith. 'Just in case we need you again.' James Bull nodded his head.

Drake shouted. 'Police. Is there anybody here?' There was silence.

'OK,' said Drake. 'The first thing to do is to establish if anyone is here who is either disabled or perhaps dead. Do a quick scan of all the rooms. You two take upstairs. I'll do the ground floor,' said Drake.

It was a tidy little house. There was a kitchen to the rear and a living room at the front with a bay window looking over the canal.

Drake opened the doors and looked into the rooms on the ground floor.

'Nobody up here,' shouted Steve.

'OK, do a thorough search now,' said Drake. 'See if you can find anything explaining the owner's whereabouts. Don't move anything that might later be used as evidence. Wear your gloves.'

Drake started with the living room. There were bookcases against nearly every wall in the small room. The other walls were covered in framed design drawings. The room had a pale, polished wood floor only partly covered by colourful patterned rugs. The space was remarkably free of furniture. There were two unusual armchairs and a couple of small side tables.

The chairs were like enormous eggs carved out on the sides. Drake thought you wouldn't so much sit on it as sink into it. They would completely envelop someone sitting in them. They were covered all over in tan-coloured leather. Drake was inwardly rather proud of himself. He knew what they were even though he had only seen pictures of them. He knew he was cheating. He remembered Cynthia telling him about the Egg Chairs designed by the famous Danish architect Arne Jacobsen. Only a designer would have such chairs! They must be expensive and difficult to obtain, but they sat in this room like modern sculptures.

One chair was facing a set of deep shelves. The other chair, partly obscured by the nearer one, was facing in the opposite direction. The shelves immediately caught Drake's attention. Displayed on them were several domestic items. A toaster, a bright red kitchen mixer, a sculptural bread bin, a couple of clocks, and several vases. They were all out of context. They sat there as if on display rather than waiting to be used. On the wall behind all these were five pictures of expensive-looking watches. Beneath all these was an extremely hi-tech-looking HiFi. Drake assumed that the house owner had designed all these items. It was looking likely that this was indeed where Professor Kuiper lived.

Drake turned his attention to some bookshelves. Three books even had Willem Kuiper's name on the spine. That clinched it. Drake was now confident they had found the house of Professor Willem Kuiper. Drake opened the door into the hall and shouted up the stairs.

'We've got the right house. Keep looking.' He returned to the living room. It was then he saw it. The second chair was no longer partly obscured. It was facing away from him. He could only see the back. However, he could also see a hand draped over the left side. His mind was already ahead. It was telling him they found Professor Kuiper. Drake went around the chair to see the occupant. He was astonished by what he saw.

It was a body as still as could be, but it did not belong to Professor Kuiper. It was not even a man. In her stationary pose, the woman was beautiful, strikingly so. She had a classically composed face surrounded by long, dark, silky hair. She wore a full-length black evening gown with a low neckline revealing a sculptural silver necklace. This necklace looked like a hand-crafted work of art. Drake bent down to feel for a pulse in the hand draped over the side of the chair. There was no pulse, and her hand was cold to his touch. She was dead and probably had been for some time. Drake slowed himself down. This was no emergency. The situation demanded a careful response. Drake went back over to the door and shouted upstairs again.

'Katie, Steve. Come down here immediately. I have found someone.'

As his colleagues came down, Drake returned to the scene of his discovery. Now, he noticed a small side table in front of the chair. On the table were a mobile phone, an empty glass tumbler, and a bottle of gin. The gin bottle was empty.

'Oh, my goodness!' exclaimed Katie.

'Who on earth is she?' demanded Steve.

'Goodness knows,' said Drake as he opened his phone and tapped on the screen.

'Professor Cooper.'

'Hello, Prof. It's Drake here. We have a body I'd like you to look at for us before we move her. It looks like an accidental death or a case of suicide. Something is bothering me. I'm not sure what it is. Can you come over to Whipcord Lane?'

'I see,' said the pathologist as he entered the living room. He bent down, pulled his glasses onto his forehead, and examined the body.

'I assume this bottle of gin was there when you found her?'

'I suppose the conclusion that she drank too much gin is too obvious.' said Drake.

'That is a possibility,' replied Professor Cooper. 'But only after the post-mortem could I reach such a conclusion. It rather depends on how much gin she drank. And just when she drank it.'

'Of course, we have no idea at the moment,' said Drake. 'The bottle could have been full originally, but equally, it could have been half full or even empty.'

'I have examined people who have died from an overdose of alcohol,' said the pathologist. 'But more often, they get extremely sick, vomit and are rather unwell but survive. That is what some of them hope, of course. But others are not best pleased when they wake up. They suffered all this pain and discomfort and failed in their objective.'

'It could be an accident,' said Drake slowly, 'but it is also possible that it is suicide.'

'This is not a common method of suicide in my experience,' said Professor Cooper. 'Do you have any reason to believe this is not an accidental death?'

'Nothing at all,' replied Drake. 'It just all seems a bit too obvious. But then it's my job to be suspicious.'

'A common feature of deaths like this is an overdose of some potentially lethal drug. They drink all the alcohol to give them the courage to down a load of pills. Have you found any empty tablet bottles or boxes?'

'No,' replied Drake. 'We have not completed a thorough search yet, but we would have seen them if they had been here. Katie, go and look for a bin in the kitchen. It might be obvious, or it might be in a cupboard. See if you can find anything that could have contained drugs.' Katie disappeared. Professor Cooper finished his preliminary examination of the dead woman and stood up. Drake spoke but was thinking aloud.

'At this stage, we have all three types of death as possibilities. It is an accident, possibly a call for help. Or it might be intended suicide, or, of course, it could be murder.'

'Correct,' replied Professor Cooper. 'My best guess at this stage is that it is either an intended or accidental suicide. Drugging someone to death is not a particularly common form of murder. We are just guessing until I have completed the post-mortem.'

Drake grunted. 'I suppose someone could have spiked her drink and then left.'

The pathologist did not comment. Katie returned, looking disappointed and shaking her head.

'There is a bin in the kitchen, and I have emptied its contents onto the table. It's all just normal kitchen refuse. No sign of any drug bottles or glasses.'

'Don't worry,' said Professor Cooper. 'We need to get her back on the lab table. If she has taken anything, I will almost certainly find some evidence. I'll let you know.' With that, he left.

'OK, Steve. I think you know the procedure. We need an ambulance and gloved individuals to take her as carefully as possible to the pathology lab.

'Yes. I'm getting the hang of it now!' Steve grinned. Drake was looking unhappy. The others waited for him to say something. He did.

'One thing that is puzzling me is how she got in here. The door was locked. We had to get our locksmith to open it for us. There is no sign of a key so far.'

'Somebody else could have let her in and then left,' said Steve.

'Excellent. Good thinking,' said Drake. 'If so, a prime candidate would be Professor Willem Kuiper, but we don't know where he is. If it was him, could he somehow have murdered this woman and left, locking the door behind him? Right, Katie, this needs to be treated as a crime scene. You need to arrange a scene-of-crime team to conduct a full search. Come back to the station with me. Steve, you remain on duty here to ensure the scene is not contaminated. Katie will arrange for you to be relieved by uniformed constables. It looks like, far from helping to solve our mystery, we have a new one to deal with.'

6

The team assembled back in the case room, waiting for Drake to arrive. After his usual struggle to find his keys, the door opened, and he shuffled in.

'Katie, is the SOCO team still at work at Whipcord Lane?' asked Drake.

'Yes. All in hand.'

'I've been thinking,' said Drake. 'Tell them I want the gardens searched too. Ask them to be sure they check anything out there that looks as if it has recently been moved. OK, Steve, bring that large-scale street map over here.'

Steve opened the map onto the table in the centre of the room.

'Gather around the map,' said Drake. 'I want you locals to help me. On the day he disappeared, Willem Kuiper was at the Centre for Industrial Design. That is here.' He pointed to the map. 'We know he was still there when Aletta van Leyden left. She isn't certain of the time but estimates it to be around ten in the evening. From what we have been told, it is thought that Kuiper walked to and from his home. From the evidence we found there, we now believe his home to be in Whipcord Lane.' He pointed to the map again. 'We believe that Kuiper made an emergency call to the 999 service at 23:13. The call was made on the mobile phone registered to him. The recording tells us he needed help but almost immediately disconnected the call. It seems a reasonable hypothesis that he was walking home. There is no sign of him at his home and no sign of disturbance. It seems probable that he ran into trouble on the way home. We found a body in his home, an unknown woman. We don't know how she might be connected with Professor Kuiper. I have decided to put any further investigation into her on one side until after the SOCO team has reported and Prof Cooper has completed the post-mortem. Is everyone agreed?'

Drake scanned around the table to see his audience nodding in agreement.

'Right, so let's concentrate on finding Professor Willem Kuiper. This is where I need local help. Can we plot a likely route for him? Remember, he was walking.'

'If I was doing that walk,' said Katie Lamb, 'I would come out of the Centre at the University and turn right along Nicholas Street. When I reached Watergate Street, I would turn left. That meets City Walls Road, just next to the Watergate. I would turn right up that road. That's quite a pleasant way to walk.' Katie turned to Drake. 'It runs parallel to the City Walls. If I remember correctly, just before it curves to the right, there is a ramp up onto the Walls. You could walk or cycle up there. That takes you over the railway. Then I think there are some steps down into Water Tower Gardens. That is a rather nice little park. Most people don't know it's there. It is right up against the City Walls on one side, and they are quite high there. From memory, the other sides are hemmed in by housing. There are only small entrances to the gardens. Go across the garden, and you're virtually at Whipcord Lane.' Katie paused and looked around.

'It's not an area I know well,' said Inspector Martin Henshaw, 'but that seems entirely logical. The route is quite direct and a pleasant walk.'

'Are there any other routes that anyone feels are more likely?' asked Drake, looking around. Nobody spoke. 'OK. We need a search party to work along the route to look for things that could be relevant. Don't be hesitant. Photograph and record things. If possible, bring in any objects that seem relevant. Report anything of significance to Inspector Martin Henshaw on his mobile phone. I want any evidence protected. While searching, also speak to passers-by who may have seen something. Grace, arrange all this as soon as possible, please. Work with Sergeant Tom Denson to allocate duties. Go in pairs. Match up uniformed branch people with members of CID. We need a maximum presence to cover such a long distance. If you meet anybody, show them our pictures of Professor Kuiper and see if they remember anything if they were there on the night in question. Katie, print the photographs we need for the search parties. We will aim to start first thing tomorrow. The distance and all those steps might be too much for me, but I want to see the route. Martin, get the Range Rover when I arrive in the morning and drive me there.'

The following morning, Martin drove Drake to The Centre for Industrial Design. The entrance was on the corner of Nicholas Street and Weaver Street. Martin turned into Weaver Street to reverse the Range Rover. The vehicle was purring gently to remind the occupants that it had just been serviced.

'OK,' said Martin. 'We are about to follow Katie's suggested route.'

'Excellent,' replied Drake.

Martin pulled out, turning right onto Nicholas Street.

'Ah,' said Drake. 'I'm getting the hang of it. There is the Vice-Chancellor's office on the left.'

'Correct,' said Martin as they arrived at the crossroads with Watergate Street. 'We are turning left here, but if we had turned right, we would arrive at The Cross in the centre of Chester. Now on the left is the little back road which takes you behind the Georgian Terrace to the car park at the back of the Vice-Chancellor's office.'

They reached one of the bridges or gates that carry the City Walls over streets.

'That is the Watergate,' said Martin. Drake noted that it was a simple affair compared with his favourite Eastgate. It was a single stone arch topped by a gently curving balustrade. There was a small opening on one side, that invited pedestrians to avoid the traffic. Martin turned right immediately before the Watergate, and they drove along City Walls Road.

They reached the beginning of a gentle ramp at the back of the pavement to their left.

'Stop here,' said Drake. 'I can manage that, and then I can find the steps down to, what was it called?'

'Water Tower Gardens,' said Martin, pulling up as suggested. 'I will drive the car around and pick you up at the other road entrance to the gardens.'

Drake shuffled his way up the ramp onto the walkway that encircles the city on the top of the ancient City Walls. He soon found himself crossing over the railway and making his way down into the gardens. They had a circular path that he followed anti-clockwise until he saw Martin waving. Drake clambered back into the Range Rover. Martin set off and immediately took a left and a right.

'We are back in Whipcord Lane,' he said, pulling up in front of Professor Kuiper's house.

'Excellent,' said Drake. 'It's all in my head now, so I know what you locals have described. We can return to the station and let them continue the search.'

Drake had returned from his assisted journey along the route when his phone rang.

'Hello, Drake, Professor Cooper here. My examination has shown evidence of a substantial amount of an opioid substance in her body. I can't be certain which one it is at this stage. The laboratory tests to detect which of a range of opioids is present are notoriously complex and rather unreliable. There is no evidence of an injection, and her nose was clean. The substance was probably ingested. As we suspected, she also had an extraordinary level of alcohol. If both the opioid and the alcohol were self-administered, she may not have appreciated the jeopardy of combining the two. The fatal combination caused her heart to give up. She might have got away with the overdose if she had not drunk all that gin. We will never know. It is as we suspected when on-site.'

'So,' said Drake. 'It could have been an accident, suicide or a call for help that went seriously wrong?'

'That sounds reasonable,' said Professor Cooper. 'Although either or both the alcohol and the opioids could have been administered by a murderer, on balance, that is less likely based on data we have. If you don't need anything else, I will write my report.'

'I must keep an open mind at this stage,' said Drake. 'As you say, it could still be that the overdose was administered by someone else, perhaps after she had already got into a drunken state.'

'I can't help you with that line of investigation,' said Professor Cooper. 'I am unlikely to be able to find any evidence either way. OK, I will let you have the report as soon as it is complete.'

'Thanks for excellent service as always,' said Drake, shutting his phone. 'Martin, look after things here for me, please. I'm going to Kuiper's house in Whipcord Lane with Steve and Katie. I want to have another look around there. Get Jimmy to go there too.'

The three police officers and James Bull, the locksmith, arrived at Whipcord Lane. The SOCO team were packing up.

'We've not found anything helpful in the house,' said the sergeant in charge. 'But my lads scoured the gardens as requested. We found nothing worthy of reporting. Drake panned around the garden.

'Is there nothing else unusual here?' he asked.

'There is one plant pot with a big bush growing in it. It was lying on its side. We've had high winds recently, which could explain that.'

'But somebody could have tipped it over, looking for a hidden front door key,' said Drake gruffly.

'We didn't find a key or any evidence to support that idea,' said the sergeant.

Drake turned to the locksmith.

'Jimmy, can you stay with us? I have a suspicion we might still need you.'

'Sure, no problem.' James Bull sat on the bottom step after Steve Redvers and Katie Lamb had gone upstairs. Drake turned his attention to the kitchen. It was a hi-tech affair with glossy white and grey fittings. The worktops looked like genuine marble. Below it were the usual kitchen appliances, including a refrigerator, a freezer, ovens, a microwave and a washing machine. All were built-in, and some were behind glossy doors. Most of the lighting was hidden behind pelmets. There were some tiny LED spotlights in the ceiling. He idly opened each of the cupboards in turn. The doors all closed slowly by themselves when he released them. He got to the last one below the sink and sucked in a big breath with satisfaction.

'Jimmy, come here, will you? I thought this must be here somewhere. There, next to the drainpipe, was a substantial safe. He gave it a push. It was rock solid. The main floor was covered in white tiles. Under the sink, it was plain concrete. The safe sat foursquare, challenging anyone to break in.

'It looks like this safe is bolted down,' said Drake. 'I'm half-expecting to find valuables here.' James Bull arrived to look over Drake's shoulder.

'Insurance companies can require fixing securely to concrete,' said James Bull.

'Have a look at this. Is there anything you can do with it?'

'Oh, dear,' said James Bull. 'This requires a different set of skills. I'll give it a go.' He bent down. 'It looks like quite a good one. It may take me a while.'

'Come and look at this,' shouted Steve from upstairs. Drake left the locksmith to his work. He stumbled up the narrow and steep staircase.

'I'm in the front bedroom,' said Steve.

Drake could hardly open the door. There, occupying a large percentage of the available space, was a king-sized double bed. Drake reckoned even he could have lain across it.

'So, this man has a fine eye for design, loves books and music, and his sleep,' grunted Drake. 'Check all the cupboards.' Drake went and looked in the small bathroom. It was as hi-tech as the kitchen. As well as a sculptural washbasin, there was a small corner whirlpool and spotlights everywhere.

'Bingo,' came the call from downstairs. Drake went to the top of the stairs. James Bull, the locksmith, was standing in the hall. 'Success,' he said. Drake half-stepped and half-hopped one step at a time down the staircase. It was easier on his grumbling hip that way. Martin followed him into the kitchen. The safe had given up the battle. It was wide open. It had three layers of shelves and was fitted out in a quilted cloth. Resting on this were five beautiful wooden boxes that looked handmade. They sat there like jewels. Drake put his gloves back on and opened one. Inside, sitting in plush fabric, was an expensive-looking watch. He opened the boxes in turn. Each one contained a precious-looking timepiece sitting in plush satin. The fifth box was sitting on the top shelf. Drake lifted it gently and opened it with great care. It had the usual space for a watch, but it was empty.

'Aha. I bet he was wearing this one,' said Drake to Steve. 'The Vice-Chancellor told us he always wore the most expensive watch. We had better take all these into custody and put them in our secure evidence store.'

'At that point, Katie Lamb shouted from upstairs. 'Come and look at this.'

Drake patted the locksmith on the back. 'Well done, Jimmy. You're a star.'

Drake and Steve clambered up the stairs again.

'In the bedroom,' shouted Katie. The two men obliged. 'Sorry, but you'll have to come right in. I need to shut the door.' Drake and Martin shuffled around the giant bed.

'This is a double wardrobe,' said Katie. 'The left-hand side has all men's clothes. They are neatly arranged in colours and styles. This room belongs to a particular sort of man, I would say. That is except for the bottom shelf. In there, we found some jeans and a jumper. It looks as if they were thrown in. They look scruffy compared to all the other clothes. Perhaps he wore them for gardening or something. We can't tell. However, the right-hand side is rather different. You said he liked his sleep. Perhaps this bed was meant for more gymnastic pursuits. Look at this.' She opened the door on the right-hand side of the wardrobe to reveal an expensive-looking nightgown made of silk and lace.

'Steve couldn't help but laugh. Katie grinned and ran her gloved hand down a long silk nightgown.

'I wonder,' said Drake. 'First, we find the body of a glamorous woman, then a huge bed and finally, some expensive-looking lingerie in the wardrobe of an unmarried man. This looks as if it is intended for a rather special visitor. I wonder what we have stumbled on here. Professor Willem Kuiper becomes more and more interesting even in death.'

7

Drake and Martin were having a well-earned cup of coffee when Martin's phone rang. He stood up and walked around the room, holding his phone to his ear. He was talking and listening while waving his free hand in the air. Finally, Drake heard him congratulate his caller.

'They've found him already,' he said. 'The body was well-hidden under some trees in Water Tower Gardens. I'm not surprised. That area would probably be quiet at that time of night. It would give an assailant maximum opportunity. He has been stabbed in the heart. No weapon is visible, but they are searching now. The body has not yet been identified formally, but they say his face matches the photos they have. There is a lot of blood. The knife or whatever was used must have gone right into the heart.'

'OK,' said Drake. 'We need someone to do a formal identification. Martin, try and get hold of the technician at The Centre for Industrial Design. His name is Frank Richards. He strikes me as the most able to do that unpleasant task. Tell our boys to make the whole of the gardens a crime scene. We will let the rest of the search continue. There might still be evidence along the route we think he followed.'

Drake picked up his phone and hit one of his speed dial buttons.

'Professor Cooper, Chief Pathologist.'

'Hello again, Prof. We have another body for you. It's in Water Tower Gardens. It appears to have been a stabbing. Do you want to see it in situ first? It would be excellent if you could get there quickly.'

'No problem, Drake. I can leave what I am doing. I will get over straight away.'

Detective Inspector Martin Henshaw drove Drake in the Range Rover. They arrived just before the pathologist. The protective blue tent had been assembled around the body. Professor Cooper headed straight for it.

'OK, Drake,' he said. 'Ask everyone to stand back, and I will have a preliminary look.'

'Put up no entry tape across all the entrances to the park,' said Drake to Constable Redvers. He took a walk around the park with Martin. The entrance from the road where Martin had parked the Range Rover gave access to a footpath. It ran past a small children's playing area with swings and a simple roundabout. Then, the path curved around a fenced-off tennis court. Next to the gate to the tennis court was another small children's playing area. This one seemed designed for even younger children. There was a slide and a climbing frame. Beside them was a single swing with a child's seat. Beyond that, and to the left, there were two bowling greens.

Over to the right, there was a pavilion, which was locked. It was painted in dark green and had a sweeping pitched roof. Straight ahead, the path went alongside the second bowling green and headed directly to the Water Tower. To the right was a circular path. It surrounded a children's climbing frame made of rustic poles. The path curved round to meet the other straight one at the foot of the Water Tower. There were several park benches. They seemed intended for parents to rest while watching their more active children.

Drake saw a second tower. Martin said it was called Bonewaldesthorne's Tower and was built in the thirteenth century. Drake could see the City Walls connecting to it. Curving around it was a flight of steps. Drake had used them to come down from the walkway at the top of the City Walls. The body was discovered under trees between the two towers and against the City Walls. The blue tent marked the spot with Constable Katie Lamb on duty outside. There was a park bench nearby looking at the children's play area. Drake walked back to the pavilion. Some seats were under the overhanging roof and in the sun where Martin waited. Drake sat next to him, deep in thought. It occurred to him that he was investigating a modern crime in a place steeped in history. It was probable that it had seen much violence over the years.

Eventually, Professor Cooper emerged from the tent, shaking off his rubber gloves. He saw Drake and Martin and made his way over to them.

'Not much more I can do here, Drake. It's a middle-aged man wearing black trainers, a pair of black cargo trousers and a black mandarin-style shirt. He has been stabbed from the front. It looks as if the knife or whatever was used has penetrated the heart. There has been a lot of bleeding. I will tell you more once I have done the post-mortem.'

'Thanks, Prof,' said Drake. 'We will arrange with your people to transport the body to your mortuary. Did you, by any chance, notice if he was wearing a watch?'

'No, but the buttons on the cuffs of his shirt were undone. I rolled each one back to make sure there was no slashing of the wrists. I saw no watch.'

'Did you see his phone anywhere?'

'No. No phone.'

'That's odd,' said Drake. 'He was making an emergency call that we have listened to. The call got cut off. We assume he collapsed. The emergency responder got no further information, terminated the call, and initiated a protocol that exists for such a situation. We were notified the next day. Presumably, the murderer took his phone.'

'There is another point to note at this stage,' said Professor Cooper. 'I did not see any weapon that could have been used. I'll call you as soon as I have finished the post-mortem. Now, I must return to the investigation I was doing when you rang. My assistant here will assist your officers in searching for clues around the area.' With that, the pathologist set off along the path to the road where Martin had parked.

'Well, that's interesting,' said Drake. 'There is no watch. The Vice-Chancellor told us that he had designed several watches. We saw pictures of them all in his house. There was one watch missing. According to the Vice-Chancellor, he always wore one worth one and a half million. I wonder if we have already found the motive.'

Drake and Grace arrived at The Centre for Industrial Design for a meeting with the staff. Frank Richards collected the visitors at the entrance and took them to a meeting room. Drake could hear chattering before he entered. He walked to the front and stood patiently. The room gradually went quiet.

'We have asked you all to come here because we have some news about our investigations into the disappearance of Professor Willem Kuiper. Unfortunately, the news is not good. Yesterday, we discovered the body of Professor Kuiper. I am sorry to say that there was nothing we could do to help him.' Drake paused and looked around. He could see many distressed-looking faces. A couple were shaking their heads in disbelief. 'There will be a post-mortem, and our pathologist already has the body and will report back to me as soon as he can.' There was a collective intake of breath before he continued.

'We are conscious that these events may disturb you. The police are used to dealing with this situation. Detective Sergeant Grace Hepple can arrange help for you if necessary. When I have finished, Grace will give you her telephone number and email. You can see her after this meeting, call her phone number, or email her. Alternatively, you may come to the Police station in person.' There was a faint murmur of people talking to their immediate neighbours. Drake waited for silence.

'We have now formally begun our investigations into Professor Kuiper's death. I am afraid that we cannot rule out foul play at this stage. To help us, we shall be asking each of you to meet with us. This is so we can learn more about Professor Kuiper's life. You may, perhaps, think you have nothing to say, but please let us be the judge. At the beginning of such an investigation, we often don't know what information might be helpful. Now, I will do my best to answer any questions. However, some aspects of our investigation must remain confidential at this stage.' Drake looked around. Walt Dickinson raised a hand. Drake nodded.

'Can you tell us where he was found?'

'It was in Chester. I am sorry, I prefer not to be more precise or say more just now.' Walt looked around. Nobody else wanted to question Drake, so he continued.

'Is it possible it was some sort of accident?'

'The evidence suggests not,' replied Drake.

'Do you think it might be murder?' asked Walt.

'There are some injuries to the body suggesting that might be the case.'

Walt spoke again and seemed to be asking questions on behalf of the whole staff. It was apparent to Drake that they respected and trusted him and saw him as their new leader.

'He always wears a ludicrously expensive watch. Have your officers found that on him?'

'I can say something about that,' replied Drake. 'We have found some of his watches in a safe at his house. There appeared to be one missing. We found no watch on his body.'

'I thought as much,' said Walt, turning to his staff. 'It seems likely that he has been mugged on the way home. He was foolish to wear that watch.'

'Perhaps you can help us with that,' said Drake. 'Do you have any idea who else might know about his watch and might therefore be responsible?'

Everyone shook their heads.

'Well, all the students know,' said Walt. 'It is sometimes a topic of conversation.'

'Thank you,' said Drake. 'If we feel it would help us to interview all the students, we will ask you to assist us. However, at this stage, I have an open mind about why Professor Kuiper has died. Now, if there are no more questions, we must get to work. Mr Dickinson, is it possible to speak with you now?'

8

Drake sat in Walt Dickinson's office, waiting for him to return with two mugs of coffee. He looked around to see shelves of books and a stack of large portfolios leaning against them. On one wall, there were some framed drawings. These were the design sketches of well-known objects. One was the lemon squeezer famously designed by Philippe Starck. It looked more like something intended to go to outer space than a kitchen utensil. Drake knew it because his wife, Cynthia, bought one. He was curious about how successful it had been and yet notoriously underused. Drake thought it was more a piece of sculpture than a designed product. He was reflecting on this absurdity when Walt returned with the coffees.

'Tell me, Walt,' said Drake. 'Why is Philippe Starck's lemon squeezer so popular?'

'Ah,' replied Walt. 'A good question. Many have written learned papers on The Juicy Salif. He designed it in a restaurant. This drawing was done on a paper napkin. Starck is known for the remarkably rapid creation of designs. He claimed to have designed a chair while the seat belt sign was on during take-off. His designs are usually sculptural objects that have functions. Starck said the Juicy Salef was not meant to squeeze lemons but to start conversations. He is a fascinating chap. Whether he is a designer is hotly debated.'

'I don't understand what you mean,' said an intrigued Drake. 'You say there is a debate about whether he is a designer.'

'Well, I suppose he might be thought to design more for himself than for clients, although many clients have been delighted with his work for them. The other question is whether he designs for his users. That is a more contentious issue. There is an argument to be made that he is an artist rather than a designer. We are all amused by his work. A lot of it is extremely clever. I suppose we all envy his success. There is probably only room for one Philippe Starck. If you asked my staff, they might not hold him up as a role model. Design as it is normally practised is more complex.'

'Fascinating,' said Drake. 'I sometimes wish I had chosen to be one of your students instead of becoming a policeman.'

'Oh, I don't know,' said Walt. 'What you do must be endlessly fascinating. There is no doubt that it is important. I'm certain we would all like to be a detective.'

'Now to work,' said Drake. 'What can you tell me about Professor Kuiper?'

'Not a lot. The Vice-Chancellor wanted him to replace me as Head of School. He and the Vice-Chancellor decided to change the name from School to Centre. I wasn't consulted. It was a direct appointment by the Vice-Chancellor. I understand what they are trying to do. Kuiper gives us much more of a research orientation. This is unusual in industrial design. I once talked to an architect friend who is a distinguished historian. He amusingly said that the trouble with trying to understand my subject is that you go to the library to find the industrial design section, and it just isn't there. By comparison, the schools of architecture, town planning and landscape have big research traditions. Industrial designers like me have always got on with the job instead of sitting thinking about it. Kuiper would argue that we live in a rapidly changing world, so industrial design must develop. Many of the objects that we design now have computers in them. He would argue that we need to understand computers much more. He would have said that we are designing robots in many cases. He is right, but I'm too old to change.'

'So, you knew little about Kuiper when he arrived?' asked Drake.

'Correct. With our usual university procedures, I would have seen his curriculum vitae and helped to interview him. I did neither. The first I knew about it was when he appeared. The Vice-Chancellor brought him to the department to start work. By and large, he has ignored me since he arrived. I think perhaps he was a bit embarrassed by it all. The Vice-Chancellor had not told him about the history of the place. Of course, he wasn't interested in that anyway. He wanted to create a different sort of department. Now, I feel it is more about research than creativity. I was taught to be a designer and have practised as a designer. I know I am not a natural leader or even a manager. I was never taught to research as it is done in the Centre now.'

'You sound a little bitter about all this,' said Drake.

'You might see it that way. I keep to myself now. In many ways, being Head of a department in a university is a tedious and often difficult job. Your colleagues often isolate you. They know you must, to some extent, decide what they do and whether they get promoted. So, you tend to lose friends. The Vice-Chancellor blames you for everything that is wrong or even less than perfect as he sees it. Life was much easier in the old art colleges.' Walt sighed and looked up at the ceiling.

Drake allowed silence to develop, and suddenly, Walt spoke again, and his mood had changed from sorrow to anger.

'I get it,' he said. 'You think I have a motive to kill him.' Drake maintained his silence. He wanted Walt to continue. He did.

'That is ridiculous,' he said, almost spitting out the words. 'Some people accuse me of having a short temper. It is certainly true that I don't tolerate fools gladly. But to accuse me of murder is absurd.'

'I haven't accused you of anything,' said Drake deliberately.

'But you do suspect me. I don't believe this. I'm already a suspect because he took my position.'

'As I often have to say,' replied Drake. 'At this stage of an investigation, everyone is a suspect.'

'Well, you must find another suspect to occupy your mind,' said Walt. 'I am away now for a few days.' With that, Walt picked up a leather bag with a long strap, slung it over his shoulder, stood and stormed across to the door, which he opened and left, slamming it behind him. He nearly knocked over Grace, who was just about to enter.

'What was that all about?' asked Grace.

'Our friend, Walt, seems a mild-mannered and perhaps rather old-fashioned chap,' replied Drake, 'But, by golly, he has a short fuse. He also has an obvious motive. He admitted as such.'

'What do you think?' asked Grace.

'Too early to say,' replied Drake. 'I tried to establish some rapport with him, and we talked about design for a while. On the surface, he seems a nice sort of chap. All of a sudden, he started to complain about me accusing him of murder. Of course, I had done no such thing. I did admittedly use the standard line about everyone being a suspect at this stage of an investigation. Perhaps, in retrospect, that was unwise. He has probably been badly treated by our friend, the Vice-Chancellor, and I imagine they don't get on too well. Walt sees himself as a traditionalist, and the Vice-Chancellor is determined to be a modernising force. They are probably irreconcilable. I got the impression that Walt is quite bitter. But he probably blames the Vice-Chancellor more than Kuiper. He says Kuiper never talked to him. The Vice-Chancellor had probably set that up. Kuiper preferred to leave him to himself rather than try to develop an understanding.'

Drake paused and reflected. Grace waited for him to speak again.

'I'm not sure that I could see him planning a murder. Maybe though I could see him undertaking a murderous act when losing his temper.'

9

Walt was away for a few days. Drake used his office at The Centre for Industrial Design to interview staff. He rearranged the chairs to allow for a more informal setting. Two together for himself and Grace, and an empty one opposite. First, they interviewed the senior students and learned nothing new. Now, they were concentrating on the major players in The Centre. There was a delicate tap on the door. Grace went over and opened it. In came Dr. Aletta van Leyden. She crossed the room with an assured elegance. She had long, shiny dark hair that framed her finely featured face. Her complexion was smooth and pale. Drake noticed she had unusually long fingers. She was dressed in the most striking clothes. She wore a dress with a halter neck and skirt down to just below the knee over black leather boots. The latter had a medium, carefully sculptured heel.

Aletta's dress was graphical in its effect. There was a combination of straight edges and curves with great blocks of pink and orange, a colour combination that is not for the faint-hearted. It drew Drake's eye and triggered some fuzzy memories. He struggled to recall what it was reminding him of. His brain was not about to be helpful. He snapped himself back to the present.

The whole effect suggested care and thought went into Aletta's appearance. Perhaps many might have considered it too cultured for work, but she carried it off with an air of inconsequence. She smiled and took the seat that Drake indicated. As she sat down, she shook her hair away from her face. Unlike Walt, she seemed entirely composed. She gave off an air of quiet competence. This was not a person likely to panic. She had struck Drake as being calm and collected on his first visit. Drake guessed she never got over-excited or depressed.

Drake took his chair. He had arranged it carefully. He had read about personal distance and seating arrangements. Not so close that it felt intrusive nor too distant to be sociable. It was then that he worked out his earlier memory. Cynthia had worn something similar.

'What a stunning dress,' he said.

'I'm glad you like it,' replied Aletta. 'Some people disapprove of so much colour at work.'

'My wife had something similar,' said Drake, 'and she said she was rebelling against the plain black everyone wore in her practice.'

'Really? Is she a designer too?' asked Aletta.

'She is no longer with us, but she was an architect.'

'The dress is Marimekko,' said Aletta.

'Ah, that's it,' exclaimed Drake. 'I had forgotten the name. It's a Finnish fashion house, isn't it?' Aletta nodded and smiled. She somehow managed to express a slight impatience with all this small talk, but Drake was not to be put off.

'Can you explain your name,' he asked. He tried as often as possible to begin difficult interviews by inviting the interviewees to talk about themselves. Over a long career, he had found this an effective way of putting most people at ease. Of course, he thought, Aletta doesn't need such careful treatment.

'Thank you,' she said, 'but I can take no credit for that. My name follows a common pattern in The Netherlands. It can feel cumbersome at times. Please call me Aletta.'

'Thank you, Aletta. I understand you came here at the invitation of Professor Kuiper.'

'Yes, we worked together before in Delft.'

'Did that make things awkward with the other members of staff? Were you perhaps seen as a foreign invasion?'

'Not at all. They have been helpful and friendly. It is a nice place to work. It will be much less so with Willem gone.'

'Aletta, please will you explain the work that you did with Willem. It is not my field, so I am trying to understand the background to his life.'

'Our work is inter-disciplinary. Willem instinctively knew that it had to be. It is one of the things he taught me. You can have an inter-disciplinary team. However, to have at least some people who bridge disciplines can make it even more effective. I am sure that is why Willem invited me to follow him here.'

'So,' said Drake. 'Can you describe these fields that you both inhabit?'

'Those of us who work here are excited about it. Once, information technology was only found in computers. Now, it is found in many everyday objects. We must have objects that have new abilities. Your heating system can be controlled when you are away using the Internet. A refrigerator can keep track of your food and order replacements from the supermarket. We are at the start of a revolution and still trying to understand all this. Effectively, people will converse with their surroundings as if it were perfectly normal. Alexa is an early example of this idea.'

'So,' interrupted Drake. 'You think this changes the context in which industrial designers work?'

'Absolutely. We will simultaneously live in real and virtual environments. Industrial designers have to work with both. Willem foresaw the importance of virtual reality. It has obvious potential for entertainment. However, when we apply it to education and training, for example, it begins to make a huge difference. Using VR, students can learn and practise skills. This has colossal benefits in areas where physical practice is difficult, such as medicine. Students can practise delicate and complex operations without endangering patients they would otherwise work on.' Aletta paused and picked up the bag slung over her shoulder. She pulled out a small bottle of water and took a sip.

'I'm so sorry,' said Drake. 'I should have arranged for some coffee.'

'No, water is better,' replied Aletta. Drake felt slightly put in his place by this remark. As well as calm, this woman was confident. She carried on with her explanation.

'Willem knew that Virtual Reality headsets are too bulky, heavy, and uncomfortable. In years to come, people will laugh at how crude they are. Internationally, there are several leading labs working on this. The target is to have Virtual Reality headsets that are no more awkward to wear than a pair of glasses.'

'I can see what you mean,' said Drake. 'So, how do you solve this problem?'

'I cannot say much,' said Aletta. 'Our work is surrounded by high security. It has huge potential. The application of it commercially could be extremely high value. The Vice-Chancellor understands this. Not so many people in his position have such foresight.' Aletta took another sip of water.

'We need to make devices that are as simple as glasses. But you cannot focus on your glasses. They are too close to your eyes. One proposal is to use holograms. The idea is to project a three-dimensional image in front of the glasses. So far, the quality of the image is poor. It is also difficult to get a wide angle of vision. Virtual Reality aims to let you see all around you, so a narrow field of view is useless. We think we have new ideas. If we can be first, we can generate valuable patents. Everyone in Blindsight is extremely ambitious.'

'Thank you, Aletta,' said Drake. 'I almost understand that.' Drake took an internal sigh of relief that she had finished her lecture. He was soon to discover that she had more to say. However, a research student entered the room looking flustered.

'Aletta, we have an urgent call for you from Holland,' he said. 'She says it will not take long, but she must speak with you now.'

'Excuse me,' said Aletta. 'I will be back.' When she had gone, Drake turned to Grace.

'Normally, she would be high on our list of suspects. She is the last known person to see Professor Kuiper alive.'

'Yes,' said Grace. 'She seems capable. Somehow, I can't see her as a murderer.'

'If there is one thing I have learned,' said Drake. 'It's that you never can tell.' The door opened, and Aletta returned.

'Was that a problem relevant to our investigation?' asked Drake.

'No. A personal matter.'

'Tell me,' said Drake. 'Did Professor Kuiper have any unusual phone calls or messages before that Tuesday? Aletta shook her head.

'Did he perhaps go somewhere unusual?'

'He had not long returned from Bali. I have no idea why he went there. It seemed to happen suddenly. I assumed it was a personal matter connected with his wife.'

'You said you had another project,' said Drake.

'Yes. We are also trying to apply artificial intelligence in this field. It would be great if skilled surgeons could wear something that recorded what they do in three dimensions. Get many surgeons to do this and make AI learn from those recordings. It could then instruct a new student in the best ways of operating. We also want to know how they use their hands. But we cannot ask such people to wear cumbersome gloves. We need far better recording devices than we currently have. It is much more complicated than my description. We are only at the early stages. We believe we are close to some important breakthroughs here.'

'It all sounds exciting but difficult,' said Drake.

'That is exactly correct,' said Aletta. 'It needs disciplines to come together. It needs creativity and enormous amounts of knowledge.'

'So, did Professor Kuiper have that?' asked Drake. Aletta laughed.

'Not really. But he understood what was necessary. He knew how to find excellent people, make wonderful teams, and raise funding. That was his contribution. Without these things, nothing would happen, so he was invaluable. Of course, he was not ignorant. He was a creative and skilled designer and had studied information technology. But he wasn't a world expert.'

'So, do you have experts in your team?' asked Drake.

'Yes.'

'Are you one of those experts?' asked Drake hesitantly.

'Yes, of course.'

'Where was Professor Kuiper working before he came to Chester?'

'We were both working in Delft in the Netherlands. There is an excellent industrial design department there. It has a worldwide reputation. We had both taken degrees there. Then Willem took a master's degree in information technology here in Chester. After that, he returned to Delft and set up a company to develop the interface between industrial design and information technology. He quickly got huge research and development grants. He invited me to work there. We did excellent work for a few years, and then he came to Chester.'

'What attracted him to come here?'

'The Vice-Chancellor has a progressive attitude. He was prepared to invest in our unit. He allowed Willem to set up a company. The Vice-Chancellor is keen to establish links between academia, the professions and industry. Some kinds of funding can be generated in a university and others in a commercial company. Here in Chester, the company and the university unit are integrated. It is an ideal arrangement. It allowed for considerable investment from the university with far less loss of ownership than would have been the case when working with venture capital companies or banks.'

'So, did Professor Kuiper bring all his Delft company to work here?'

'No, just me and a few research students. He let the other senior people in the Delft company take it over. Some left, of course. Those who remained thought the company needed a new identity, and they renamed it VV.'

'VV?' asked Grace. 'Is that their full name?'

'No, sorry, they always go by the snappy letters. It stands for Virtual Virtue. It is a clumsy name, so I'm not surprised they abbreviate it.'

'A rather different question, Aletta,' said Drake. 'Do you have any ideas about people who might want Professor Kuiper out of the way?'

Aletta sat quietly, looking up at the ceiling. Drake waited until she spoke.

'You must understand that he and I had a close working relationship. However, I appreciate that many people found him difficult. If you disagreed with him about matters that he thought important, you would find him at best remote and at worst antagonistic. Several commercial competitors would prefer him not to be in the game. Whether any of them would go so far as to kill him, I cannot say. This is potentially a multi-billion-pound business. That makes it a dangerous business. Because we work on the Internet, we are always vulnerable to hackers. We have high-security arrangements that usually defeat them. They may turn to more physical interference. One can never tell.'

'Can you give us any names?' asked Drake.

'I prefer not to make accusations. Willem had a laser-like intensity about business matters. This did not always make him friends.'

Drake turned to Grace and nodded.

'Has he made any other enemies?' asked Grace. 'Perhaps people he knew personally rather than commercially?'

'Well, I suppose I have to say his ex-partner. The separation was unpleasant, and they had many aggressive interchanges.'

'How do you know this, Aletta?' asked Grace.

'Willem told me. He was upset about it. The aggravation went on for some time.'

'Where does his ex-wife live?' asked Grace.

'I've lost track, I am afraid,' replied Aletta.

'When they were first together, they moved to Delft. I think his wife came over when Willem moved here. I'm sure she frequently went back to Delft. I don't know if she still has a place in Chester.'

'Why did they split up?' asked Grace.

'I guess they drifted apart. She had her own business that was going nowhere. He helped her to develop it to become international. Once he had done that, he lost interest in it. That was one of his characteristics. He was a restless soul, always wanting to move on and tackle new problems. Then, some people say there was another woman. That probably made her give up on him.'

'Where does this other woman live?' asked Grace.

'I don't know her name, and I have no idea where she lived.'

'What about Professor Kuiper's wife,' asked Grace. 'Could she have wanted to murder him?'

'I know little about her,' replied Aletta. 'I suppose Willem has made enemies in the Centre here.'

'Who in particular?' asked Drake.

'Walt is unhappy, and I can understand that, but Willem had no interest in helping him.'

'Did Professor Kuiper have a laptop computer?'

'Yes, of course.'

'Would you expect him to be carrying it home?'

'Occasionally, he might leave it behind, but usually, he carried it in a bag over his shoulder. Why do you ask this?'

'There was no computer or bag with him. We have not found a computer at his home. Perhaps he was murdered for his belongings,' said Drake. 'His phone and watch had gone, and no laptop was found.'

'How dreadful,' said Aletta. 'It was just a mugging then?'

'Possibly, possibly,' said Drake.

Aletta suddenly looked at her watch.

'Please excuse me, I have an important meeting. I'm sure we can find another time if there are more questions.'

'Of course,' said Drake, as Aletta left.

'What a fascinating person,' said Grace. 'I wish I understood more about design. It seems such a wonderful world to be in.'

'An unusual combination of considerable intelligence with creativity,' said Drake. 'I think we are going to need to speak to her again. It feels as if she could tell us much more. I wonder what that phone call she took was about.'

'She said it was personal.'

'But what she said didn't feel quite right,' replied Drake. 'It was the way she spoke. Is she hiding something?'

'I wish I could have detected that,' said Grace.

'Professor Kuiper appears to have lived an interesting life,' said Drake. 'I am getting the impression that he was focused on the success of his projects and didn't mind what happened to people he thought were less important. Aletta mentioned another woman. Was it the woman found in Kuiper's house? If so, did she go to his house to commit suicide? Or perhaps Kuiper was responsible for her death? We have a double mystery on our hands.'

10

Everyone was busy at their work. Martin was writing a formal set of notes about the search for and discovery of the body in Willem Kuiper's house in Whipcord Lane. Once he had finished that, there was Professor Willem Kuiper's body to report on. Grace seemed to be answering a continuous stream of phone calls. Various people rang with sightings of one kind or another. So far, none of them seemed relevant. Drake was reading his notes about his interviews with Walt Dickinson and Aletta van Leyden. Eventually, he shuffled them all in a neat pile and struggled to his feet. This morning, his hip was being less helpful. It seemed further than usual to get out of his chair. He limped across to the case boards erected in the centre of the room.

Drake had used these boards for every murder he had tackled. They played a central role in his method, which had proved successful over many years. His method had evolved, and now he depended entirely on them to order and review his thoughts. Now that he had almost mastered his iPhone, he always had images of them with him. He often took his phone out and scrolled through them on car or plane journeys.

The arrangement of boards was such that they could be erected in several configurations. His favourite was a long straight stretch with two wings at either end. Drake called this his letter "I" layout. It was in use for this case. The case boards were not so popular with other members of the team. They dominated the case room, which increasingly felt too small for many cases. Most of the boards were an off-white colour and consisted of a soft enough material to allow for things to be pinned on them. A couple of boards were white and shiny. A small shelf adjacent to them held a collection of coloured felt-tip pens. The boards were about the same height as a doorway. With his six and half feet height, Drake could easily reach the top of the boards, but sometimes, as on this day, he struggled to bend down to the bottom.

'Katie, Steve,' called Drake. 'Come here and let me show you how we use these boards.'

Detective Constables Katie Lamb and Steve Redvers dropped what they were doing and met Drake standing by the first board. When Drake was sure they were paying attention, he began his lesson.

'The first board is where we put any new information as it comes in. The important thing is to get information up. We can arrange it later. So, this board looks a little chaotic when we have a busy or complex case, as we do now. On the next board, we put all the people involved in the case. This includes photographs, interviews, things others have said about them, and so on. On the third and fourth boards, we have a timeline. It runs from the earliest event that we have information about, through the estimated time of death of the victim, to the discovery and then on through the investigation. We try to establish links between all these items. We use a solid line for firm information and a dotted line for uncertain information.' Drake paused as he saw Grace joining the lecture.

'I think you know all this, Grace,' he said.

'Yes. Of course. I thought you might like to know I've just received a call from Professor Cooper's assistant to say that he has completed the post-mortem examination of Professor Kuiper and wonders if you would like to go over there to discuss it before he writes his report.'

'Excellent,' said Drake. 'This is the most important information that we are expecting right now. Get the Range Rover, and we'll go straight away. Martin, perhaps you could finish explaining about the case boards.' Martin grinned and scratched his head. He looked at Katie and Steve and shrugged his shoulders. He wondered why he had been singled out for this impossible task.

Drake found his coat and pulled it on as he set off for the front entrance.

A quarter of an hour later, Drake and Grace arrived at the Pathology Lab.

'Ah, good,' said Professor Cooper. 'I know you always like to hear all the facts rather than waiting for the final report.' Drake nodded his head. The pathologist led the way to the mortuary.

'We have a middle-aged man of average height. No glasses or hearing aids and, as far as I can tell, in generally good health. He appears unshaven for perhaps two or three days. He has received a stab wound to the chest that has punctured his heart. The only way he would have survived this injury is to have a fully equipped cardiovascular surgeon at his side. People can sometimes survive heart stabbings if they get immediate expert attention. That is not what happened in this case.' Professor Cooper paused to make sure his audience was with him so far.

'As I am sure you know, the heart is a multi-cellular organ. This means that stabs into the heart can take many different forms. Mostly, the seriousness of a wound is determined by three things. Firstly, the size of the weapon. Generally, the larger the weapon, the more quickly blood will be lost. The next factor is whether the weapon is withdrawn or left in place. If it is withdrawn, death will usually follow extremely quickly. If the weapon is left in position, it reduces the blood loss. This effect can be a considerable increase in survival time. If ever you get stabbed in the heart, do not pull the weapon out!' Professor Cooper laughed at what he thought was a good joke. Drake had heard it before and a weak smile fluttered across his lips.

'The third factor affecting survival is where the weapon has been plunged and entered the heart. So, we can investigate all three factors in this case. The weapon's size is relatively narrow and long enough to penetrate the chest. I estimate the blade used is about two centimetres wide and probably up to one centimetre thick. These are, however, approximate estimations, and I give them as a guide only. The stab did not damage the back. Either the weapon was less than about 20 centimetres long, or the stabbing action stopped short of the maximum length. I cannot tell which. The second factor I cannot tell you much about. The weapon was not in place and has not been found. Therefore, it must have been removed. If it had been removed immediately after the stab, the victim would probably have died quickly. It probably only took a matter of seconds. If it was left in place, he could have lived longer. Perhaps a few minutes. If it had penetrated the right ventricle, the injury would have almost certainly caused what we call a tamponade. This means that the pericardial sac fills with blood. This prevents the heart from expanding. It would result in almost immediate death. However, in this case, the weapon penetrated the left ventricle. This is fortunate for the victim, who stands a slightly better chance of survival. This is because this part of the heart tends to be thicker and more able to seal itself around the weapon. I estimate the victim survived the stabbing by only a few seconds if the weapon was withdrawn immediately or for a matter of several minutes if left in place. If he remained upright and calm and had not been further molested, he could have survived a little longer.'

'So,' said Drake carefully and slowly. 'In the case of an attack by a murderer, it is likely he died in just a few minutes or a much shorter interval if the blade was withdrawn immediately.'

'That is a reasonable estimate,' replied Professor Cooper.

'We have a recording of an emergency call made to 999,' said Drake. 'He called for an ambulance, and the recording went dead. It would presumably take time to get out a phone, dial, get a response, answer the question about the service required and then begin to speak.'

'Of course, my findings cannot prove that, but they are compatible with that scenario,' said Professor Cooper.

'The body was found lying under a tree,' said Drake. 'Is there any way you can tell if it was moved?'

'Logically, I am sure you will conclude that it must have been moved,' said Professor Cooper. 'That is unless the victim and murderer crawled under there together or somehow the murderer persuaded the victim to go there. These are unlikely scenarios.

There was blood around on his clothing. It could indicate the body was moved after death, but it doesn't prove it. We found some blood on the nearby bench. It is possible that the stabbing was carried out there, but again, we cannot prove that. It is also possible that the attacker transferred some blood after the event. Between the bench and the tree where the body was found is rough grass. We were not able to find any evidence there. Are there any questions so far?'

'No,' said Drake. 'It seems fairly clear.'

'Not quite,' said Professor Cooper. 'There is one further matter to discuss. It concerns the location and angle of penetration of the stab wound. The attack was from the front. His back is unharmed. The point of penetration is just to the left and below the sternum. The angle of the wound is slightly to the left and upwards.' Professor Cooper paused.

'Is that special in some way?' asked Drake. Professor Cooper stood immediately in front of Drake and raised his right hand. He lowered it in a stabbing motion towards Drake's chest.

'Look,' replied the pathologist. 'Assuming that I raise my hand first, you can see how my hand is moving downwards. Creating a wound that goes upwards is almost impossible. By the time I have reached just below the sternum, my hand is falling significantly.'

'So how could this wound have been created?' asked a puzzled Drake.

'The murderer could have made an upward movement from a relaxed arm. The data tells us that this is possible but rare. Perhaps the victim was not standing,' replied Cooper. Perhaps he was prone. The attacker may have been kneeling beside him or even with a knee on his face. There are no injuries or marks to suggest this, though. Another possibility is that the victim was standing, and the attacker came from behind.' Cooper signalled for Drake to turn around. 'Look, if I come from behind and wrap around you, my angle of attack is slightly upwards. There is one more factor I need to mention, but I cannot be sure about yet. The victim has a small amount of material inside his mouth and on the teeth. He could have been eating when the attack came. This might have partly reduced the sound of any cry of surprise and pain. I have the material sent for a particular analysis. Once I have the results, I shall inform you. We can discuss this then. I have a slight suspicion this may prove important. I prefer to say no more about this until we get results.'

PC Katie Lamb drove out to Whipcord Lane. As she suspected, several cars were parked on the same side of the road as the houses. She remembered there was parking pretty solidly along this section of the road. On the opposite side, against the canal, the road was clear. Before coming to work with Drake, she had done a stint in traffic. It had given her an idea. She had shared it with Inspector Martin Henshaw while Drake was out with Grace. Attention had been focused on Professor Kuiper, but somehow, she could not get the image of the dead woman in his house out of her mind.

She parked and walked down the road, taking down the registration numbers of all the parked cars. Once back in her car, she put all these details through the Police National Computer (PNC) system. She short-circuited the Automatic Number Plate Recognition software and typed the numbers in from her notes. As she expected, the cars were all properly registered, taxed and had their MOT certificates. She looked up the names and addresses of the registered drivers. One by one, the computer came up with addresses in Whipcord Lane. All except one. It was a car that she had noticed a couple of times. It was parked poorly, with one front wheel on the pavement. This was registered to someone with an address in Commonhall Street. She knew the place. It was a backstreet just off Bridge Street, in the city centre. The car was registered to a female with the name of Sophia Hamilton.

Back at the station, Katie Lamb was keen to talk to Drake when he and Grace arrived.

'Yes, Katie,' said Drake as she hovered by his chair.

'I have reviewed all the vehicles parked in Whipcord Lane. Only one is registered to someone not living there. It belongs to a female living in one of those dinky two-up, two-down houses on Commonhall Street. She was Sophia Hamilton. I may have tracked down the woman you found dead in Kuiper's house. I can't be sure of this, but I think the car has been there all the time we have been going.'

'Well done, Katie. This is interesting,' said Drake. 'So, you think Sophia Hamilton had arrived in her car?'

'That's the logical conclusion,' said Katie proudly.

'Let me just call our pathologist.' Drake tapped away on his phone and switched it to speaker so Katie could hear the conversation.

'Professor Cooper, pathologist.'

'Hello, Prof. It's Drake here. I have another question for you now about these two recent deaths. That is Professor Willem Kuiper and Sophia Hamilton.'

'Yes, go ahead.'

'Can you tell us which of them died first?'

'I think I know the answer, but let me check my reports.' Drake tapped his pencil on the table in a curious sort of rhythm. Katie was trying to work out if it was intentional or random.

'Hello, Drake. You're probably not going to like my answer to your question. The answer is no. To amplify a little, in neither case can I pin the death down to a date that I am happy about. Each could have preceded the other by up to a day either way. Of course, this also means they could have died on the same day. I cannot be more precise, sorry.'

'OK, thanks for your help as always,' said Drake. 'That leaves us with one more thing to think about.' Drake put his phone down and turned to Katie. 'One possibility is that they are unrelated, but that seems unlikely. Another possibility is that Sophia Hamilton killed Kuiper and then committed suicide. It is also possible that some third person killed them both.'

Katie stood looking at him, wondering what to say. 'We need to go to this address in Commonhall Street,' said Drake. 'Why don't you take Steve Redvers and go over there?'

11

Drake was prowling around his case boards and grunting. Dave was busy trying to hack into Sophia Hamilton's phone and getting progressively more frustrated. He had found several suggestions from people on the Internet. So far, nothing proved successful. Steve and Katie had gone to Sophia Hamilton's house on Commonhall Street. Martin was working on his computer. Grace was still a relative newcomer to the city of Chester. An idea wormed its way into her head. She leant across the table to where Martin was working.

'Where is this Commonhall Street?' she asked. Martin was tapping away on his keyboard, looked up and waved a hand in her direction. Perhaps she had interrupted him. The idea was not so good after all. She opened her laptop and started looking at maps of the city centre. A minute later, Martin came around the table.

'Sorry,' he said. 'I was just finishing a complicated edit on my report. You have become so much a part of the team that I had forgotten how new you still are to Chester.' Grace smiled. Martin picked up the map that was lying on the table. He unfolded it and pointed to Commonhall Street.

'It's here, look. It's an amazing little place. It's right in the centre of town. A sort of hidden gem. There is some redevelopment going on. A lot of people are a bit concerned about it. Look, you get to it off Bridge Street. It's opposite the entrance to the Grosvenor Shopping Centre.'

'Do you know, I've never had a look around that. I might go down there, do a bit of mooching, and catch up with the others in Commonhall Street.' Her idea was working, after all. Martin seemed more attentive. He seemed more anxious not to put pressure on her. If so, he had matured during his time in Hong Kong.

Half an hour later, Grace parked the police squad car in its reserved spot by the Town Hall. She walked down Bridge Street looking for the shopping centre. There it was. The grand flight of steps up to the level of The Rows and the entrance to The Grosvenor Shopping Centre. She looked across the Street. There was a sign for Commonhall Street. Excellent. Once in the Shopping Centre, she was in what seemed to be the largest mall, St Michael's Row. This was not the usual modern mall. It was flanked by old and rather elaborate facades. She was only a short way along it when a shop window caught her eye. Standing in the middle was a black suit that would suit her nicely. Her current one was now getting on and showing its age. She needed to perk up. The black suit always worked. She looked up. The shop was LK Bennett. She knew their shop in Canary Wharf and had bought things there. She had not been aware that they had a shop in Chester. It was all absurdly expensive, but she told herself she would get a lot of wear from it. She soon carried her bulging and posh-looking carrier bag across Bridge Street. Her credit card had taken a hammering, but she was pleased with herself.

Steve and Katie pulled up outside the house on Commonhall Street. It was odd to find such a small-scale set of dwellings just off the main central Street of the City centre. They had approached it from Nicholas Street. This made Steve more aware of how close they were to the Centre for Industrial Design. They were looking at a short terrace of six houses. Each had their front door and one ground-floor window looking onto the street. The half-dozen doors were brightly painted, and the whole place looked neat. These houses might be relatively small, but they looked cherished by their owners. Katie pressed the doorbell, and they heard it ring inside. There was no response. Several more bell pushes later, there was still no response.

'What do we do next?' asked Katie. 'I've got a strong feeling this is where our dead woman lived.'

'We need to enter, but we must get a search warrant. We will have to go and talk to Drake.'

'I'll call him,' said Katie, impulsively. Steve wandered down the street to see if there was any way of getting access at the back. As he came back, Katie was getting excited.

'Drake says he will take responsibility just like Whipcord Lane. He's on his way over.'

Half an hour later, Drake arrived in the Police Range Rover with the locksmith, James Bull.

'I see,' said Drake as he slid out of the car. 'We have another small house. It looks even tighter than those in Whipcord Lane. OK, Jimmy, get to work.' The locksmith opened his tool bag and pulled out his lock-picking tools. Drake took a short walk down the street. Katie had told him that there was a way through to Bridge Street.

Commonhall Street narrowed towards the end and had a small bridge across. For a moment, Drake wondered what this was for. When he reached it, Drake admonished himself for being so stupid. Of course, it carried the upper-level Rows walkway that ran down Bridge Street. He emerged from under the bridge into the street. There were steps to his right leading up onto The Rows. He looked to his left, where he could see The Cross. It marked the junction of the four main streets of the city. To live in Commonhall Street was to have a privileged location in the historic quarter. For a moment, he stood asking himself whether he would rather live here or where he was on The Groves. It was a pointless question. He was not about to move.

Drake reached Sophia Hamilton's house just as the locksmith straightened himself.

'The problem with my profession,' he said, 'is that I am permanently bending down. Sometimes, I kneel, but that brings other problems. My back and knees are complaining.'

'I feel for you, Jimmy,' said Drake.

After a couple of minutes, James Bull was grunting to himself. 'This is an easy one,' he said as the door opened. The small party of police officers entered.

'Oh, I say,' said Drake. The narrow hallway was made to seem wider by a staircase made entirely of glass. Drake ran a hand across the end of one of the steps. He went to the back and looked up inside the flight of stairs. The effect of its transparency combined with reflections was quite dizzying. It was a functional object made into a fascinating sculpture. Drake wished he had the imagination to think of such ideas. The floor was black-stained wood, which carried through right across the house. Drake decided that a wall had been removed to create such a space.

'I detect a designer's hand here,' said Drake. 'This is not just any old interior. The person behind it knows what they are doing. It could be by the same designer who did Kuiper's house.'

There were two lounger chairs of a design Drake immediately identified. They had curved and veneered plywood back and seat panels with black leather seats and back pads. Next to each one was a black leather stool designed to match.

'These are the famous chairs designed by the husband-and-wife team of Charles and Ray Eames,' said Drake to his colleagues. 'They were Americans and during their career became famous. You can still buy these chairs from a limited number of retailers here. My wife Cynthia was always telling me about Eames and partner.' Drake halted for a moment as if listening to his wife's voice. Katie and Steve had seen this before and just waited. 'Sorry,' he said. 'I just get these flashbacks. She is always with me, ready to intervene when I see something interesting. For some reason, these stools are always referred to as ottomans. I've never quite understood that; they look like stools to me. They are soft and comfortable. Surely, an ottoman is more solid and probably has storage below the hard seat.' Steve raised his eyebrows to

Katie at the long lecture. They both wanted to get on with learning about Sophia Hamilton, not Charles and Ray Eames.

Drake looked around. This was not a room filled with books. There were, however, many magazines spread around on the floor by one of the chairs. Popular titles included The World of Interiors, Homes and Gardens, and Grand Designs. It seemed likely that the occupant had created this interior. She was probably a professional interior designer. Drake was in no doubt that she had a fine eye for design of all kinds. He looked around further. A series of ceiling and freestanding light fittings were beautiful pieces of sculpture. The fabrics hanging by the window were a riot of colour. In one corner of the room was a drawing board tilted at an angle and covered in sketches of objects and spaces. Katie disappeared and soon came into the room, looking pleased with herself.

'In the kitchen is an empty plastic drug bottle. It has Sophia Hamilton's name on it. The prescription is for Myloxifin. We have the address of the chemist on the label. They are only just around the corner.'

'OK,' said Drake. 'I need to be sure of this. Go there now and get whatever information you can about the drug and the patient. If they are reluctant to disclose information, see if they will give you the prescribing doctor's name.' Katie set off with a distinct swagger. Drake was amused to see that she was rather enjoying herself. That was excellent.

Katie Lamb clutched Sophia Hamilton's drug bottle, now sitting in its transparent evidence bag. She surveyed the label and set off looking for the dispensing chemist. The pharmacy was soon found. She entered, accompanied by a ring from one of those mechanical bells triggered by the top of the door.

'I am a police officer,' she said, showing her ID. 'I would like to speak to the senior dispensing pharmacist, please.'

'That's me,' said a man in a long white coat behind the counter. 'What's the problem?'

'Can we go somewhere confidential?' asked Katie. The pharmacist took her into a small room off the main space.

'This is where we do injections and interviews,' said the pharmacist, pointing to a chair. 'People outside in the shop can't hear us talking.' He sat opposite her across a small desk.

'We are investigating the death of Sophia Hamilton,' said Katie. 'We believe she has been prescribed Myloxifin. It was dispensed here.'

'Correct,' said the pharmacist, 'She has been a patient collecting prescriptions from us for many years. I'm distressed to hear that she has died. She was relatively young.'

'The circumstances are such that we need to investigate,' said Katie. 'Can you confirm that you have dispensed something called Myloxifin for her?'

'Yes, I'm pretty sure you are right. We do not have many patients taking this drug. It is potentially addictive and also dangerous if taken in excessive quantities. We only dispense small amounts at any one time. Let me check our records.' He turned to the computer at his side and worked away rapidly on the keyboard, staring intently at the screen.

'Ah, yes,' he said. 'I remember now. She takes it occasionally for severe migraine. She tried all the other painkillers and specialist migraine drugs, and none seemed to work reliably for her. Looking at our records, she seems to have been ordering more than usual recently, but not beyond the amount restricted by her doctor. There is nothing to worry about there. It is a strong painkiller and can be used as an anaesthetic. We don't dispense it often. It is strong and habit forming.'

'Can you tell me what it contains?'

'Yes. The main constituent is oxycodone, which is the most dangerous and addictive bit. It is also the main drug. It is a semi-synthetic opioid. Myloxifin also contains Naloxone, which is present essentially to attempt to block some of the worst side effects. Taken in larger quantities, Naloxone can also be used to try to counteract the effects of an overdose. Have you reason to believe she took an overdose? If so, we would be extremely concerned.'

'It is a case under investigation at this time,' said Katie. 'But I don't suppose it hurts if you know. The pathologist who completed the post-mortem reported the presence of an opioid and considerable quantities of alcohol. There was an empty gin bottle beside her.'

'Oh, my goodness,' said the pharmacist. 'We are always careful to warn about that. You will see on the label we print instructions not to consume alcohol. The instructions in the box would also say this. I'm also sure that her doctor would have stressed the need for great care with this drug. Do you think it was an accident?'

'I can't answer that now, but I expect, in due course, we will review the situation with you. Can you give me the name of Sophia Hamilton's doctor? I need to get someone to identify the body.'

The pharmacist passed Katie a small card showing the doctor's details. Katie had been writing everything down in her notebook. She checked the spelling of the drugs with the pharmacist, thanked him for his help and left.

Katie was walking back to Sophia Hamilton's house on Commonhall Street when she bumped into Grace.

'I thought I would come and look around,' said Grace. Katie pointed at her carrier bag.

'You've managed to fit in a shopping spree. I bet that's a bit special from there.' Grace winked and grinned. Once back at Sophia Hamilton's house, Katie briefed Drake on her visit to the pharmacy. Drake nodded and smiled. Katie was coming along nicely, he thought. She will get promoted eventually.

'First thing, Katie,' he said. 'You need to get someone to do a formal identification of Sophia Hamilton's body. We don't know any relatives. Get on to her doctor and ask him to go and do it.'

'Yes, of course,' said Katie, bristling with pride at the tasks she was getting to perform.

'Right,' said. Drake. 'Let me just bring our pathologist up to date. He took out his phone, put it on speaker and hit a speed dial key.

'Professor Cooper, pathologist.'

'Hi, Prof. It's Drake. I have an update for you on the woman found in Professor Kuiper's house in Whipcord Lane. She is called Sophia Hamilton. Her doctor will come and make the formal identification. Constable Katie Lamb is arranging it. She has prescriptions for a drug called Myloxifin, and we found an empty bottle here in her house. It contains something called oxycodone.'

'Oh, my goodness,' said the pathologist. 'That is a dangerously strong opioid. Taken together with an excess of alcohol, it is likely to be lethal. Effectively, the alcohol amplifies the drug's side effects. They include breathlessness and severely reduced heart rate. She could easily have just stopped breathing sufficiently to get enough oxygen. The reduced blood flow from the heart would carry it around the body less effectively. That is not a good combination. I will finish my report. I think we can conclude she died of an overdose.'

'Thanks, Prof,' said Drake. 'So now we know how she died. We need to discover the circumstances.'

'Over to you, Drake. Goodbye.'

'Bye.'

Steve was examining Sophia's computer. He looked up.

'Well, her computer doesn't have any security on it. I have opened her email, and it looks like she exchanged messages with Kuiper frequently.'

'One more matter,' said Drake. 'I checked her clothes in the bedroom wardrobe. They were nearly all size twelve.'

'That lingerie in Kuiper's house was size twelve,' said Katie.

'So,' said Drake. 'We have provisionally established the link. We still don't know how she got to Kuiper's house because although you found her car, we haven't found her keys. Did someone else drive her there, possibly in a semi-drugged state? Was it Kuiper, and if so, why? The business of the missing keys might turn out to be important.'

12

The following morning, Drake and Grace returned to The Centre for Industrial Design. They were using Walt Dickinson's room and were waiting for Frank Richards to arrive. Grace got out her notepad. Drake thumbed through a book from the shelves. It was full of beautiful drawings and photographs. At precisely the appointed time, there was a tap on the door. Frank entered in his brown lab coat and took the seat opposite them.

'Thanks for coming, Frank,' said Drake. 'Can we begin by hearing how things changed when Professor Kuiper arrived?'

'Sure,' replied Frank. 'It turned out that everything changed. All the original staff call it "The Big Change." He was appointed out of the blue. None of us, not even Walt, knew about it until one morning, he walked into the School with the Vice-Chancellor. Walt had been told the afternoon before to have all the staff present for a meeting with the Vice-Chancellor. None of us knew that he was bringing in a new head. The Vice-Chancellor told us that the good news was that we finally had a professor. No School member had previously held that title, though we all knew Walt was Head. Some people thought this was a good thing. Some others weren't so sure. Then the Vice-Chancellor said he had agreed several things with Professor Kuiper. The first was that he would immediately take over the leadership. The second was our title changed from a School to a Centre. This meant that we would offer more post-graduate degrees, become more international and do far more research. Then he left.' Frank paused and looked at Drake and Grace.

'So, all that was a sort of bombshell, was it?' asked Drake.

'Absolutely,' replied Frank.

'Has it been a good thing?' asked Drake.

'I'm not one for change,' said Frank. 'So, to start with, I was rather opposed to it all. I prefer continuity. I think most of the staff felt the same way. I think everyone was sorry for Walt. As time has passed, I feel there have been a lot of positives. We have a significantly larger departmental grant. We've got lots of new equipment. We've made several new appointments. I've got a better workshop.'

'So, what did Professor Kuiper say at this meeting?' asked Grace.

'Not a lot,' replied Frank. 'I've since understood that he prefers ideas and actions to words. I respect the fellow. He was in a difficult position. I guess he feels the less he says, the better it will be. But he talks to me quite a lot. Perhaps I don't have a position to argue about. I'm sorry, I'm talking about him as if he was still alive. I can't get used to him not being around anymore. It's awful.' Drake scratched his head, and the others waited for him to say something.

'From what you've told us, it all seems to be an improvement, doesn't it?' Frank nodded, then tilted his head from side to side.

'What worries some staff is the new emphasis on research. Many of them feel their skill lies in designing and teaching design students. There are other worries for some. The emphasis is on the design of objects that include a significant element of information technology. This is probably how the world is going, but this can seem threatening to those unfamiliar with IT. To be fair to Professor Kuiper, he graduated on the innovative master's IT course. It's specifically designed for people with non-information technology backgrounds. He has offered to create sabbaticals for staff who want to take the course. Rumour has it that one or two of the younger staff are considering it, but the senior and older staff are not interested. That's understandable. I want to do it, but I don't think Professor Kuiper liked that idea. I was originally a mechanical workshop supervisor, but in recent years, I've had to learn a lot about computers. The School, oops sorry, the Centre, needs me to be able to do basic computer maintenance. Mainly software and operating systems. Nothing too technical.'

'Who are the new appointments?' asked Grace.

'Dr Aletta van Leyden, who you've met and two new research assistants who work with her.'

'They work mainly in the same area as Professor Kuiper?'

'Exclusively.'

'So, they don't interfere with anybody else?'

'Exactly. They are no threat. We were about to advertise more posts, but I've no idea if that will happen now.'

'Perhaps we could change tack a little,' said Drake. 'We need to know more about Professor Kuiper. I understand he came from The Netherlands. Is that correct?'

'Yes,' replied Frank. 'He is Dutch and came to us from TU Delft, one of their leading universities. Then he came here and took that master's course in IT. None of us knew him then, of course. After that, he went back to Delft and started up a company. Dutch industrial design has an international reputation. He was happy there and doing well, as I understand it.'

'So, why did he come here?'

'We don't know what our Vice-Chancellor offered him. We do know that a key part of it was the ability to operate commercially and academically. He has set up a company that he calls Blindsight.'

'That's an odd name,' said Grace. 'What does it mean?'

'He explained it to me once. I don't remember it all. As a teenager, he had rapidly deteriorating sight and nearly went blind. He eventually had operations that restored good vision, but the whole experience had a profound effect on him, as you can imagine. It is typical of him that he immediately researched all about human vision. Apparently, and I find this amazing, some blind people report seeing things. It's called blindsight. It's beyond my understanding. He began to take an interest in ways to support human vision. That has taken him on to virtual reality and artificial intelligence. I'm now at the end of my expertise. I can't explain more. Anyway, Professor Kuiper thought it was a great name for a unit involved with virtual reality. A VR headset makes you blind to the real world but allows you to see a virtual one. Not many people would have come up with that idea. He was a clever man.'

'We understand that he was married,' said Grace.

'Yes, he had a wife or partner. She came to the UK with him. I'm not sure if they were formally married. They certainly lived together. They separated almost immediately. I don't know anything about it except that he has admitted to having an affair with another woman. I don't know more than that. I think it was all rather acrimonious.'

'Does his wife still live in the UK?' asked Drake.

'I think so. He told me one day that she moved to a flat in that development by the Shot Tower over on the canal in Boughton.' Grace made a note.

'Do you know her name?' asked Drake.

'Only vaguely,' said Frank. 'She comes from some country in the Far East. I can't remember, and she has an odd name. He used to refer to her as Nimade.' Grace was making more notes.

'Is there anything else you can tell us that might help us?' asked Drake.

'I suppose you ought to know about his competitors. As far as I understand it, he had started a company in Delft that was supposed to be researching and developing virtual reality. When he came here, he gave the company to his old employees. But they tried to keep developing his ideas, which he wouldn't allow. He became almost paranoid about them.'

'Who are they?' asked Drake.

'I can't remember the name, something like VV. They are based in The Netherlands. They took over the commercial work he was doing in Delft. When he left, he shut down his operation there, and his staff created a new company. Legally, they were banned from using any of the intellectual property in the previous company. Unfortunately, they seem to ignore this. Willem was sure they were using all his ideas. He was trying to find legal help to stop them. It is in a different country. That could be extremely expensive. I think he had almost given up.'

'Is there anybody else you would suggest we need to speak to,' asked Drake.

'Not that I can think of,' replied Frank. 'Actually, I think Prof Kuiper was rather a lonely man. He certainly didn't have a large circle of friends. He told me once that he only really had one true friend.'

'Who was that?' asked Grace.

'He didn't say. I got the impression it was someone back in Holland. Now I think about it, I remember him saying this friend was partly responsible for him coming to Chester.'

'Thanks, Frank,' said Drake. 'You have been a great help to us.'

'It's the least I can do. I had grown to like the man. This business has upset me personally. I also now worry about where the Centre will go.'

'I'm sorry we can't help you with all that,' said Drake. 'But we will do our best to bring whoever is responsible to justice.'

Drake had called a meeting to discuss the next steps in the investigation, but there was no sign of him. Everyone was sitting around the large rectangular table chatting. Eventually, Drake arrived.

'Sorry for the delay,' he said. 'I had to report on progress to the Super.'

'Hard luck,' said Martin. Others smiled knowingly.

'Yes,' said Drake. 'It's not easy. The university Vice-Chancellor is putting pressure on him. They want it sorted out as soon as possible. I've told him we are still working on it. We need to progress a few lines of enquiry. Firstly, Martin. Take Steve and go to the housing development by what is called the Shot Tower. What does that mean, does anybody know?'

'It's quite a piece of history,' replied Martin. 'It's a tall round tower down by the canal in Boughton. I used to fish there as a kid. It was used to make the lead shot. They poured molten lead over a sort of sieve at the top. The lead fell through in pellets that formed perfect spheres as they dropped to the bottom, solidifying on the way. Then, they dropped into a big vat of water, where they rapidly cooled off.'

'Why did we need so much lead shot?' asked a curious Drake.

'For muskets, originally anyway,' replied Steve.

So, this Shot Tower is quite old then?' asked Drake.

'Not sure. Probably a couple of hundred years,' replied Martin.

'So,' said Drake. 'We believe that Professor Kuiper was married and then divorced. It is thought his ex-wife lives in a new development by this tower. Does that make sense?'

'Absolutely,' said Martin. 'it's quite large, lots of flats, looks quite posh.'

'Now the problem you have, Martin, is that we only know the wife's first name. She is called Nimade, and I don't know the correct pronunciation. She is from the Far East, and there is some complication about her name. That is the only information I have. Quite obviously, we expect her to be able to help us with our investigation, as they say. I think the divorce was somewhat acrimonious. Does that give her a motive? It may be a long shot, but at the least, she should be able to tell us more about Professor Willem Kuiper. If you can make contact, ask her if we can go and talk to her. Frank Richards and Aletta both told us there is some other woman involved. Was it Sophia Hamilton? If not, who?' Martin was making notes and nodding his head.

'No problem. We will get on with it right away.'

'Now, Grace. Take our technician, Dave and track down a company called VV. It is short for Virtual Virtue. It's Dutch. It may or may not be in Delft. They are serious competitors for Professor Kuiper's company, Blindsight. There is some possibility of industrial espionage involved. The first task is to identify and find them. At this stage, though, do not approach them in any way. No emails or use of a website, please. I do not want them to know we are interested in them.'

'Actually,' said Dave. 'I can look at their website using a VPN. They will not know who it is then.'

'Remind my old brain what a VPN is,' groaned Drake.

'It stands for Virtual Private Network,' said Dave. 'It means that you don't go on a website yourself. You send instructions on an encrypted line to another place to do it for you. It's pretty well secure. It means the owners of the website that you are visiting cannot get the address of the real user.'

'Oh, I see,' said Drake. 'Actually, I'm not sure I do. But I understand the clever result. Go ahead.'

'I've got another idea,' said Dave. 'We never found Professor Kuiper's laptop, which might have contained information. Because he was so well informed about Information Technology, I strongly suspect he will have his files backed up. That is quite likely to be in the cloud. We might be able to access them if we knew his email address and password.'

'Now I live in Chester, I know only too well what a cloud is. But I don't understand what you are saying,' said Drake.

'It's nothing clever,' replied Dave. 'It's a range of computer sites where you can put your data on high-capacity discs. As long as you are connected to the Internet, you can put files there and retrieve them. If your computer fails, you can still get all your data back. Is there anyone at The Centre for Industrial Design who might be able to help with that?'

'Yes,' said Drake. 'Good thinking. Try Dr Aletta van Leyden.'

13

'The new housing development by the Shot Tower is called Robinson Way,' said constable Steve Redvers. 'It is right behind the award-winning new supermarket. I'll drive up to Broughton.' Detective Inspector Martin Henshaw sat looking out of the window. He had heard about this place before. It had been in the news and won several awards, but he had not seen it yet. He was looking forward to exploring it. He glimpsed the Shot Tower as Steve pulled into the car park in front of the supermarket.

'It's on the other side of the canal. I don't see a way round to it,' he said.

'There's supposed to be a bridge over the canal,' said Steve. 'I'm sure they built a new one.' Steve set off around the supermarket with Martin in tow.

'I think it's only a footbridge,' added Steve. 'But it would be a long way to the next road bridge. Let's leave the car here. It should be an interesting walk.'

The two police officers walked down the left-hand side of the supermarket. They could see the Shot Tower straight ahead in the near distance. Then, as they got to the canal, there it was. A footbridge over the canal took them into a piazza. The footbridge tapered and became narrow as they crossed it. Once over, they found themselves up in the air.

'I think the footbridge had to be high enough to give headroom for canal boats,' said Steve as they descended a short stairway. Then there they were, between two blocks of new apartments. The Shot Tower stood at the far end of the piazza. It was slightly off-centre between two modern blocks. The block on the right went just past the tower. The block on the left stopped short and connected to some old industrial buildings.

'They must have been part of the old leadworks,' said Steve. 'There were many more in my childhood, but I think they were in pretty poor condition and had to be knocked down.'

'Let's look at the Shot Tower,' said Martin. 'I've never seen it before.' It stood at the other end of an axis from the footbridge and was framed by the apartments.

'What a thoroughly charming place,' said Martin. He walked up to the bottom of the tower. It was circular in plan and had arched windows dotted around it at various heights.

'It seems to taper slightly as it goes higher,' said Martin, 'or is that a trick of perspective?'

'I think it tapers,' said Steve. A large bird flew over and landed on the roof.

'I saw something about that on the news,' said Martin. 'We are lucky to see it. They've built something on the roof to encourage peregrine falcons to nest there. It looks as if it has worked.'

'The whole thing is looking handsome now, isn't it?' said Steve. 'Recently, they have taken a nasty outside lift off the tower and tidied the whole place. Nearly all the old lead works buildings have been knocked down. I don't know when it was built. Quite a long time ago. Maybe about 1800, I think. I believe it's the oldest one left standing. There are a couple of others somewhere. There were lots of them around the country once. I read that the earlier process was unsatisfactory. It didn't make the shot balls sufficiently spherical for use in muskets. These new towers were seen as a significant advance in technology.'

'How fascinating. I'm so glad they've saved it,' said Martin. 'I suppose there's a staircase inside, and the windows must illuminate it.' They walked around the tower. Just beyond the left-hand apartment block was an industrial, warehouse-type structure. It was linked to the tower by a bridge. A sign announced that this building now housed some large and luxurious apartments.

'It looks like this building has been preserved,' said Martin. 'Do you know what it was?'

'I assume it is part of the old leadworks,' replied Steve. 'I think this bit was an engine house.' The leadworks were quite extensive but run down and neglected.'

'Drake would like this,' said Martin. 'You can see they've tried to reflect the industrial nature of the place in these new apartment blocks.' Steve looked at him, and they laughed. It could have been Drake lecturing colleagues about architecture.

'I imagine these apartments in the two new blocks must be quite expensive,' said Martin. 'I can't imagine anyone coming here unless they were comfortably off. It all looks as if it will become a sought-after location.'

'Yes,' replied Steve. 'Our friend Nimade must be alright financially even if she has separated from Professor Kuiper.'

'OK,' said Martin. 'You take the left-hand ones, and I'll take the right-hand block.' They separated and disappeared into their chosen blocks.

Detective Inspector Martin Henshaw and Constable Steve Redvers met in the piazza between the two blocks after a fruitless day searching the Robinson Way housing development next to the Shot Tower. Nobody had heard of a Nimade or knew anyone with an oriental appearance. Just as they were about to return to their car, a woman walked across the footbridge over the canal carrying a Waitrose bag. It looked like she had been shopping for provisions at the nearby supermarket.

'Go quickly, Steve, and see if it's her,' said Martin.

Steve fell trying to get out of the car and disappeared from Martin's view. Martin was sniggering. Steve just managed to intercept the woman before she went inside the development.

'Excuse me,' said Steve, holding out his ID. 'I'm a police officer, and we are looking for someone called Nimade.'

'That's me,' said the woman. 'Have I done something wrong?'

'No, of course not,' said Steve. 'I assume Nimade is your first name. Is that correct?'

'Yes. In a way.'

'And would your second name be Kuiper?' asked Steve.

'I don't have a second name, but that is a long story. I have used the name Kuiper in the past,' said Nimade, 'but I don't use it anymore.'

'Am I correct that you were the partner of Professor Willem Kuiper?'

'That is correct. We have separated. Why all these questions? What do you want to know?'

'It's nothing to worry about,' replied Steve, 'but we want to talk to you about an ongoing investigation. Could a couple of my colleagues come to see you? We think you might be able to help us with this investigation?'

'Is it about the argument between Willem and Laurence?' asked Nimade.

'Who is Laurence?' asked Steve.

'Laurence Bailey. He's joined me and left Willem's company,' explained Nimade. 'They are having a dreadful dispute over it. I've told Laurence to leave it be. Willem is behaving stupidly.'

Martin had arrived and overheard the conversation.

'What we want to talk to you about may be related to this issue,' said Martin, 'But I think it's too complicated to discuss here.'

'Of course. Do come in. How rude of me not to have invited you earlier.' said Nimade.

'We would like to send two colleagues over tomorrow morning. One of them will be female, the other is our Chief Inspector.'

'No problem. I'll be in all morning. I do hope Laurence isn't getting into trouble.' said Nimade.

'Not as far as we know,' said Martin.

Martin and Steve reported back to Drake at the station.

'OK,' said Drake. 'Grace and I will go and see Nimade tomorrow as arranged. In the meantime, Martin, you and Steve go up and down Whipcord Lane and knock on doors. We need to know if anyone saw or heard anything on the night Kuiper disappeared. See what you can discover. Sophia's exact whereabouts on that Tuesday night are important to our investigation, not just of her death but possibly also of Kuiper's.'

Martin and Steve arrived in Whipcord Lane early the following morning. Martin had decided they should go in time to catch people going out to work.

'You go knocking on doors,' said Martin. 'I will keep an eye out for anyone going out that you might miss.'

Steve began at the end of Whipcord Lane by the canal. His attempt to find someone to speak to was fruitless until he got to Willem Kuiper's house. Martin was standing at the next house waiting. Steve knocked on the door. It was the woman who had pointed them to Kuiper's house. She spoke as quickly and as incoherently as before. Martin was about to ask her to repeat slowly when she disappeared inside her house, leaving the front door open. Martin and Steve looked at each other in puzzlement. They heard some frantic rattling from deep inside, and the woman reappeared. She held out her hand, and Steve put his underneath. She dropped a set of keys into his hand. She then took Martin by the hand and walked over to the planting between her property and Kuiper's house. She gestured wildly up and down at the bushes.

'I've got it,' said Martin. 'You found these keys in the bushes.' The woman nodded her head, sighed, and disappeared inside her house. The two policemen stood wondering what was coming next. She appeared yet again carrying a bag of seeds. She went over to the bushes and threw a handful of seeds down.

'I see,' said Martin. 'You found the keys when feeding the birds.'

The woman let out another sigh and nodded. She was exasperated by their inability to understand her in this game of charades. She turned and went back into her house again. This time, she shut the door. Steve and Martin looked at each other and laughed. Martin went out into the street and back into Kuiper's front garden. He tried the keys in the front door. One key opened it immediately.

'Look,' he said to Steve. 'This one looks like a car key. I bet it fits Sophia Hamilton's car. We can't test it now because our SOCO team have taken it away on a trailer. She must have arrived and opened the front door. Then, for some reason, she threw them into the bushes.'

'Well,' said Steve, 'it seems likely that she was not in a good state by then. Her overdose was already taking effect if she took the tablets at home.'

'Excuse me,' are you police?' asked a voice. Martin turned to find a young man standing at the gate.

'Yes, Sir,' replied Martin. 'Can we help you?'

'I live a door further down. We know there has been an incident here. The other evening, a man was hammering loudly on this door. I heard the noise and came to look out of my window. I saw him banging and standing back. He looked up and then banged again. So, I went to my front door to see if he needed help. By then, he had disappeared, and I saw a car rushing to leave. The tyres were screeching.'

'Could you describe this man?' asked Martin.

'I knew you would ask me that,' said the informant. 'I can't. I didn't get a good look at him.'

'What time was it?' asked Martin.

'Oh dear. I really cannot say. I didn't check my watch. I would say early evening. I couldn't be more precise than that.'

'Was there anything on the television then?' asked Martin, hoping for better information.

'I didn't have it on. I was working. Yes, early evening, I would say, getting dark.'

'Thank you,' said Martin. 'Do you mind if Constable Redvers takes your name, address and phone number? We may need to speak to you again.' While the man obliged and Steve made notes, Martin tried to call Drake, but he was not answering his phone.

'Of course,' said Steve, having finished his notetaking. 'He will be at Nimade's apartment by now.'

'I think he will want to know. We have now established that a man tried to contact the occupant of this house on that Tuesday evening. Was he trying to raise Professor Kuiper or Sophia Hamilton?'

'And of course', said Steve. 'Who the heck was he? Could it have been Kuiper?'

'Unlikely. We know it was early evening, and Aletta has told us Kuiper was in the Centre for Industrial Design until much later. Anyway, he would have his keys. So, who was this man, and has he got anything to do with our investigation?'

14

The following morning, Drake and Grace arrived at Robinson Way. As they walked between the two housing blocks, Drake couldn't help standing and taking in the new architecture. He guessed that Cynthia would have thought it was clever. The footbridge was on the axis between the two blocks that framed a view of the Shot Tower at the far end. The buildings were domestic in scale, but the overall structure was quite industrial. Although covered in a cladding rather than the local brick, the colours respected the surroundings.

His still nascent architectural analysis suggested it was a good job. He "heard" Cynthia reminding him to distinguish between architecture he liked and architecture he admired. He quite liked this place, and he certainly admired what the architects had tried to do. It was thoughtful and clever. They took the lift to the first floor and rang the bell of Nimade's apartment. The door opened to reveal a vision of oriental dress. She bowed slightly in acknowledgement of Drake's greeting.

'Good morning,' he said, holding out his ID. 'I am Detective Chief Inspector Drake. This is my Detective Sergeant, Grace Hepple.'

'Please come in.' Nimade moved aside rather than leading them in. She stood while the two police officers entered the living room.

'What a charming dress you are wearing,' said Grace in breathless admiration.

'Thank you,' said Nimade. 'It is part of my national dress. It makes me feel at home.'

She wore a long, slim-fitting sarong-style skirt in a mainly green floral pattern. Above this was a white lace top bound at the waist with a long bright yellow sash hanging down to her knees. Drake estimated she was less than five feet tall. She gestured to the chairs facing the floor-to-ceiling window, which looked onto a balcony with a view of the famous Shot Tower.

'Would you like a cup of my special tea?' asked Nimade. Both Drake and Grace nodded and smiled. While Nimade was busy, Drake looked around. He had settled into a wicker chair with patterned fabric-covered cushions on the seat and back. He had been somewhat cautious about sitting in such a chair, but it welcomed him by sympathetically settling around him. He remained more nervous about how easy it would be for him to climb out of it. The room was full of bamboo and coloured fabrics. On either side of the doorway onto the balcony were two fearsome-looking creatures carved in pale, smooth wood. Intriguingly, they sat facing slightly towards the doors and mainly looking out. The whole place was calm and yet full of interest.

'I'm interested in your two sculptures,' said Drake as Nimade put their tea beside them.

'Yes,' answered Nimade. 'They deter evil spirits from entering the room. It is traditional where I come from.'

'That explains why they are looking out instead of into the room,' said Drake.

'Exactly,' said Nimade. 'They could not do their job if they looked inward.' She gave Drake a stern look and then broke into gentle laughter. Drake smiled back. She was teasing him. Nimade sat bolt upright and looked quizzically at her visitors.

'Nimade,' said Grace when Drake nodded to her. 'I'm sorry to say we have some sad news. Your ex-husband has been found dead.' The response surprised Drake and Grace.

'That is not sad,' she said so quietly that Drake wondered if he had heard her correctly. Could this mild-mannered and charming woman mean such a harsh judgment? Drake and Grace remained silent. This was partly out of respect but also astonishment. Nimade spoke again.

'Perhaps I shouldn't have said it like that. Of course, it is sad when anyone dies. Although our relationship began well, it became unhappy. He was quite nasty to me. He cheated me. But enough of that. Thank you for coming to tell me. I appreciate it. I followed him here from Holland. We had a company that we ran jointly, but he cheated me. I have now started again, and I run it myself. All is well.'

'Tell me,' said Grace, following Drake's pattern. 'Where are you from originally?'

'I am Indonesian. I am from the beautiful island of Bali.'

'Are we correct to address you as Nimade? Is that your first or family name?' asked Drake.

Nimade let out a charming little giggle.

'No,' she said. 'In Bali, we do not use family names. I don't have one. On our island, we only have four basic names. They tell about the order of birth. My name is Made, which means I am the second born. My older sister is called Wayan. My younger brothers are Nyoman and Ketut. Boys and girls use the same names, but boys sometimes put "I" first and girls "Ni," so I am Nimade. You are not pronouncing it well. I always tell English people that my name is Knee Ma Day.'

'Forgive me,' said Drake, 'but doesn't that get confusing? You must have so many people with the same name?'

'Not really. We also get nicknames. But those usually vary from family to friends or work. You can have several nicknames. Everyone in any situation knows who you mean.'

'So, what appears on your passport?' asked a puzzled and fascinated Drake.

'I didn't travel until I met Willem, so I used Kuiper after that, but I don't like to use it now. May I correct you? We were never actually married. We met and fell in love in Bali. I love the island of my birth, but it can be a little old-fashioned and inflexible. To hold a wedding in Bali, you must be of the same religion. I am Hindu, and Willem was a non-practicing Christian, so it was not possible. We moved to Holland and then the UK. Marriage no longer seemed to matter.'

'Nimade,' said Drake. 'I must tell you that there is a possibility that Willem was murdered. Have you any idea who might be responsible?'

'Oh, dear. Of course, I am sorry he is dead, and it's awful if he was murdered. The least he deserves is justice. Any number of people might want to get even with him. I don't think I know anyone who would kill him. How did he die?'

'I'm sorry,' said Drake, 'but I can't tell you that. It is part of an ongoing investigation.'

'Of course, I understand.'

'Can you tell us more about your situation? How did you come from Bali and meet him? Was it in The Netherlands?'

'No, he was on a visit to Bali. The Dutch once ruled my beloved island. We have no great affection for that period of our history. But there are still many contacts with the Dutch. He's a designer, he came to my shop, and we talked. In Bali, we value contact that can bring us trade with European countries. He said he would help me set up a business in the Netherlands. It went on from there. I suppose I was young and easily starstruck. I must tell you that he was a brilliant man. He was extremely clever to work out the need to combine industrial design with information technology. He could also put great collaborative teams together and lead them. He was inspirational. He was a genius. The world needed Willem Kuiper. But I was wrong to think I needed him. I do not need him.'

'So,' said Grace. 'Was your shop for industrial design things?'

'Not really. In this country, you would probably call it interior design, but that makes no sense in Bali.'

'Can you explain that, please?' asked Drake.

'It is difficult for people who have never been to Bali to understand. You would see this more easily if you visited. We don't make a distinction between interior and exterior. What you call architecture, interior design, and even landscape design are all the same to us. Our climate is different. We need to be shaded from the sun, but we do not need to be separated from the outdoors as in this flat.'

'That is fascinating,' said Drake. 'My wife was an architect, and now that she is gone, I am trying to understand architecture.'

'A typical traditional Bali house is nothing like yours. When we get a plot to build a home, we first make a wall around the site with an opening for an entrance. We almost always build a wall across but setback from the entrance. That also keeps evil spirits away.' She giggled, winked at Drake, and continued.

'The plot is almost always rectangular, and the long axis must point to our sacred volcano, Mount Agung. Then, inside this wall, we build a series of small pavilions. Most of them will have at least one side open. We use each pavilion for its specific purpose. One is for cooking, one for eating, several for sleeping, and others include perhaps a shrine and places for relaxing and entertaining. There are no corridors in Balinese buildings.'

'That sounds wonderful,' said Drake. 'I must try to visit your wonderful island.'

'You will always be welcome,' said Nimade. She clasped her hands together, pointing skywards and bowed slightly before continuing. 'So, it makes little sense to distinguish between interior design, garden design, and architecture. They are all part of one thing.'

'So, what was your business?'

'It was called Design East. I can source wonderful things in Bali, such as fabrics, ceramics, furniture, carvings, art, and sculpture. My shop supplied all these and could commission special designs from artists and craftspeople. We make things out of local materials. Wood, bamboo, weavings. All these things I can supply. My shop had become well established and popular with locals who wanted to improve their residences. It is in the town of Ubud where all the local artists and craftspeople work.' Nimade paused, grimaced and looked out of the window. Drake thought she was recalling something she would prefer to forget. She continued.

'However, Ubud is also on the tourist trail. Many visitors from Europe and Australia would want to buy things and have them packaged and sent to their homes. That part of the business was not my strength. Then, an Australian living in Bali, Laurence Bailey, started to help me and soon took over the management of the overseas trade. I would never have been able to expand the business without him. Then, one day, Willem came to the shop. He was fascinated, as I can see you are. Many people from Holland or England come to Bali and feel the same.'

'So, what did Willem do to help you?' asked Grace.

'He had a business dealing with his specialist area in Delft. There was an empty shop next door. Willem used my money and his local knowledge to open the shop in Delft. It is a marvellous location right in the main market square. It was so successful that Willem sponsored a shop in Amsterdam. Since then, we opened in The Hague and Eindhoven. Inevitably, we soon developed an Internet business selling online. Willem got more interested in that than the shops. We were about to start another here in Chester, then probably London. I could arrange the selection of objects and materials. Laurence arranged the packaging and the transport. To buy and transport Bali art to Delft cost us a fraction of the price we could sell them for in Europe. Many craftspeople in Bali work for low wages. I pay them well over the minimum wage. They are all happy to get paid so well. It was a successful business and highly profitable.'

'You said Willem cheated you?' said Drake. 'What happened?'

'I was naïve. He got a much better job here in Chester. I came with him. But he was having a relationship with another woman. I felt I could not trust him. We separated, so continuing the business was not possible. Willem wanted me to buy him out, but I didn't have the money. So, we sold it, and each kept half of the money. A man called Damien Bewick bought it. To begin with, I thought I could work with him. He was horrible to me and treated me like a junior employee. I had to leave. I am starting again. I withdrew all my contacts in Bali, so Damien Bewick, who bought the business, was furious. I think he lost a lot of money. I told him it was Willem's fault. He was even more cross when Laurence Bailey decided to stay with me. He works mainly in the shops in Delft and Bali.' Nimade dabbed her eyes. 'He has helped me to find the right place for our new shop here in Chester. I would be lost without him.'

'So,' interrupted Drake. 'Why did Willem want to break up your company?'

'I don't think he thought about it like that. He just wanted to move on. He needed more money for his new company here.'

'You are talking about Blindsight?' asked Drake.

'Yes. I don't understand what they do. I know it is clever and potentially could make a lot of money. Willem had lost interest in my company. He got involved with virtual reality and all sorts of futuristic things. He wanted to be the first to design things that would eventually be in every house. One of the wonderful things that initially attracted me to Willem was his wish always to move forward and do new things. But I have since seen the downside of it all. Of course, he needed money to fund his new enterprise. I have lost most of the shops in The Netherlands. I kept the one in Delft because it was in my name. It was my money that we used. I have opened one here in Chester. It is a wonderful city. I have a new business called Bali Style.'

'Does Damien Bewick live in The Netherlands?' asked Grace quietly.

'No,' said Nimade. 'He lives here in Chester. That is how Willem met him.'

'Do you know where he lives?' asked Grace.

'I don't have his address, I'm afraid. I think it is in Curzon Park somewhere.'

'How does he run Design East, which is mostly in The Netherlands?' asked a puzzled Drake.

'He has put local people in charge of each shop, but they know nothing about the Bali end of the business. It's a disaster. Recently, he came to my shop. He tried to persuade me to work with him. He was quite threatening, telling me how dreadful things would happen to my business if I didn't. He kept looking around the shop. Not so much at all our delightful things but at the shop itself. I wondered if he was going to steal things or smash the place. I didn't like him. I told him to leave.'

'If he threatens you, please let us know, and we will visit him,' said Drake. 'You have been most helpful. I am sure it was difficult to talk about all this. We wish you all the best with your new business. Before we leave, please give Grace any contact details you have for Damien Bewick. It would be helpful to have details of the shops involved in Design East.'

Grace drove Drake back to the station. He remained silent throughout the journey. In the case room, Drake sat in his chair. It rocked creakily. He sat silently with his eyes closed. Grace made herself a cup of tea but left Drake to his own devices while she dealt with her emails. Suddenly, Drake interrupted her train of thought.

'Isn't Nimade a charming person?' said Drake.

'She is so gentle and talented,' said Grace. 'She has a slightly strange combination. She believes in tradition, but she is also innovative and creative.'

'So,' said Drake, 'the upshot of all that is we have yet another line of investigation. Has Damien Bewick lost so much money buying Design East that he wanted to take it out on Willem Kuiper? From what Nimade tells us, he sounds like a rather unpleasant chap. Could he be responsible for the murder?'

15

The case team were all at their laptops except for Dave. Drake was rocking gently in his favourite chair. He alternated between the crossword and reading his case notes with the occasional grunt. Occasionally, his eyes would close. Strangers might think he was nodding off, but Grace knew better. He was turning the case over and over in his mind. The peace was broken by Dave coming in with his laptop.

'We've tracked down VV,' he announced to the room. 'It is rather oddly named, as was suggested. The full name is Virtual Virtue.' Drake opened his eyes. He had been listening all along.

'Where are they?' he demanded.

'They are in Delft in Holland,' said Dave. 'They seem to have some relationship with TU Delft, formally known as Delft University of Technology. It is highly regarded. They sell the Artificial Intelligence capability that they have developed. Strangely, Willem Kuiper is mentioned on their website.'

'Good work,' said Drake. 'Right. Let's all review the case.' Everyone gathered around the table. Drake immediately went to the case boards and entered the information for VV. He spoke as he crossed the room to the table.

'We now have three mysteries to deal with. The deaths of Sophia Hamilton and Professor Kuiper and the break-in at The Centre for Industrial Design. They could all be connected, or only two connected or all entirely separate events. Firstly, there is Sophia Hamilton. She was found dead from a combination of excessive alcohol and an overdose of Myloxifin in Professor Kuiper's house. How did she get there? Her car was parked in the street, but her keys were under a bush. Did she drive or someone else? The second question is whether she committed suicide or whether some unknown person administered the dose, probably after she was drunk on an excess of gin. Perhaps it was a call for help that went disastrously wrong. Drake paused and took a sip of his lukewarm coffee. Everyone waited silently for him to continue. Grace was sure this explanation was not for their benefit as much as a rehearsal for his own.

'We have just heard from Kuiper's ex-partner, Nimade, that he had at least one other woman, maybe more. She doesn't know any names. Was Sophia Hamilton one of these other women? There was a mobile phone on the table with a gin bottle. Dave, have you managed to break into it?'

'Not yet,' said Dave, 'but I haven't had much time. It is an old Android phone, which gives me some hope. iPhones are notoriously secure, but people have had success getting at the data on Androids. I know where to get information on how to do this, so, given time, I hope to produce results.'

'Secondly,' said Drake dramatically. 'We have the death, almost certainly murder, of Professor Willem Kuiper. We already have several lines of investigation. He seems to have been extremely clever but rather good at making enemies. People with at least a theoretical motive include his ex-partner, Nimade, who broke up with him acrimoniously and, she claims, he cheated on her with another woman. Grace and I have heard that because they broke up, they had to sell a company she started, and she has had to begin again. It was a substantial business called Design East that Nimade claims she started. Kuiper sold it without consulting her and even keeping all the money. He sold it to a Chester chap called Damien Bewick, who has since discovered it doesn't work when Nimade is not involved. He has probably lost much of his money, so he has reason to be angry with Professor Kuiper. We must investigate him. Their most senior employee deserted the company and joined her in a new venture called Bali Style. His name is Laurence Bailey, and he is also pretty angry with Kuiper.' There was another pause as Drake sipped the last of his coffee.

'Then there's Walt Dickinson, who Professor Kuiper pushed out of favour at Deva University. We have seen he has a terrible temper. Then there are the people at "Virtual Virtue," who feel he stole ideas jointly developed with him. Another possibility that keeps pushing itself forward in my mind is Sophia Hamilton. Could she have killed him for some reason and then committed suicide? We need to get to the bottom of all this somehow. Perhaps none of that matters at all, and Professor Kuiper was mugged for the watch missing from his safe. The Vice-Chancellor told us that he always wore it, but there was nothing on either wrist of his body. It was worth over a million, so mugging is a distinct possibility. Who might have known about it?' Drake paused and looked around at his attentive audience before starting again.

'Finally, there is the puzzle over the break-in at The Centre for Industrial Design. Who did it and why? The computers and hard discs were not stolen but damaged. This might suggest the thieves were not after the data. However, as we know all too well from many thefts, computers are easy to sell and quite valuable. It is hard to understand the motive for the break-in.' Drake paused.

'So, where should we turn our attention to?' he demanded. The lesser ranks all turned to look at Martin, who seemed unprepared for the attention.

'I suppose we could work on more than one line of investigation,' he said.

'Good thinking,' said Drake. 'Perhaps the first thing to do is to find the people we have not yet had access to. That means Damien Bewick, of course, but we could also try tracking down some relatives or friends of Sophia Hamilton. The other thing to do is to put out information about the missing watch. Steve, will you do that? I think there are images of all the watches on the wall in Kuiper's living room. You should be able to identify the missing one. Martin, perhaps you and Katie could try to trace people connected with Sophia Hamilton. Grace, you can help me with the University people in general. Maybe we can either eliminate or focus on Walt Dickinson. We need to go back to The Centre for Industrial Design. I would also like us to find out more about Damien Bewick. We know that he bought the old company Design East from Professor Kuiper. He has found it unworkable now that

Nimade and Laurence Bailey have left and set up their own company, Bali Style. We understand from Nimade that Damien Bewick is angry about this and that she found him impossible to work with. He sounds as if he ought to be a prime suspect for Kuiper's murder.'

'There's one more thing,' said Dave, the technician. 'As we all know, Kuiper had his phone with him when he died. It's an iPhone. I suspect it has the latest operating system and is secure. It was not on him when we discovered the body. If the murderer took it, they are unlikely to be able to open it. However, we accessed his call record from the mobile phone company. There's not much we can learn from that. One possible piece of information is that his most frequently called number was in the Netherlands. We have found the name of the person it is registered to. Strangely, it's a rather grand English-sounding name but a Dutch number.'

'What is the name?' asked Grace. Dave opened his notebook and flipped through several pages.

'Justin Makepeace,' he said.

'Martin, try and find out more about him,' said Drake. 'You never know, it might be important.'

Steve Redvers went to the evidence store. He knew the four watches found in Kuiper's safe were stored there for safekeeping. He took each wooden box out and opened it to reveal the watch inside. He then photographed the watches on his phone. He set off for Whipcord Lane in a squad car, taking the key that had been found with Sophia Hamilton. Police cones were outside the house so he could park directly by the little gate. He ducked under the blue and white "Do not cross" tape to enter the front door. The safe had been left open when the watches were removed. He went back to the living room where Sophia Hamilton's body was found. On the wall behind the shelves were drawings and photographs of five watches. He studiously compared his phone pictures with the images on the wall.

One took centre position on the wall and was the watch he had no phone picture of. This must be the one that was missing. He took photographs on his phone of all the images on the wall. He wrote the name of the manufacturer in his notebook. He pulled out his iPad and discovered the house Wi-Fi was working, but it needed a password. He wandered around the house looking for the network router box. It was in a cupboard with a sloping top under the stairs. A tag hanging off the box had a password on it. He was surprised that Willem Kuiper was not more safety conscious.

He sat in one of the Egg chairs, which were more comfortable than he expected. He searched on his iPad for the watch company website. It was full of watches at prices he could not imagine paying. Most were in the tens of thousands of pounds. He found one with no price on it. It was the watch he was interested in. All watches in this limited edition had been sold. He searched on his iPad for websites dedicated to expensive watches.

He found a site listing the highest prices watches had sold for at auctions. Everything was priced in US Dollars. The one at the top of the list fetched over thirty thousand dollars. He sat staring at it in disbelief. He scrolled to the bottom to find the most costly of these absurd watches. It had been sold for over two million dollars. He started to work his way up. Then, suddenly, it was on his screen. It was identical to the photograph he had just taken on his phone. The Vice-Chancellor had told Drake that this watch was worth one and a half million pounds. Steve was astonished to discover one of the ten made had been sold at auction a couple of years ago for over three million dollars. He opened a little currency app on his phone. It was worth one and a half million pounds.

Grace wondered what the best way might be to track down Damien Bewick. Her line of thought was interrupted by Sergeant Denson bringing the mail. She suddenly saw a possibility. She would follow it up tomorrow. It was already too late to do it now.

The following day, Grace drove out of town. She went over the bridge by the racecourse and steered the squad car into the outside lane. She wanted to be ready to navigate the notoriously tricky junction ahead. It was known as Overleigh Roundabout. She had driven here many times before. She had missed her turning on several occasions. In particular, the turning off into Curzon Park was tricky to find. She managed it and let out a sigh of relief. She was soon driving along Curzon Park North, parallel to the River Dee. To her right, set behind trees, was a selection of grand houses, which most people would describe as mansions. To her left would be a series of turnings into quieter roads, some of which had more modern homes. In most of Chester, these would still be regarded as large and expensive houses, and she guessed this would be a likely place to find Damien Bewick's home. But she had a trick up her sleeve. The first turning she took was fruitless and a dead end. She tried a couple more before seeing what she was after. A red Royal Mail van. She pulled up behind it and waited. Sure enough, a postman wearing his trademark shorts and carrying his enormous bag appeared from down the road. Grace was out of the car quickly enough to intercept the postman as he opened the rear door of his van. She held out her ID and a street map.

'Can you tell me where I might find someone called Damien Bewick,' she asked.

'Mr Bewick, Yes, of course, Sergeant. I deliver to his house almost every day. He lives here,' he said, pointing to the map.

'Thank you,' said Grace. She set off for the location the postman had given her. Grace was sure that Drake would want to be involved in an interview with Damien Bewick, so she remained in her car and took a couple of photographs on her phone. It was a grand house set back from the road behind a gravel forecourt. There was a central door with windows on either side. It had an altogether traditional and unremarkable appearance. Given the location in one of the more recently developed parts of Curzon Park, she guessed it would fetch a pretty sum on the market. She sat and checked her pictures and watched the house. There was no sign of movement. It looked very much as if Mr Bewick was out. Considering her task complete, she returned to the station.

16

The following morning, Drake arrived just after Grace. He did some circuits around his case boards and looked disappointed. He had not seen anything new. He then went over to the coffee machine. He made two cups and took one over to Grace, who was working on her laptop writing her report.

'I've found Damien Bewick's house,' said Grace as Drake put her coffee down and looked over her shoulders at the pictures she had loaded onto the laptop.

'He must be pretty well-off to afford a house like this,' said Drake. 'From this picture, it seems to have a sophisticated security system. We need to proceed carefully on this. I would rather have more information about the chap before we interview him. Arrange a watch on the place for a few days, and let's see what we get.'

Martin came in, looking frustrated. Drake gave him a sympathetic smile.

'I've been using that list of Kuiper's calls that the phone company gave us. I was trying that Dutch number that Kuiper had been calling so much. It belongs to a fellow called Justin Makepeace. He never answers it. I've left a message on his answering service to get him to contact me. So far, I've not had any luck.'

Steve Redvers arrived and immediately started showing his photographs of the drawings and pictures of Willem Kuiper's watches.

'Right then,' said Drake. 'Get on to the manufacturers and see if the watch he was given has a serial number. Once we have that, then we need to put out a general notice to all police authorities about a potential theft. I imagine whoever has it won't be able to sell it for much. Such an expensive item will have to go to a proper auction. See if you can discover the places likely to run such an auction and alert them to the situation. Hopefully, whoever has it will be sufficiently greedy and stupid to try to recover its full value.'

Drake took his cooling coffee back to his chair, dug out his wrinkled copy of The Times, unfolded it to the crossword and began his work. Martin's phone pinged, breaking the peace and annoying everybody except Martin. It was a text message, and it came from the Dutch mobile of Justin Makepeace. Martin read it and showed it to Drake.

'That's interesting,' said Drake. 'He says he is in Delft. He says he's doing some research there.'

'Yes,' replied Martin. 'He wants to know why we are after him. He says he has no plans to be back in the UK soon. What shall we do?'

'OK,' said Drake. 'Try to call him again, and if there's no answer, send another text. We will have to tell him what's happened. I'd rather do that face-to-face, but if it's the only way of getting his attention, then so be it. Say we believe he might be able to help us. Let's see where that gets us.' Martin walked away, tapping on his phone. It was only a few minutes before he returned.

'He has sent me another text. He didn't know about Willem Kuiper being stabbed, and he is appalled and says he was a lifelong friend. He is working every day in the library at Technical University Delft. He says he can arrange a meeting room there. He says that this is important to him. He will spend as long as we want with us.'

'OK,' said Drake decisively. He called Katie Lamb over from her desk.

'Katie, look at flights to Delft for me, please. I'm not sure if they have an airport. I doubt it. My Dutch geography is poor. Try and arrange a trip over. I can go and see the Bali Style shop there too.'

'Certainly,' replied Katie. 'When do you want to go?'

'Just as soon as you can arrange it,' said Drake. Technician Dave came over to Drake with some more thoughts.

'I overheard you talking about going to Delft,' he said. 'I've tracked down this company that is Kuiper's main competitor. They are called VV. They have an office in the main square in Delft. Perhaps you might visit them too?'

'I've got a better idea, Dave. Why don't you come with me? With your knowledge, you would be much more able to understand them.'

'Great,' said Dave. 'Thanks, that sounds as if it would be interesting.'

Drake and Dave settled into their seats on flight KL1074 from Manchester to Amsterdam. Katie told Drake that a train ran from Amsterdam Schiphol Airport to Delft. Drake stood back and pointed to the window seat.

'No,' said Dave, 'Higher ranking officers should have the window seat.' Drake laughed and pushed him forward.

'Don't be silly,' he said. 'I need the aisle seat to stretch out my legs. I'll get the cramps in ten minutes sitting in the window seat. How long is this flight anyway?'

'It's only an hour and twenty minutes,' replied Dave. He was not used to accompanying his boss and was anxious that he did not develop one of his grumpier moods. Seeing Drake stand in the aisle of the plane dramatically illustrated his height. He could easily reach to put their bags in the overhead locker. Dave thought there were many benefits to being as tall as Drake. He could dominate a recalcitrant miscreant. He could see over a crowd. He could put his bags in the overhead locker.

Dave still had his boyhood enthusiasm for everything to do with planes. He appreciated watching the happenings at a busy airport. Drake had already opened his iPhone and was scrolling through all the notes and pictures he had accumulated about the case. The Times newspaper was on his lap. It was folded open at the crossword, covered with Drake's usual hieroglyphics. Dave judged it was best to leave him in peace and sat looking out of his window.

'Doesn't flying drive you mad?' grumbled Drake as they plodded on through their taxi to the runway. 'You have an hour flight and half an hour at each end touring the airport. Add on the two-hour check-in and all that dreadful security stuff, and you've wasted most of the day.' Dave thought an answer was not required. He nodded and smiled. By the time they had landed and docked at Schiphol, Drake was even grumpier. With Dave's guidance, he discovered that the airport station was on the way from Amsterdam to Delft, so they had a short journey. It took a brief walk through an obligatory shopping centre. They took an escalator down to the railway booking office. 'This is a bit easier than Heathrow. Why can't we design things like this? I'm beginning to like Holland.' was Drake's comment as Dave got two tickets from a booking clerk who spoke perfect English.

'The trains run every half an hour and take forty minutes,' said Dave, handing Drake his ticket. Their luck was in. No sooner had they reached the platform when a train arrived. Dave was fascinated by the coaches, which only had doors at the ends. There was then a split staircase with one flight going down and the other going up. This took passengers to each of the two levels in the coach. Dave wanted to go upstairs to get a better view. Drake trailed along behind, lowering his head to get through the door.

They soon found a table with two empty seats on one side, and only one woman sat opposite. She smiled and nodded to them as they arrived. They stored their bags and sat down with Dave again in the window seat. Drake looked at his watch, thinking it might tell him the time. He glowered at it and tapped the screen to encourage it to move on, but it didn't. Dave suggested the time difference in Holland might be responsible. Drake grunted and felt silly.

'It's disgraceful,' said the woman opposite, who had seen Drake's encounter with his watch. She spoke with a Dutch accent but had heard them speak in English. Drake was becoming impressed with the language skills of this naturally helpful nation.

'Excuse me?' asked Drake.

'This train. It's already two minutes late.'

Drake turned to Dave, and they both laughed.

'What's funny?' asked the woman. Drake tried to explain how grateful you would be in England to have a train only two minutes late. The woman did not seem to find this helpful, and the conversation ended.

They soon arrived at a brand-new station. It had a grand and lofty station hall with great sweeping curved roofs. Drake lectured Dave about this architecture and wanted to look around. Dave humoured him for a few minutes.

'I've got some half-understood memory of this,' said Drake.

'We should just about get to the university by two,' said Dave as they got into a taxi.

'Excellent,' said Drake. 'How do we find Justin Makepeace?'

'I will text him when we get there,' said Dave. 'He has a room we can use.'

The taxi stopped almost as soon as Drake had pulled out his phone.

'Good gracious,' he exclaimed. 'This is another fascinating building. What an amazing place Delft is. I knew it was a historic city. I didn't expect such futuristic architecture. You have to admire how the Dutch invest in the public domain. Dave, look at this building. The architects have taken the ground right over the roof in a great sweep of grass. Higher on this roof, there is a simple white cone. I'll take a bet that it floods the interior with daylight. Then, you need to ask what sort of building warrants this approach. A library is likely to be a deep-planned building. In any case, you don't want to glaze the walls. They need to be solid for shelving. It's clever, appropriate and artistic. It's just marvellous! This is already an interesting trip.' Dave was amused to see Drake so enthusiastic as he wandered off, trying to get better views of the building.'

Dave was busy texting Justin. He got a reply back straight away to say he would meet them at the entrance. He managed to persuade Drake to go inside the vast interior. It had a slopping ceiling with a great hole in the middle.

'Sure enough,' said Drake. 'The cone distributes daylight in the centre of the space.' He looked around to see Dave talking to someone else. His little lecture on architecture had fallen not so much on deaf ears as missing ones.

'This is Justin Makepeace,' said Dave.

'Hello, I'm Drake. I'm just admiring this extraordinary building.'

'Yes,' said Justin. 'It's pretty special. We're lucky to have a famous international firm of architects here. They designed this library and the railway station.'

'Ah,' said Drake. 'I wondered if the same architectural hand was responsible for them both. Who are these wonderful architects?'

'They're called Mecanoo,' replied Justin. 'The name sometimes causes people to confuse them with toys, but it's a single letter "c" and a double letter "o" unlike the toy.'

'Of course, of course,' said Drake. 'I remember now. My wife occasionally mentioned them.'

'Your wife?' enquired Justin.

'Yes, Cynthia Drake.'

'Wasn't she the D of PDS?'

'Yes, Porter Drake and Simpson,' replied Drake proudly.

'Well, yes, we know of their work. It's quite impressive.'

'I'm sad to say she is no longer with us. Justin patted him on the back and smiled. Dave was warming to this sympathetic, urban individual.

'But I understand my best friend in life has been murdered,' said Justin. 'I'm finding that hard to believe. Willem Kuiper and I have been close friends since we were students. I hope I can tell you some things that might help you bring his murderers to justice. There are certainly some possibilities.' He looked left and then right, finally spinning right around.

'But, come with me. I cannot talk about things like that out here, where there may be prying ears and eyes. What Willem was doing was confidential. Recently, he told me they were making great progress. It had to do with the way they made use of AI in the design of virtual reality headsets. He was not one to exaggerate. Strangely, I was worried that he might be harmed. It is a cut-throat business. I thought he might only be kidnapped to get a ransom reward. I think his life was probably worth a great deal. A pity his murderer didn't understand that.'

17

Drake and Dave followed Justin through the airy and spacious library. He opened the door to a small office. The wall opposite the door was fully glazed flooding the room with daylight. They sat around a small circular table where Justin had put some water bottles.

'Shall I tell you first how we found out about you?' Drake asked. Justin nodded his head.

'We found Willem Kuiper's body under a tree in a small park. He had been stabbed. We know he made an all too short call to our emergency services, which we believe was terminated when he died. His phone was missing when we found him. Although we don't have his iPhone, we did get a record of his calls from the phone company. Your number was, by a long way, the most frequently dialled. We know he told one of his colleagues that he only had one real friend in life. We presume you are that friend.'

'Yes, indeed,' said Justin. 'We met here in Delft when we were students.'

'Sorry to interrupt you,' said Drake. 'Why were you here in Delft?'

'It has a huge reputation. I wanted to be an industrial designer, and they have a world-famous school here. They all speak English so well. I fell in love with Dutch culture. I describe it by saying, "The trains all run on time, and you can take drugs on them." Of course, I don't mean that seriously or literally. Things here are well managed and reliable, but there is a freedom that we in the UK can only imagine. I love it here. This wonderful building in a historic city like Delft is a good example. History is respected and preserved, but society is open to new ideas too.'

'So, you studied industrial design together?' asked Drake.

'Yes. We found ourselves sitting at adjacent desks on the first day. He spoke wonderfully good English, so I suppose I naturally graduated towards him. We got on famously right from the start. We were both what you might call natural designers and did well. We found the course stimulating. Although it was challenging, we understood all the issues it raised. When we graduated, some of the best students decided to do a master's course. Willem and I discussed the challenge to industrial design created by the information revolution. We foresaw that many products would eventually have computers in them. We felt this was a new direction that we should follow. Because I am from Chester, I knew about the innovative master's course at Deva University. It is specifically designed for students with undergraduate degrees that are not in computer science. We moved to Chester for a year and then came back to Delft. For a while, we worked together as conventional designers. Willem always wanted to develop ideas rather than do traditional practice. Miraculously, he got funding to start a research and development unit. He was brilliant at finding good people and putting together a multi-disciplinary team. I worked with him for a while but gradually began to write more. I've finally decided, late in life. I'm doing a PhD.' Justin paused and sipped his water.

'Thank you so far,' said Drake. 'That is all interesting. We interviewed Nimade. She told us that she met Willem at her shop in Bali. How did that come about?'

'While I was working with him, we started to design interiors to earn money. We were interested in handcrafted materials, and I bought this wonderful book about design in Bali. Willem had been to Bali on holiday and loved the place. The Dutch were involved in the history of the place, so there is a natural connection. He went there to see if he could source materials to give us an edge. Willem has always had a commercial angle to his work. He found Nimade's shop, and they got on marvellously. He had the idea of opening a shop jointly with her in Delft. It is still here. It's called Bali Style now. It's in the old Market Square. The Dutch name is Markt. Anyway, the business went from strength to strength.

Willem raised money to open more shops in Amsterdam, The Hague and Eindhoven. Willem was never one to stand still. We used our understanding of the Internet and information technology to create a website and an Internet business. Willem got more interested in designing the website and the Internet business. Nimade had hired an Australian guy, Laurence Bailey. He helped to run the international business. He manages the shop in Delft. Willem promoted him to oversee all the shops in the Netherlands.'

'We understand that Willem and Nimade fell out,' said Drake. 'Can you tell us anything about that?'

'Not really. By then, I was getting more work writing about design and reviewing places, shops, and objects. It just grew and has kept me busy ever since. I do know that Willem had what you might call a roving eye. We never talked about his women. He didn't volunteer anything, and I wasn't interested. I understand that Nimade discovered one of them, and they fell out. Nimade has a strong sense of fairness. I think it's a Balinese thing. Willem could be focused like a laser beam when dealing with business matters. I think he had moved on to his research and development work in his company, Blindsight and was no longer interested in Nimade's business. She calls it Bali Style now. He probably wanted all the money he could muster for Blindsight and left her with a raw deal. It was probably unfair, but I don't know the details. He told me that he was angry that Laurence Bailey sided with Nimade over it. She still has the shop here in Delft. It's in the Central Market. I've seen Laurence a couple of times. He seems to run it now. It's a good combination. She has all the design flair and can source material in Bali. He knows how to deal with all the packing and transportation business. He is an excellent manager and keeps the show on the road.'

Following Justin's advice, Drake and Dave took a taxi to the centre of old Delft. Justin had called for it, and almost as soon as they had left the library, it was there to collect them. Justin told them it was quite a long and complicated walk, and it would be easy to get lost. The taxi driver was talkative.

'Getting around the city,' he said, 'is made more complicated by all the canals we have. You need to know where the bridges are to plan a sensible route. You will enjoy the city centre. It is a lovely old place.'

The taxi pulled up just outside a quaint old hotel. Drake could see from his map that they were only just off the edge of the space known locally as Markt. They checked in and navigated their way up a narrow winding staircase to their adjacent rooms. They dropped their overnight bags. The two policemen freshened and set off, following Drake's map.

They walked a short distance down Voldersgracht and came to a little street that crossed over a narrow canal. Almost immediately, they were in the expansive, rectangular place that was Markt. Drake had been reading his tourist guide and pointed to one end of this market square, where there was the grand town hall.

'That's Renaissance architecture,' said Drake, 'so not as old as all the buildings around. At the other end of the square is the main church of the city, which looks gothic to me.'

'I don't know how you can tell all these things so quickly,' said Dave.

'One obvious clue in this case is to look at the windows,' replied Drake. 'If you look at the church, the windows are small openings with pointed arches. Now look at the town hall. It has windows with curved arches over them. It's simple.'

Dave muttered his appreciation of the lesson in architecture.

'Now,' said Drake. 'We haven't come here to enjoy the architecture. If we walk across there, we should find Nimade's shop, and next door are the offices of Virtual Virtue. They are one of the main competitors for the Chester Blindsight unit.'

The shop had a sign that read Bali Style. The sign looked like it had been made quickly and put over an earlier name board.

'It was called Design East when Willem Kuiper was in charge,' said Drake. 'The windows are crammed with beautiful objects. It is a feast for the eyes. Let's go in.'

Suddenly, as the door closed behind them, they had left the hustle and bustle of Markt behind and were now in a haven of peace and calm. A young lady approached them. She was as beautifully dressed as the shop window. She bowed and smiled, touching her hands together as if in prayer.

'I'm beginning to fall in love with design from Bali,' said Drake.

'I am from Bali,' said the shop assistant. 'How can I help you?'

'We are just looking around,' replied Drake. 'But we were told to ask for Laurence.'

Their host looked genuinely crestfallen.

'Oh dear,' she said. 'I'm afraid he is in Bali right now. He goes there often to find things for us to sell. I'm afraid he isn't expected back for some time. He has to supervise all the packing and crating. Most of our items are precious. We don't want things to be damaged in transit.'

'So, are you in charge in his absence?' asked Drake. Their host smiled and bowed again. Dave could tell she had charmed his usually more detached superior.

'May we look around?' asked Drake.

'Of course,' said their host, backing away from them. She made a sweeping gesture of invitation with her right arm.

Drake started to tour the shop. There was bamboo everywhere. There were wood carvings in abundance. Drake remembered the ones in Nimade's apartment. They all had the same florid and detailed style of carving. Mostly, they were figures of exotic-looking animals and humans. There were masks by the dozen. Drake found some light fittings that cast beautiful shadows around them. The sofas were all colourful and inviting.

Drake and Dave had come to the end of their tour.

'I'm sure,' said their host, 'Laurence would want me to show you our fabrics. Please follow me upstairs' She walked right to the back of the shop and began to climb some rather rickety steps.

Drake followed her unsteadily up the winding staircase. Dave came behind, nervously watching that Drake did not stumble. They arrived in a surprisingly large space under the roof with tall dormer windows. Everywhere they looked, there were fabrics of one kind or another. There were curtains, rugs and coverings for seating. Brightly coloured cushions were scattered everywhere.

'These are all woven in Bali using local materials. We never quite know what Laurence will bring back next. It depends on what the craftspeople in Bali want to make. We can, however, usually get a repeat made up if requested. So, if you had bought a rug and wanted another to match, you could bring in a photograph. We can get it copied for you.'

'Is that the end of our tour?' asked Drake as their host started back down the staircase. At the bottom, they came to a doorway.

'What is through there?' asked Drake, not wanting to miss anything.

'Oh, it's just an emergency escape. We keep it locked for security, but we all have a key.

'I could fill my home with all these things,' said Drake. 'But I am anxious to find the VV offices before they close.'

They said their goodbyes and thanks to the shop assistant and left.

'Oh look, Dave,' said Drake, 'Nimade told us VV was next door, and it is.'

'Yes, and on a corner with a side street going through and over the canal,' said Dave. He pointed to the door, where there was a small VV sign.

'Oh, dear,' said Dave. 'It looks closed already.' He tried the door, but it was firmly locked. Drake walked on to see if he could look through the windows, but they had plain white blinds pulled down. Across the little side street was an inviting-looking café.

'Let's have some coffee. We need to rethink our plans,' said Drake.

No sooner had they moved towards the café than a waiter with a long apron came out and pointed to a small table with two chairs, each having an absorbing view of the square. Dave ordered coffee, and they sat in silence, taking in their beautiful surroundings and all the bustle of people going about their business. The waiter brought a tray of coffee and biscuits. Dave had done relatively little travelling. It all seemed charmingly foreign.

'I wonder if you can help us,' said Drake. 'We hoped to see the people next door, but it looks closed, and there is no sign on the door. Would you happen to know when they open?'

'I would like to know myself,' said the waiter. 'It has been that way for several weeks now. It's bringing down the tone of the place. We like to have everywhere open here. It brings customers.'

'So, do you know what has happened?' asked Drake.

'Well, there are many rumours. Some say they had a break-in, and everything was taken. It's hard to believe people could get away with it. Others say the company went bust. They have gone out of business. They were always a bit secretive. We never understood exactly what they did. They didn't join in around here. It's all a bit of a mystery. I see people there from time to time. If you knock on the door, somebody might answer.'

18

Drake and Dave thanked the waiter and crossed the narrow street back to the VV premises. Dave thought he heard some movement inside.

'Let's give it a try,' said Drake. Dave was busy reading some posters in the shop window.

'It all looks most interesting,' said Dave.

'OK, if we get in, you do the talking as I don't stand much chance of understanding what they are doing.'

'What shall I say?' asked Dave. 'This isn't what I am trained to do.'

'Just tell them you are interested and ask if they will show us around. See where it takes us. If I feel the need to, I will chip in.'

Dave read a notice in small print on the door. It invited people to come in and find out about VV. He shook the door violently and was about to bang on it when it opened. A woman appeared wearing half-glasses with her hair tied back in a ponytail. She wore old-looking jeans and a white blouse. Drake thought she looked business-like.

'*Goedendag!*'

Dave made his introduction in English.

'Come in and look around,' responded the woman in perfect English, 'My name is Gudula. 'I'm afraid there are not many people around today.' She turned and waved to a man standing at the back of the shop. He left, and she continued. 'We are in transition. We were originally a major research company, but we lost our funding and turned to retail until we could re-establish ourselves. Unfortunately, that has not been a success so far.'

'Your work is in Artificial Intelligence?' asked Dave.

'Yes, but not purely AI. We are developing applications of AI that also need designing and manufacturing.'

'That is fascinating,' said Dave. 'I have dealt with a company in the UK with similar objectives called Blindsight.'

'Oh, yes,' said Gudula. 'We know them. Or should I say in English, we know of them.'

'So, what is your angle?' asked Dave. He was already worried whether he was right to mention Blindsight. He looked at Drake and saw no expression of concern on his face. Perhaps more one of gentle amusement.

'Look at this poster here,' said Gudula, pointing to a chart hung on the wall over a computer on a desk below.

'We are interested in helping people with epilepsy or other similar problems. These people may not just be classical epileptics but may have a TBI.'

'What is a TBI?' interrupted Drake.

'Sorry,' replied Gudula. 'It is easy to fall into acronyms in our business. A TBI is a Traumatic Brain Injury. An instance of concussion might be a more minor thing. A TBI might be the result of a car accident or some serious things like that. These are caused by the sudden movement of the brain within the skull. The problem we are currently trying to help is usually diagnosed as photosensitive epilepsy. People see flashing lights of some kind and suffer a fit. They may fall over and lose consciousness. The effects can be the result of something like repeated camera flashes. You might notice that the television companies often warn when a sequence is about to include them.' Drake nodded his head. He was surprised and glad to be keeping up so far. Gudula continued with her explanation.

'Traditionally, people with these problems are often advised to wear certain types of glasses, but this is only a poor partial solution. They don't always work. It is rather hit-and-miss. They also reduce vision when the lighting is poor. We need a kind of optical device that evens out the flashing effect. I cannot say anymore because we have international patents on the technology, and it is a valuable commercial secret. Imagine wearing a device that looks and feels like ordinary glasses that effectively measure the light and shield the eyes appropriately. One of our teams has been testing various devices and giving patients a button to press when they feel affected. We hope the data gathered by these experiments can be used to train Artificial Intelligence to make the devices work for everyone. It seems there are many ways of reacting in these situations. People are not all the same.' Gudula stopped and pointed to the wall chart that explained what she had been describing.

'Another of our research groups is trying to connect AI more directly. It seems these flashing lights cause changes in gamma oscillations in the brain. You can think of these as brain waves or unnatural electrical impulses in the brain. We can measure these by using electro-encephalograms. The kind of things you might get in hospital if you are suspected to have some problem with the brain. However, EEG kits for normal medical use are cumbersome and uncomfortable. That doesn't matter in the controlled environment of a hospital, but for everyday use, it is hopeless. People cannot walk around with all that stuff on their heads. So, our other group are trying to design new ways of doing this in nothing more unusual than a simple hat or cap. These measurements can then be used directly to train AI to spot unusual behaviour and correct intelligent glasses.'

'This all sounds exciting work,' said Dave.

'Yes, thank you,' replied Gundula.

'So, what are the main obstacles to your work?' asked Drake.

'In a word, funding,' replied Gundula. 'We originally had several research grants, but our work lies somewhere between research and commercial development, and it is much trickier to find people to fund it. It is also expensive. We need powerful computers and other equipment. Then, we must have highly trained research staff. I have had to lay off staff until the next grant application succeeds. It is a competitive business. We are not guaranteed success.'

'Your work does sound remarkably similar to that going on in Blindsight,' said Drake.

'Yes, we do similar but parallel things,' replied Gundula. 'We know about them because the director of Blindsight, Willem

Kuiper, did some of our early work before going to the UK and setting up his new company. I have had meetings with Aletta from Blindsight, and she is extremely interested in our work. She thinks they could get funding for it. We even discussed whether we might merge and where we would operate. They are already bursting at the seams, and the University won't give them more space. We need technical and other support, so we looked at some science park types of places.'

'Were these in Chester?' asked Drake.

'One was. The other was nearby. It was near the airport. It seemed promising. I think Aletta has put the idea to Willem Kuiper, but he won't hear anything of it. He has become antagonistic to us and is preventing any collaboration. So, he has become the obstacle. I'm unsure if anything will come of it now, but Aletta remains positive. I've no idea how she proposes to overcome the obstacle.'

'So how are you existing at the moment?' asked Drake.

'We have had to let a lot of staff go, and we have a minimal company left. We have an Internet business. It sells our basic virtual reality headsets and AI software. We also do some consultancy work with companies wanting to apply AI. I don't know how long we can survive like this. I am hopeful, but the situation is serious now. Aletta has said she has some ideas about unblocking the situation, but we have no idea what they are or how she is doing. I shouldn't be talking about it. It is all rather hush-hush. Please forget that part of our conversation. I don't suppose you gentlemen can help us?'

'I'm afraid we can't,' replied Dave. 'We are not in that sort of business. We are just interested in it.'

'I see you have a stack of crates and boxes at the back of the shop unit,' said Drake. 'So, it looks as if you are doing some business.'

'We get a minimal income from allowing our neighbours to load and pack material here. They import a lot, and their shop is not designed to receive large crates.'

'You mean Bali Style bring goods in through your premises?'

'Yes, they don't have a side entrance on the road, which we do, and we now have space to spare. It's all efficient and doesn't cause us any problems. Laurence Bailey comes round and unpacks everything. If he isn't here, it stays locked up until he arrives. Most of it goes into the Bali Style shop, but some parcels are destined for other customers around Holland. Laurence takes those away with him.'

Dave looked at Drake and pointed at his watch. Drake nodded.

'Thank you for a most interesting discussion,' said Dave. 'We must be going. I hope you sort out your funding issues. It is most worthwhile work.'

'Let's see if that helpful waiter will call a taxi for us,' said Drake. Dave called him and asked. The waiter stood in the doorway and waved his arms in the air.

'There's always one waiting over there on the other side of the square,' he said as Dave looked puzzled. 'It will be here in just a minute.'

During their taxi ride to the station, Drake sat in silence. He seemed to be looking out of the window. Dave was worried that perhaps he had let Drake down in Virtual Virtue. Once they were on the train, Drake became more vocal.

'Well done, Dave,' he said. 'You brought her out beautifully. People usually like talking about themselves, and she said much more than she felt she should have. So now we have a new angle to our mystery. It seems Aletta has been going behind Willem Kuiper's back by talking to VV. Gudula more or less implied that Aletta was trying to get Kuiper out of the way. This is not the picture she painted. She seemed to idolise Kuiper in my original conversation with her. The mystery deepens again. Nobody is quite what they seem in this case.'

19

The following morning, Dave arrived early and told Grace, Martin, and the others about his trip with Drake to Delft.

'It all feels inconclusive,' he said, 'but Drake seems quite happy with it.' Grace smiled. Drake had probably seen a new angle and was working on it in his head. Her phone rang.

'Hello, Detective Sergeant Grace Hepple.'

'Hello, Grace. This is Professor Cooper. I've been trying to call Drake, but he isn't answering his phone. I have some new information to discuss. I was planning on calling in on my way this morning. Do you know when he will be around?'

'I was expecting him first thing. He has just returned from a whirlwind visit to Delft. I would guess he is a bit tired, but I'm sure he will be here soon.'

'OK, then. I'll call on my way and hope he is there. It could be quite important news.'

Grace had not long put her phone down when Drake arrived, looking less than alert.

'I'm not jet-lagged,' he said. 'A one-hour time shift shouldn't make much difference, but I confess all that travel was tiring. The Dutch railway is impressive compared with our ramshackle affair.' He made his first coffee and settled down with his Times newspaper. He was still only halfway through his drink when Professor Cooper arrived.

'Good morning to you all,' he said as he entered the case room. Drake and his colleagues gathered around the central table. They looked expectantly at the pathologist.

'You may remember,' he said, 'that I found some material in Willem Kuiper's mouth. I wasn't sure what it was. Perhaps he was eating something when he was attacked. If it was what I half suspected, then it needed more detailed analysis than I could do in my lab. I have just had the results. We have found some DNA in Willem Kuiper's mouth.' He paused partly for effect and partly to see what reaction he was getting.

'I don't understand,' said Drake. 'Surely, you can pick up their DNA in anybody's mouth?'

'Of course. Of course,' replied the pathologist impatiently. 'But this is not Willem Kuiper's DNA. It belongs to someone else. Now, there could be a perfectly normal explanation. He might have been kissing someone quite recently. However, I found some actual material. That does not suggest that an ordinary kiss was responsible.'

'So, this DNA might belong to his assailant?' asked Drake.

'Of course, I cannot say that. We don't know. If, at some point, you find a suspect, and their DNA matches, this might give your barrister a great angle in court.' Everyone looked at Drake, who sat thinking.

'I am interested in putting this together with your point about the stabbing action being upward,' he said eventually. Drake slowly levered himself out of his chair and beckoned Steve Redvers and Martin to do the same. 'Turn around, Martin,' commanded Drake. 'Now Steve, you have a knife in your right hand. You are coming up behind Martin to stab him. How would you do it?'

'I think I see what you mean,' said Steve. 'I guess I would put my left arm around him, pull him towards me, and then bring my right hand round to stab him in the chest, and that would cause a slight upward movement.'

'Excellent,' said Drake. 'But there is one thing you might have forgotten. You are creeping stealthily and silently in order not to make any noise. Does that make a difference?'

'Yes, of course,' said Steve. 'I would put my left hand over his mouth.'

'Exactly,' said Drake, 'and I think, Martin, your instinct would be to bite the hand over your mouth.' Martin nodded.

'Well,' said Professor Cooper. 'I'm glad you have worked it out. This was what I thought. Of course, it is all supposition, but it does seem likely. If you find a suspect fairly quickly, I can look for a wound on the hand. It would certainly be pretty convincing in court. If we're lucky, we might get a DNA result. So far, all I can say is my findings would probably be compatible with this hypothesis.'

Once Professor Cooper had left and the team had settled down, Drake called everyone to order.

'This case seems to be getting more complex by the day,' he said. 'By my count, there are at least half a dozen possible suspects in the murder of Professor Kuiper. We cannot prevent new information or events from distracting us, but we do need to impose some order on our investigations. We need to probe the people surrounding Professor Kuiper in more detail. I prefer not to interview suspects until I know more about them. In this case, we have no alternative. So, I want to start with the person who seems to be the least likely to have a motive, the technician, Frank Richards. Carrying out interviews at the university could spread rumours. We will invite them here. Martin, please go to the CfID and ask Frank Richards to join us. Sometimes, a female presence can lubricate the proceedings. Grace will join me in the interview.'

That afternoon, Inspector Martin Henshaw arrived with Frank Richards in tow. Martin showed him to an interview room and made him some tea. A few minutes later, Drake and Grace arrived. Martin left to get on with other work. Drake and Grace settled down to interview Frank again.

'Thank you for coming, Frank,' said Drake as he sat opposite alongside Grace. 'I hope we haven't interrupted anything important?'

'You have, but I'm grateful,' replied Frank. I was doing the insurance claim for the computers. Thank goodness Aletta thought of taking out the policy. It's tedious. I think they try to discourage you by making the forms so complicated.' Drake laughed.

'Can we begin on the day before you discovered the break-in?' Frank nodded and smiled. 'So that is the Tuesday. Were you in the Centre that day?'

'Yes, I was there all day. It was busy. Some of the undergraduates are getting near the end of a design project. I love all our students, but they are a different breed to me. They cannot seem to manage their time well. At the beginning of a project, they sit around chatting and larking about. Then, there is a mad panic towards the end. Then they want the studio to be open all night. It happens almost every time. They have to produce design drawings and often models, and that means using my workshop. I am responsible for their safety, and they can use dangerous tools. It could be a chisel, or it could be a huge electric bench saw. It depends on what they are doing, but their models can be full-size or to a scale. Sometimes, their projects might be some domestic product. One group have just been designing air fryers. They are the latest thing, so the tutors like them because there aren't many established solutions yet. Students always seem to get marked up for being original. Sometimes, this applies to the higher-level students. They might have to design something as big as a garden ride-on mower or a mobility scooter. In these cases, they might make scale models.'

'Would Professor Kuiper be involved in tutoring these students in the studio?' asked Drake.

'Not often. He is more concerned with the research side of things. Sometimes, he wanders around the studio, and the better students love him. They know he has proved himself as a designer, and not all their tutors have. He often helps the better students to be creative. The less good students are a bit frightened of his reputation. He can be extremely challenging.'

'Does this ever break out into a confrontation with a student?' asked Grace.

'Not usually. Are you asking if any student might want to cause him harm?'

'Has that ever happened?'

'Not to my knowledge. Strangely, you might think, it is more likely with one of the tutors. I know one or two have got upset about Professor Kuiper suggesting a design angle they don't like.'

'Surely that wouldn't lead to demolishing the Centre or even murdering Professor Kuiper?' asked Drake.

'Oh, no,' said Frank. 'I can't imagine that.'

'So, I think you are telling me that you cannot imagine anybody from the Centre being responsible for murdering Professor Kuiper.'

'No, I can't imagine any of us doing it.'

'What about Walt Dickinson? He seems angry and bitter about the way he has been treated.' Frank sat silently, thinking for a moment.

'I know what you are saying. Walt has a short fuse, and he has been badly treated. I think, at the beginning, he was indeed angry. Because where I mostly work is near the Head's office, I sometimes overhear things from there. I have heard voices that sound raised in anger on two occasions. I'm afraid one of those times, it was Walt. He was shouting at Professor Kuiper. But I still can't see it turning to violence. I'm sure it didn't on that occasion.'

'You said there were two occasions when you heard raised voices,' said Drake. 'Do you know who the other one was?'

'I can't be certain, but I think it was Max. He was an awkward chap. He was a fiery individual, but he left a while back.'

'Thank you,' said Drake. 'Can I go back to something you said a moment ago? You said that you think Walt is happier now. What do you mean by that?'

'I think now, he has come to terms with it. He has settled back into doing what he most enjoys.'

'What is that?' asked Drake.

'Oh, designing and tutoring design students. He loves those parts of his work. I think he found the job of being Head of School rather tedious at best and stressful at worst. He is pleased to be free of those problems and is OK with life now.'

'Thank you, Frank,' said Drake. 'I'm going to tell you something. I need you to undertake not to mention this conversation to anybody else. The only reason for doing this is that we have another enquiry going on in parallel with the murder of Professor Kuiper and the vandalism of the Centre. We are trying to see if there is a connection between these.' Drake paused to get Frank's reaction and assess it before continuing.

'OK,' said Frank. 'If I can help, I should be only too pleased.'

'The fact is, Frank. We have another person involved in our investigation.' Drake studied Frank's face.

'I don't understand what you mean,' said Frank.

'Do you know a person called Sophia Hamilton?'

'Yes. Of course. She worked here.'

'Really?' asked Drake. 'You mean she was a member of the academic staff?'

'No. She was Professor Kuiper's PA.'

'Aha!' said Drake. 'I'm glad I asked you. Can you tell me more about her?'

'It was probably all a terrible mistake,' said Frank. Drake turned to Grace and nodded his head.

'In what way was it a mistake?' asked Grace.

'Well, this is not my area of responsibility,' said Frank. 'I don't know all the facts. I suggest you ask Walt about her. He would know much more than me. I don't have anything to do with appointments.'

'You say she worked here,' said Grace. 'Does that mean she doesn't work here now?'

'Yes, she disappeared some time ago. I haven't heard anything of her since then.'

'Why did she disappear?' asked Grace.

'I don't know. I would prefer you to ask Walt.'

'Walt is away, isn't he?' asked Drake.

'No. he's back today. He's in the Centre.'

'Thank you, Frank. We prefer that you don't discuss the details of this interview with your colleagues, please,' said Drake.

20

About an hour later, Martin had collected Walt Dickinson, the previous Head of the School, and sat him down in the interview room.

'OK,' said Martin. 'Your next victim is here!' Drake and Grace went to the interview room, where Walt was waiting.

'Apparently, you want to talk to me again,' he said.

'Yes, please don't worry about it,' said Grace.

'We are trying to establish the relationship between Professor Kuiper and someone called Sophia Hamilton. Can you help us with that?' asked Grace.

'To a limited extent,' replied Walt.

'We understand she worked in The Centre for Industrial Design as Professor Kuiper's PA,' said Grace.

'Yes. It was a complicated situation. I think Professor Kuiper made a couple of mistakes. It is easily done when you lack experience.'

'Can you explain what you mean?' asked Grace. Drake deliberately allowed Grace to continue this line of questioning. The one thing they did not need at this point was for Walt to fly off the handle again.

'Not long after Professor Kuiper joined us, our Vice-chancellor gave him a new post to fill. We advertised, and Max Hamilton applied. He was interviewed and appointed.'

'Sorry,' said Grace, 'was he Sophia Hamilton's husband?'

'No. Max Hamilton is Sophia's brother. He is an industrial designer based here in Chester. A few weeks later, Professor Kuiper persuaded the Vice-Chancellor that he needed a personal assistant. We used to call them secretaries. In the modern world, that is seen as disrespectful. Of course, they don't sit typing anymore. We all do our typing these days with our computers.

They help to do a lot of the administration. They arrange meetings, timetables, and exams. They do all that sort of thing. Max told me, his sister, Sophia, was qualified to do that job, and he recommended her. I'm not saying there was anything improper because there were some interviews, but I think Professor Kuiper was anxious to make a quick appointment, and she could start immediately. We discovered that earlier in her career, she was an interior designer. I think Professor Kuiper liked that. I have always been rather suspicious about appointing closely related people. It can cause all sorts of problems. Anyway, to start with, it seemed OK. Then, after a few weeks, the problems started with Max.'

'What problems were these?' asked Grace.

'Well, Professor Kuiper thought he had appointed someone to work with him, but Max didn't see it that way. He wanted the normal academic freedom to develop his research. Professor Kuiper wanted to tell him what to work on. Max told me he thought Professor Kuiper was barking up the wrong tree. He thought other better ideas could be developed. Professor Kuiper didn't want to hear that. He was an extraordinarily focused person. The relationship went downhill pretty quickly. Max is a rather hasty and awkward chap, anyway. I think most people found him a bit prickly. By comparison, Professor Kuiper just ignored people who didn't interest him. He ignored me. That suited me. I am happy doing what I always did before I became Head of the School.'

'So is Max still here in the Centre?' asked Grace.

'Oh, no. It didn't work out. It has always been difficult for universities to dismiss poorly performing staff. Partly, it is again a matter of academic freedom. We don't want people to be dismissed because other staff disagree about their ideas. It puts an understandable and desirable restraint on what a head of department can do. On the one hand, that is good, but sometimes it isn't. Then you get someone underperforming and taking up a post without contributing much.'

'So, are you saying Max Hamilton was dismissed?' asked Grace.

'In a way. It's more complicated than that. This university is a bit of a tyrant in some ways. We usually have to appoint a new academic to a time-limited post. It can be six months, a year, or even three years. This means that at the end of that probationary period, they can have their contract terminated if it isn't working. Otherwise, they can be appointed to a permanent post. Max was on the shortest possible probation of six months. Professor Kuiper let him go after that. It was quite abrupt. I think there was a bit of a row about it. We haven't seen him since.'

'What about Sophia then?' asked Grace.

'She was pretty cut up about it, but she stayed on. Then, all of a sudden, she just disappeared. Nobody was told what happened. Some people think she had a huge row with Professor Kuiper. Other people think the opposite. There is some suspicion they had a tempestuous affair. I don't take an interest in all that gossip, so I have no idea if that is true. From what people say, Kuiper had an eye for women. She is an attractive woman. So, it might be true. Perhaps she found it difficult to work with Professor Kuiper. She probably thought he had been unfair to her brother. As I said, it's not good to appoint relatives. I had a husband and wife once, and it was a nightmare trying to manage them.'

'How long ago was this?' asked Grace.

'Oh, I don't keep a diary,' said Walt. 'Perhaps two or three months. That is all I can tell you, I'm afraid. Some other staff might know more. Dr Aletta van Leyden is much closer to Professor Kuiper. Maybe she could help you.'

'We have heard reports of a shouting match between Max Hamilton and Professor Kuiper,' said Drake. 'Are you aware of that?'

'I didn't hear it, but the story has done the rounds,' replied Walt. 'I don't think Max would kill anyone, at least not deliberately.'

'So,' asked Drake, 'could he do it accidentally?'

'I can imagine him maybe grabbing someone in an argument and throttling them,' replied Walt.

'On that theme,' said Drake, 'We have also heard that you had a shouting match with Professor Kuiper.'

'Maybe I got angry with him once,' admitted Walt. 'But I didn't murder him.'

'Perhaps you could tell us where you were that Tuesday evening.'

'At home.'

'Could someone verify that for us.'

'Yes, my wife.'

'Thank you,' said Drake.

After Martin had set off to take Walt back to the Centre for Industrial Design, Drake and Grace sat down with a cup of coffee.

'Wow,' said Grace. 'It gets more interesting. Walt is still in the frame. He has now admitted losing his temper with Kuiper.'

'Yes,' said Drake. 'He is a suspect. Somehow, I can't see him deliberately going out to kill someone. A fight on the spur of the moment, maybe. I'd like you to arrange to see Walt's wife and get that confirmation he was at home.'

'Yes,' said Grace. 'I agree about Walt. Was Sophia Hamilton the other woman Nimade mentioned to us? When you were in Delft, Justin Makepeace talked about another woman. If Sophia had an affair with Professor Kuiper and then it ended, maybe she did commit suicide. He seems to have been the sort of person who might dump somebody abruptly.'

'On top of what happened to her brother,' said Drake.

'Perhaps,' said Grace slowly, thinking as she spoke. Then she stopped and started again. 'Did she go to his house to commit suicide and make a huge problem for him? He would have found her dead when he got back.'

'What a ghastly thing to do,' said Drake. 'There is an alternative scenario. Did she perhaps kill Professor Kuiper and then return to his house to commit suicide? Both these are plausible. We cannot judge between them. We must not allow ourselves to jump to conclusions. What worries me right now is that we may never know what happened. They are both dead.'

21

Drake asked Martin to find Grace and come to an interview room. When they arrived, there was no sign of Drake. Eventually, after a short wait, he turned up.

'I have a couple of jobs for you,' he said.

'Is it on the Willem Kuiper case?' asked Martin.

'It certainly is,' replied Drake.

'Great,' said Martin. 'I need to get my teeth into it, and it will be good to work with Grace again.' Drake thought they might have winked at each other, but he wasn't sure. He hoped so. He was deliberately trying not to look at them. As well as gathering vital data, this would be an experiment to see how these colleagues got on. He remained uncertain about his skills on personnel issues and hoped for the best.

'The first thing is to track back along the route we believe that Professor Kuiper took on his way to Water Tower Gardens. We presume he was on his way home. I particularly want you to see if you can find any evidence of anyone walking with him or, more likely, following him. You might try to find security cameras with video of that Tuesday evening.'

'Excellent,' said Martin. 'It could cut through a lot of hard work if we come up trumps.'

'Exactly,' said Drake. 'The second task is to do some more searching. When Dave and I were in Delft, Gudula, the woman running Virtual Virtue, said she had discussions with Dr Aletta van Leyden about merging the Centre for Industrial Design with VV. She said that Kuiper had blocked the idea and was seen as an obstacle. This is news to me. Certainly, Aletta did not mention this in our interview with her. We need to interview her again. However, before we do so, I want some corroborative evidence. Otherwise, Aletta could deny it. Gudula told us she and Aletta had looked for possible places to house the merged units. See if you can work out where these might have been. She said they were like science parks, and one was near the airport.'

'There isn't an airport in Chester,' said Martin.

'That's what I thought,' said Drake. 'See what you can work out.'

'I'll cheat,' said Grace. 'We can park in that convenient little spot at the back of the Vice-Chancellor's office.

'At least we haven't got Drake with us, so we don't have to use the Range Rover,' said Martin. 'It lurches around too much for my liking.' He was preparing a set of large-scale photocopies of the route they believed Professor Kuiper had taken to walk home from The Centre for Industrial Design. He busied himself getting all these ready while Grace drove. Once parked, they walked back along the backstreet to Watergate Street. They turned up Nicholas Street and were soon at the Centre.

'I can't see any cameras here,' said Martin. He had a pair of binoculars hanging around his neck while Grace was holding the clipboard with all the maps on. They walked back along Nicholas Street along the charming Georgian Terrace, where the Vice-Chancellor's office was.

'I can understand why Drake likes this terrace,' said Grace. She was looking up at the houses. 'I think secretly he'd like to move at least plain clothes here! Look, there's a camera over the doorway to the Vice-Chancellor's offices. Whether it would pick someone up on the other side of the street is another matter.' Martin was scanning that side of the street with his binoculars, where there were newer buildings.

'Nothing,' he said as they reached Watergate Street. They turned left onto the bottom section of the Street.

'Bingo,' said Grace. 'Look, there's a traffic camera on a post right here. She put a cross on her map and made a note alongside it. They resumed walking down to the Watergate. They arrived at the junction without seeing any new cameras. A short distance up City Walls Road, they found a camera over the entrance to a house on the right-hand side. Again, Grace made a note. Martin checked the address. Because they were following the City Walls on the left, there were no buildings on the left-hand side of the street.

'We've come to The Queen's School,' said Martin. After looking around at the various buildings, they admitted defeat. They reached the gentle ramp on the left that took the pavement onto the City Walls. There were some buildings set back on the right. No cameras were evident.

'Let's just get as far as the point where the road bends to the right,' said Martin. 'That's where the ramp goes straight on and over the railway. After that, he would have gone down the steps into Water Tower Gardens.' There were only a few lampposts to the left and buildings a long way back on the right.

'Looks like we've only got those three then,' said Grace.

'I'd be fairly confident we might find tapes on them,' said Martin. 'We need to set Dave and Steve onto searching through them for that Tuesday night. Let's check down in Water Tower Gardens. Surely, the SOCO team would have told us if they had found any. But we could walk on to Whipcord Lane. I doubt it will help us much.' They spent a fruitless half an hour searching but found no more cameras.

'OK,' said Martin. 'Let's go back to the car. First, we need to get this information back to Dave so he can take a constable and get the videos from their owners. Then we will go somewhere else. I've had an idea.'

A quarter of an hour later, Grace followed Martin's navigation to get them to Wrexham Road.

'Oh, no. Not this dreadful place,' said Grace after they crossed the River Dee. They had reached the complicated roundabout she had navigated to get to Curzon Park.

'No problem,' said Martin. 'We're just going straight on. After a while, they passed The King's School on the left.

'This is a relatively new campus,' said Martin. 'They used to be next to the cathedral in town.'

'I bet that was fun,' said Grace.

'But too cramped, I think,' said Martin. They drove around what Grace thought must be a roundabout. No doubt the traffic people would call it an island. It felt more like a continent. Eventually, they turned off onto a dual carriage leading into the country.

'We're technically out of Chester now and in Wales,' said Martin. 'Look, there's the place I was thinking of.' They pulled up in front of a building that seemed half offices and half factory. 'It's a sort of research centre. But we are right next to the Airbus factory where they make parts for Airbus planes. Many years ago, the De Havilland Comet was made here.' Grace looked puzzled.

'What was that?' she asked.

'Oh, it was the earliest commercial jet. Quite groundbreaking in its time,' replied Martin. 'My Dad used to work there in those days. That's how I knew there was an airport here. It is more of an airfield. They use it for transport planes. They take Airbus parts over to Europe. It's the wings, I think. There are no commercial flights from here, as far as I know. That's why we didn't think of it. I guess that Gudula heard an aircraft taking off. They are great big things, very heavy transporters. You certainly hear one taking off.'

'What shall we do?' asked Grace.

'I think we should go in and see if anybody can talk to us and tell us if Aletta van Leyden and Gudula came here.'

It was a brief interview. The manager was about to go into a meeting, but he confirmed they had discussions with two people who they thought were from Deva University about taking some accommodation.

'It would be a bit different but an excellent fit for us,' he said.

Detective Constable Steve Redvers arrived at Curzon Park for another shift observing the house of Damien Bewick. He had not been seen since the investigation began, and Drake was getting more impatient with the situation. Steve reminded himself of the case by reading his notebook. Professor Kuiper's ex-partner Nimade had told them that Damien had bought the old Design East company from Professor Kuiper. Nimade had left the company, and she found it impossible to work with Damien. Her assistant, Laurence Bailey, had also left to join Nimade's new company, Bali Style. This had left Damien with a hollowed-out version of the company he bought since Nimade's knowledge of Bali was no longer available. But he was now angry with Kuiper and demanding some compensation.

Steve and his colleagues had taken care to use different cars each day to avoid suspicion. He was, however, now getting frustrated and bored by the observation job. He looked up from his notebook to see a large and expensive-looking Mercedes arriving and turning into the forecourt of Damien Bewick's house. Steve had a good view of the front of the house set behind its imposing gravel forecourt. The Mercedes scrunched across the gravel and stopped by the front door. Steve watched as a large and imposing figure climbed out of the car, dug a travel bag out of the boot and went inside the house. Steve phoned back to Martin in the case room to update him.

'Detective Inspector Martin Henshaw.'

'Hi Martin, it's Steve.'

'Someone has finally just arrived at Damien Bewick's house. I have filmed him, and he has gone inside. He had a suitcase, so presumably, he is returning from a trip somewhere, perhaps overseas.'

'OK, Steve. Keep watching and follow him if he comes out again. Drake would prefer more information before meeting him for an interview.'

'I only have one car here, so I can't guarantee to stay behind him when following.'

'I know you should have two, ideally three, for the proper procedure. Just do the best you can. Meanwhile, I'll try to rustle up more cars for you.'

'OK, will do.'

Steve thought through the situation. If Bewick did go out again, he would probably go back in the direction he came from. This was the main road into Curzon Park. Steve decided to turn his vehicle around to point in the same direction. He parked just short of the house and settled back in his seat for what he guessed might be a long wait.

About half an hour later, just as Steve was in danger of nodding off, Bewick came out of his house, got into the car and drove out and down the road just as Steve had anticipated. He followed at a reasonable distance but was increasingly worried about the traffic lights at the end of the road, where it opened onto Grace's most hated roundabout. What if they got separated? Would he jump a red light to keep with his target?

Luckily, the light was red, and Steve pulled right up behind the Mercedes. The lights went green, and they both set off. Just as Steve had half-expected, they turned left straight off the roundabout and over the river, passing the Roodee where the racecourse was on their left. Steve smiled as he remembered recently reading about the history of the Roodee. In particular, the name of the first Mayor of Chester, Henry Gee, to introduce horse racing there. Horses became known as gee-gees after his name. They drove up Nicholas Street, where the Centre for Industrial Design was on their right and were soon on the inner ring road system that took them clockwise around the city centre. They eventually reached the circular road next to the city centre and took a left onto the continuation of Foregate Street. They were only two hundred yards from the Eastgate, which had become Drake's favourite spot.

Soon, they were driving along a street called Boughton, and the quality of buildings and shops became markedly lower than in Eastgate. They were on the dual carriageway heading for Boughton and would come to the Supermarket next to where Nimade was living by the Shot Tower. Suddenly, the Mercedes pulled into one of many empty parking spots along the street. Bewick left the car and went into a women's clothing shop. Steve had pulled up just before it, and he got out to walk past the shop and look in. He paused for a short while, looking in the window. This was a cut-price affair and popular by the look of it. There must have been half a dozen customers inside. Then Steve caught sight of Damien Bewick talking animatedly to a female who, Steve guessed, was a shop assistant. She had her back to him, and Bewick was waving his arms around and appeared to be giving this poor woman a telling-off.

Steve considered going into the shop but decided it would be better to be back in his car. This was a good move, as Bewick soon emerged, and they both set off again. They came to traffic lights where the Mercedes performed an illegal U-turn. Steve instantly weighed up the situation and reluctantly followed suit. They travelled back to the rotary system and around the inner ring road to Sealand Road, where they took a right. Steve was struggling, trying to keep his target in sight. He deliberately held back so he would not be rumbled. They drove on down Sealand Road. It was some time since Steve had been this way. It was now a car-makers showroom world. Many of the most well-known brands were represented. Steve had to allow a car to cut in and struggled to keep sight of his target. They drove out into the countryside. Steve wondered if this would be a long journey when the Mercedes pulled off the road into a second-hand car sales lot. He pulled up and watched as Bewick left his car in the middle of the lot and strode into the portable cabin at the back. Perhaps a quarter of an hour elapsed when Bewick pulled out again and set off towards the city. Steve had to do a quick U-turn and try to catch him up.

They were soon back on Nicholas Street, across the river and into Curzon Park. It appeared that Bewick had done whatever he wanted, and Steve expected he might stay indoors for a while.

'Well done, Steve,' said Drake after he had been briefed on Damien Bewick's little escapade. 'How do you interpret all this?'

'Well, and I suppose this must be guesswork, that he had returned from a major trip, perhaps abroad. I was surprised he went out again so quickly. It suggests his trip was important to him. He didn't buy anything. The way he spoke animatedly to the shop worker made me feel she was his employee. The way he parked in the middle of the second-hand car lot suggests that perhaps he owns it. I guess he was checking up on a couple of companies he owns.'

'Sounds good,' said Drake, 'It seems he deals in cut-price goods. But we must keep our minds open to other interpretations. I want you to go with Grace and see if you can get anything from the people at the shop and car lot. Report to me. I expect then we will call Damien in for a chat. He seems an interesting character. Nimade said she felt he treated her like an employee in her own company. This character may not keep prisoners. We need to tread carefully with him. He could well be a key player in this mystery after all.'

22

The whole team were assembled in the case room, waiting for Dave to finish setting up the large screen. He was becoming a dab hand at these revelatory showings of security camera films. It was his moment in the spotlight. He turned to face everyone. Drake nodded, so he began.

'Martin and Grace found three cameras along the route from The Centre for Industrial Design to Whipcord Lane. I've managed to get the videos for all three on that Tuesday evening. Information from Dr Aletta van Leyden suggests that Professor Kuiper might have left at about 23:00 hours. We have the emergency phone call positioning him in Water Tower Gardens at 23:13. We have suspected that Professor Willem Kuiper walked this way when going home on the fateful Tuesday night.'

Dave pressed the play button on his computer and began to provide a commentary.

'This is the view from a camera over the Vice-Chancellor's office doorway. It looks towards the building on the other side of Nicholas Street, where The Centre for Industrial Design is. You might catch a fleeting glimpse of someone walking behind cars and a van. It is not clear from this image that it is Professor Kuiper. However, the following video is a short time later. It is from a camera on a post just around the corner on Watergate Street.' The screen showed an empty street. Almost immediately, a man appeared, walking briskly. Dave paused the film.

'It is dark, and the detail is not all that clear. I have enhanced the images as much as possible, but we remain dependent on the camera's resolution. If you look carefully, you can see that this figure is wearing the collarless mandarin-style shirt that he was discovered in. We are reasonably confident that this is him. It is also interesting to note that he has what looks like a laptop bag slung over his shoulders. Dr Aletta van Leyden told us he usually carried his laptop this way. We have not so far found the bag or laptop. Next, you will see he stops and looks around. Another man joins him. We think this other man had called out to him. They immediately set off walking together out of view of the camera.'

Dave pressed the play button again. He rewound and repeated this fragment of the video several times.

'Next, we move to a camera just around the next corner on his route. This camera is mounted over the door of a house. We had to obtain the video from the owners. Luckily, their disk holds data for some time. The two men appear and walk out of view. We only have a brief glimpse of them. The accompanying man is gesturing wildly at Professor Kuiper, who seems to be looking straight ahead rather than at this other man. It looks like the man who joined him on Watergate Street. He is wearing a cap and an Argyle sweater with a distinctive blue and orange diamond pattern.'

'Do you know?' said Martin. 'He looks as if he is playing golf. That jumper and the baseball cap are fairly typical attire on the golf course.'

'Perhaps he has just come from playing golf and not had time to change,' said Grace.

'Good idea, Grace,' said Drake, 'but surely, it is rather late.'

'Perhaps he was in the club bar for a drink or two,' said Martin. 'We call it the nineteenth hole.'

'If so,' said Drake, 'perhaps he has had to come out quickly.'

Dave again pressed play and rewind several times.

'That is the final image before Professor Kuiper would have reached the footpath up and over the railway and then down into the park. You might think that the man who has joined him and appears to be gesturing wildly could be the murderer. However, we chose to keep running the video for several more minutes. We now see two more things. Firstly, another person appears, following some distance behind Professor Kuiper. The light is not all that good, but it looks as if they are dressed all in black or at least dark clothes. We have no idea who this is or whether they then joined Kuiper. However, a few seconds later, we can see the first man returning across the field of view. We can see the cap and the sweater again. He has left Professor Kuiper, while the second person may be catching up with him. Could they be the murderer? We don't know, of course. We kept looking at the video for a quarter of an hour. Nobody else appeared. That is all we have.'

There was a round of applause, and Dave bowed ironically. As it died down, everyone turned to see what Drake would say.

'This second person,' said Drake. 'They are walking alone, so it is difficult to gauge height. However, I would guess they are shortish.' He paused and let out a sigh. 'Oh, my word. Whenever we think we have new information, it turns into another dimension of the mystery. So, we know two people were around when Professor Kuiper was walking home. We don't know who they are, and we don't know if one, or perhaps both, or neither of them committed the murder. We also now know he was carrying his laptop, which we assume the murderer took. This provides more evidence about that. Thanks, Dave. Excellent work. OK, we need to bank this and get on with our other strands of work.'

Grace had obtained Walt's address from the University Human Resources Department. She then called Frank to confirm that Walt was at The Centre for Industrial Design. His house was somewhere down the Tarvin Road. It was a straightforward drive. She was soon knocking on the door.

'Yes,' said a woman opening the door. Grace assumed she would be near Walt's age, but this person looked younger. Grace held out her ID.

'I am Detective Sergeant Grace Hepple. I assume you must be Mrs Dickinson. There is nothing to be concerned about. We think you may be able to help us with an investigation. Could I come in for a few minutes?'

'Yes, of course,' said Mrs Dickinson hesitantly. She took Grace to what she guessed was the main living room. There was no doubt that it was the work of a designer. Everything was coordinated, colourful and orderly. Mrs Dickinson sat upright on the edge of a black leather sofa, and Grace sat in an armchair opposite.

'I think you might know that Professor Willem Kuiper was murdered on the way home late on a Tuesday night.' Grace held up a calendar and passed it to Mrs Dickinson.'

'Yes, of course. Walt told me about it the following evening. It's terrible.'

'We would like you to tell us where Walt was that Tuesday evening,' said Grace. 'Can you remember that particular evening?'

'Yes, because he told me all about it the next evening. I remember it only too well.'

'Where was Walt that Tuesday evening? Did he come home from work at the normal time?'

'It depends on what you mean by normal. He got in after midnight. I couldn't tell you the exact time. I had gone to bed.'

'So, is that normal for Walt to come home so late?'

'It happens all too frequently. Since this new Head arrived, they have all worked late on some project.'

'I see,' said Grace. 'You are certain about that?'

'Absolutely. Why do you want to know?'

'It's just a check we are making with Walt and his colleagues,' replied Grace. 'Thank you. That is helpful. I don't need to trouble you more.'

Grace reported back to Drake.

'Oh my,' he said. 'There are two problems here. First, Walt told us he spent the evening at home. He said his wife would confirm that. She has contradicted it. Secondly, she says he often works late. This is supposed to be because of Professor Kuiper, but our information is that he has nothing to do with Professor Kuiper's work. What is going on? Let us see Aletta again. We need to get her take on the discussions with Virtual Virtue. But we also need confirmation that Walt was not in the Centre that Tuesday evening.

Let's get her to come in. In the meantime, I want to see Nimade's new Chester shop. Perhaps you would come with me.'

23

Grace drove the Range Rover down into town. Drake knew the Bali Style shop was somewhere on Pepper Street. They went along the inner ring road, around the Roman Amphitheatre, and along Pepper Street. Suddenly, there it was on their left. Just past was the loading bay where Nimade had said they could park. Drake went to look at the window displays while Grace got them to open the gates. He was entranced by the room settings in one window. The colours, materials and arrangement were all spectacular. He remembered the shop in Delft being wonderful. This looked even better. Grace arrived, and they went in. Nimade was standing just inside to greet them. She took up the now familiar hands together bow, and Drake felt the need to bow in return, at least as far as his back would allow.

'You have come at a good time,' said Nimade. 'We have finished fitting the shop out in a better way. My partner, Laurence, is here. He will show you around. I must take a video conference call from Bali before they leave for the evening.' She waved to a man standing at the back of the shop, who came forward and held out a more conventional Western hand.

'Laurence Bailey.' He spoke with an Australian accent. 'I manage the Bali Style shops for Nimande. You are most welcome. What are you interested in?'

'We would like to look around at all your wonderful things,' replied Drake. 'But first, perhaps you would explain to me how the operation of Bali Style works.'

'Of course,' said Laurence. 'We rely on the fantastic local knowledge and expertise of Nimade in finding things for us to sell. She sources everything for us from craftspeople in Bali. I doubt anyone else in the world could do the amazing work she does. We sell everything in our shop in Ubud in Bali. Are you familiar with Bali?'

'No, but I would love to be,' answered Drake. Laurence smiled.

'If ever you manage to visit, we would be delighted to show you around. Let me show you over here.' Laurence pointed to a map on one wall to one side of the shop. Drake and Grace followed him over.

'Bali is part of Indonesia. This country is not so well known and understood in the West. Indonesia is the fourth most populated country in the world. It is also unique in being composed of seventeen and a half thousand islands. More than half are populated. The main parts of the country are Sumatra and Java, which are immediately to the west of Bali. Bali is a volcanic island. Mount Agung is the largest, which plays a part in how the people of Bali design. When building a house, you must align your property so its longer dimension points to the sacred mountain. The centre of the island is mountainous. A great deal of it is devoted to agriculture. There are extensive terrace systems of rice fields on the hillsides, which are very beautiful. The main town of Denpasar and its airport are to the south. On a small area south of that is the main tourist area, which we call Nusa Dua. To the north but still south of the main mountains is the town of Ubud. That is where our shop and headquarters are. Ubud is a major centre of the arts and crafts of Bali, so we need to be there. There are countless galleries and workshops. So, Ubud is most definitely on the tourist trail. There are also hotels around there. It is there that Nimade finds a great deal of the material that we sell. Please sit down.' Laurence pointed to a group of beautiful rattan chairs near the map.

'Originally, and before I knew her, Nimade sold mainly to locals and a few passing tourists. However, her shop gradually grew in popularity with people from overseas. Nimade was struggling to deal with this business. Exporting things from Bali is not straightforward. Since I joined her, the business has expanded significantly. We can now finance shops overseas. This means that as well as tourists buying things in Bali, we can sell to the UK and Dutch home markets. We can transport goods from Bali to our shops over here. Because of the historical connection with the Dutch, we had shops in the Netherlands. They are in Amsterdam, Eindhoven, and Delft. We lost these shops except for Delft when Nimade split up with her partner Willem. We have recently opened this shop here and are looking to open one in the home counties. As you can imagine, the tasks of packaging and shipping our goods are considerable. I look after all that. And I supervise the shops in Ubud, Delft and Chester.'

'What are the largest things you can transport?' asked Drake.

'Sofas, some tables and even double beds would be the largest. They are not usually the most delicate. A lot of our carvings are extremely delicate and awkwardly shaped for packing. Because they are carved locally, they do not come packed in boxes. What I do is a kind of work of art. I have to create methods of packing all shapes and sizes of items. We cannot afford to have things broken and customers disappointed. The easiest things to package are fabrics.'

'How do you transport things to the UK from Ubud?' asked Drake.

'Everything has to be transported to the airport or the port. So that is south of Denpasar or to the coast where we use the port of Benoa.'

'What decides if something is air freight or goes by ship?'

'A whole host of things. It depends on the urgency, the size and weight and the availability of flights and ships.'

Nimade arrived, having completed her video conference.

'Do you like all our lovely things?' she asked.

'It's all beautiful,' said Grace. 'I wish I could completely decorate and furnish my flat from here.'

'It's not as expensive as you might think,' said Nimade, laughing. 'Although we have to pay for the freight, we get things in Bali for prices that are fair to them, but they look cheap to us. Bali, like so much of Indonesia, has a low-wage economy.'

'So, this is your latest shop, Nimade?' asked Drake.

'Yes. It took a long time to find the right place. Thank goodness I have Laurence.' She looked across and patted him on the arm.

'It's not straightforward,' said Laurence. 'We need a large floor area, preferably unobstructed open space. Then we can arrange things as we wish. Our stock is worth a great deal and is very easily stolen so we need a secure building. We need to be near the city centre. There is a car park just next door so customers can take things they can carry home with them. We also need a loading bay. Our delivery trucks are medium-sized, but we need to move the goods into a space separate from the shop where they can be stored and unpacked. If they are to be transported elsewhere in the country, we always check for damage before sending them on. Quite large objects may stand waiting for transport. We were lucky to find this place. We like the location. Although we would have loved to have an old Chester building, this one is inoffensive and works. This location is cheaper than on one of the city's main streets. They also would not be as easily accessible for deliveries. This is a good compromise.'

'Laurence was brilliant,' said Nimade. 'He knows all these things and kept his eye on the market. The minute this became available, he put a marker in for it until we could measure up and decide. Now, would you like us to leave you to look around?'

'I think we have asked all the questions we had, so it would be lovely to browse,' said Drake.

Drake and Grace moved slowly around the shop, pointing out things to each other. Grace thought Drake was like a little child in a toy shop. She had rarely seen him so animated. As they reached the room settings in the windows, Drake stopped. He picked up what looked as if it might be a short sword in its scabbard. It was lying on the top of a chest of drawers.

'May I look at this?' he asked.

'Oh, yes, of course,' replied Nimade, 'but please be careful. It is sharp.'

Drake withdrew what turned out to be a dagger from its protection. It had a wavy blade, which was narrow and sharp on both curvy edges.'

'There are two of them,' said Nimade, 'Each one is unique. They are just for show. We don't expect to sell them here. They are wonderful examples of a Balinese craftsman's art. They are all handmade and unique.'

'Really!' exclaimed Drake. 'I thought the Balinese were a peaceful nation.'

'Oh, we are,' replied Nimade. 'In Bali, these are used for ritual purposes only. They are used for ceremonies, not warfare. They are believed to have magical properties and are handed down from generation to generation in families. They are called Keris or Kris.'

'Yes, now I remember encountering these in Malaysia. Would they be the same thing?'

'Essentially, yes, you find them around Southeast Asia. But ours have much more significance to us. You will see that the hilt or handle of these is made of a representation of one of the Hindu gods or heroes. Such a design is characteristic of Bali, which is a Hindu Island. In Muslim countries such as Malaysia or even the vast majority of Indonesia, the representation of a figure like this would be frowned upon. In Bali, we celebrate it. As you can see, it is less than optimal as something to get hold of. This is not a dagger made as a weapon to kill but a Keris made for ceremonial purposes. It is special to Bali. That is why we have them in the shop.'

Drake took a photo of the Keris with his phone and returned it to its protective sleeve. After expressing their thanks, Drake and Grace left.

'Are you thinking what I am thinking?' asked Grace as they drove back to the station.

'Probably,' replied Drake. 'I have photographed it and will send the picture to our pathologist.'

24

Drake called Martin and Dave over to the central table.

'I've been thinking about the first man in our videos,' he said. 'We have little to go on except for the clothes. I want us to follow up on the golfing idea. Dave, please extract images from your videos to produce the best quality pictures possible of this person. Perhaps a couple of his front and maybe another of his back as he returns. Martin, you are a bit of a golfer.'

'I only wish,' replied Martin. 'This job doesn't give me time for rounds of golf.'

'Even so, you are ideally suited to this job. Take Dave's pictures and make a poster asking people if they know who this person is. Get them to call or text your number. You could give an email as well. Go to all the local golf clubs and courses you know and get permission to stick it up on their notice board. It's worth a shot.'

'As good as done,' said Martin. Dave went over to his computer and tapped away on the keyboard.

'I've been thinking,' said Grace. 'The other person dressed in dark clothes. When we went to the Bali Style shop, I noticed Nimade wasn't wearing her colourful Balinese outfit. She was wearing a black trouser suit.'

'Perhaps she was trying to copy you,' said Martin to a round of laughter, but Grace persisted.

'You thought that the second person in the video was short and wearing black. Nimade is short and sometimes wears black.'

'Oh my,' said Drake. 'Yes, I reckon less than five feet tall. What if it was her? We need to think about how to tackle that one. It could be a bit tricky.' Everyone settled down to their tasks. Suddenly, Dave called Grace over to his computer.

'What did you say Damien Bewick's shop was called?'

'Fashion Bargain,' replied Grace.

'I thought so. Come and look at this.' Grace walked over to Dave's desk. On the screen was a website for Fashion Bargain. 'Look,' said Dave. 'You can buy online.'

'Oh, well done,' said Grace. 'Let's have a look at some prices.' Dave shuffled over, and Grace began browsing.

'I can't say I think it looks too stylish, but it's cheap.'

'There's more,' said Dave. 'There are lots of shops. I searched. There must be a dozen. They are mostly in northern cities.'

'That's amazing,' said Grace. 'It's quite a big business. Our friend Damien must be worth a penny or two.'

'Look,' said Dave proudly. 'I did a bit of searching and found a Facebook Group. It seems to be for managers of the shops. It's a private group, so we can't see what's in it unless we join. I tried just putting in a name and one of our email addresses, but they want you to give the address of your shop. Do you have the address of the Chester one?'

'Yes, here it is,' said Grace, opening the address book on her phone. Dave hammered away on his keyboard.

'Bingo, we're in. Presumably, the Chester shop manager is already a member. Perhaps it doesn't check for duplicates. It seems basic all-round.'

'Oh, I say. Look at this.' Grace leant across to see the screen.

'It just seems to be one gripe about the owner after another. At least, I guess it's the owner. They call him "The Moaner" and don't pull their punches. They all seem pretty unhappy.'

'Surely Damien can log on and see all this?'

'Yes, but look, they all use nicknames, so he probably can't work out who they are.'

'Looking at the topics,' said Grace. 'They seem to have low salaries with a commission based on overall sales. It doesn't seem to work in their favour.'

'There are complaints about bullying,' said Dave.

'I wonder where all these clothes are made,' said Grace. 'We've seen the prices. Damien has bought a business partly in Bali. I wonder what he wanted to do with it. He has made a foolish purchase if he wanted to run the business as Nimade and Kuiper did because he was highly likely to lose Nimade and Laurence Bailey. Maybe I'm just making too many guesses.'

'Why don't we ask Nimade or Laurence what they think?' said Dave.

'Good thinking,' said Grace. 'From what she said, Nimade found him a pretty objectionable sort. I'm not quite sure how we should approach this. I'd better consult Drake.'

Grace drove around the now familiar inner ring road to the road leading to Boughton. She parked outside the Fashion Bargain shop. She went inside and found plenty of browsers rummaging through clothes. She picked a cardigan off the rack and examined the collar. Grace pulled out the label. She struggled to see the point of it. It refused to tell her anything apart from a silly unpronounceable name. There was another label attached to near the hem. It was also uninformative. She began to appreciate that none of these labels were prepared to admit anything about their origin. She made similar checks on several items with a similar lack of success.

'Can I help you?' asked the shop assistant.

'It's just a matter of interest,' replied Grace. 'Where are these clothes made?'

'They mostly come from Indonesia, where wages are low. That's why we can sell them at such a good price.'

'Thank you,' said Grace, rather pleased with herself. She would report to Drake and ask him what they should do next.

'Well done,' said Drake when Grace told him about their discoveries. 'Why don't you go and see Nimade again? See what she knows about Damien's whole setup. We need to interview him now, but I would rather be as well-informed as possible first. Just before you go, Martin has just brought Walt back in. I would like you to join me in questioning him again.'

Grace followed Drake to the interview room. Walt was pacing around the room in an agitated manner.'

'Sit down please, Mr Dickinson,' said Drake. Walt looked startled but did as he was told.

'Last time we spoke, you told us that you were at home on the Tuesday evening when Professor Kuiper was murdered. Do you want to think about that again?'

'Why should I?'

'Because we now have information that suggests otherwise,' said Drake.

'It's my wife. You bullied her into saying something wrong.' Drake looked at Grace.

'On the contrary, Mr Dickinson,' said Grace softly. 'We just asked her a simple question.'

'She had gone to bed. She doesn't know.'

'So why did you say she would confirm you came home at the normal time?' asked Grace. Drake sat motionless, letting Grace take over.

'I did get home at the normal time.'

'What time do you call normal?' asked Grace.

Walt Dickinson sat tapping his fingers on the table in front of him. Grace had learned from Drake. She waited for Walt to speak again. Eventually, he did.

'I suppose there is no absolute normal,' he said. 'Sometimes I am later than others.'

'Is that a recent development, or has it always been like that?' asked Grace. Drake liked the way Grace was handling the situation. She kept putting the onus on Walt to talk but kept her voice down and emotionless.

'I suppose it has happened more recently.'

'So, what time did you get in that evening?' asked Grace.

'I don't know. I don't remember looking at my watch.'

'We believe you got in after midnight,' said Grace.

'Maybe. I don't know. I don't remember.'

'Why did you tell us before that you had got home much earlier?' This time, Walt sat in silence, looking down at his lap.

'OK, OK. I was late, but that is not unusual.'

'The explanation you gave your wife was that you were working on a project Professor Kuiper was leading. Is that true?' Again, Walt sat speechless. Eventually, he just nodded his head.

'Are you telling us you worked on Professor Kuiper's projects?' asked Grace. 'That is not the impression we have gathered from you or your colleagues.'

'Look,' said Walt in exasperation. 'I'm seeing someone else. I didn't want my wife to know that. It would have upset her unnecessarily.'

'Can this other person corroborate this new story?' asked Drake.

'I expect he would, yes. Neither of us wants this to be known generally. We are both in marriages we don't want to disturb.' The three sat in silence. Then Walt spoke again.

'I suppose you disapprove, but it's not what it seems.'

'We don't either approve or disapprove,' said Grace. 'We are just here to establish the facts. Here is some paper and a pencil. Put the name and contact details here please.' Walt sat hesitating.

Drake turned to the voice recorder. 'Let the record show that Mr Walt Dickinson passed details of this other person to Detective Sergeant Hepple.' He turned the recorder off.

'I think you had better help us now,' said Drake. 'You have a sheet of paper on the table. Write down the required details and pass it to Detective Sergeant Hepple.' With that, Drake pushed his chair back and stood up. He walked over to the door, and then Walt spoke again.

'What happens now?' he asked.

'You are, of course, free to leave. You are helping us with our enquiries. However, if you try to go now, I will arrest you, and you will be required to remain until we have followed up our investigation. Drake left the room, giving Grace a dramatic wink as he did so. This was not the first time Drake had deliberately not followed the approved procedure. Grace thought Drake was not just a policeman. He was a humane person.

Grace came into the case room and looked for Drake. He was standing behind his case boards.

'It's an infuriating puzzle,' said Drake.

'What is?' asked Grace.

'I still cannot make the connection between Sophia Hamilton's death and that of Professor Kuiper. She is found in his house, but why?' Grace waited for Drake to turn and face her.

'I've called Walt's new contact, and he will see me now,' said Grace as Drake prowled around, contemplating the new information. 'He lives out in Boughton. If I get confirmation, I will phone you. Then I'll go and see Nimade.'

'Excellent,' said Drake. He scratched his head irritably and walked off around his boards.

About an hour later, Drake's phone went off. Or at least that is what everyone in the case room assumed. Drake started a familiar ritual of patting all his pockets in a fruitless attempt to discover it. Eventually, it was found under the Times on his table. It was Grace calling.

'As I expected, and I think you did too, we have confirmation of Walt's alibi. The person involved was terrified. I'm pretty sure he was telling me the truth.'

'I thought so,' replied Drake. 'If only people would tell the truth the first time.' Drake got up and started to fiddle with his case boards again.

Grace was getting better at navigating her way around Chester. It was a relatively small city and certainly much better than London, where she had worked previously. The much-loved pedestrian centre made it slightly more complicated for the driver. She parked the patrol car next to the Shot Tower and walked between the two blocks of modern housing. She was soon at

Nimade's door. She heard a charming little oriental jingle. She had recently seen a television programme about music in the Far East. She guessed it was a recording of a gamelan. Nimade opened the door and stood aside for Grace to enter. They had to go sideways to get into the room. Nimade had already explained this aspect of Balinese design. They sat opposite on either side of the large balcony window. Grace instinctively patted the head of the carved creature next to her chair. Nimade smiled. Grace was becoming rather fond of this gentle person.

'We are trying to find more information about Damien Bewick,' she said. 'He seems a little elusive.'

'What do you want to know?' asked Nimade. 'I don't know him well, but I'll try to help.'

'He took over your old company, Design East. You felt he treated you disrespectfully.'

'Yes, he was rude and abrupt. I didn't like him at all. I knew I couldn't work with him. But it was also what he wanted to do with the company. I had no time for his plans at all.'

'What were his plans?'

'I didn't understand it. He wanted to use it to make cheap clothes. He wasn't interested in what Bali could offer. He just wanted to find a way to make a profit.'

'I don't understand why he wanted to buy Design East from Willem Kuiper,' said Grace.

'Nor do I,' said Nimade. 'He has some plans, but I don't know what they are. Perhaps Laurence Bailey might know more. I think he tried hard to work with him for a while. In the end, Laurence decided to work with me in Bali Style. I think they had a terrible row and have remained enemies. At one point, Damien went to see Laurence at our shop. I think he threatened him in some way. Laurence didn't want to talk about it. Laurence hates Damien even more than I do. He is not a nice man. For some reason, Willem got on well with him. Willem likes people who have ambition. I don't think it is the only important thing. Damien doesn't seem to treat the people around him with respect. Damien then became angry with Willem when Laurence and I left. So, in the end, we get on making a success of Bali Style.'

'Would Laurence be at your shop?' asked Grace.

'Oh, no, he has just left for Manchester airport. He is going back to Bali. He is needed there urgently to avoid causing delays in shipping a new consignment for us.'

'How long will he be there?' asked Grace.

'I don't know. He has a lot to do there, and he hasn't even made plans to return for a while. Now that he has found our new shop and got it up and running for me, it's not too important that he is here.'

Drake and Grace returned to the case room. Drake looked for Dave and found him characteristically crouched over his computer.

'Dave, I have another job for you,' he said. 'I've been thinking we might have missed a trick. Those video clips you played us the other day showed three people. The first, we believe, was Kuiper. Then, he appeared to be joined by another man wearing what might be golfing clothes. He turned back and left Professor Kuiper before they reached the Water Tower Gardens. We concentrated on the next person to follow Drake. What if we look at the other two cameras to see where the possible golfer went? Could you do that?'

'Sure,' said Dave, 'It's no problem. We should have the original video covering at least the next quarter of an hour. Would you like to wait while I play it back? It should only take a couple of minutes.'

'Excellent,' said Drake as Grace brought a mug of coffee. Drake returned to his case boards and stood staring at them in an accusatorial sort of manner. He felt they should be revealing something he was missing. He was not in luck. They admitted nothing new.

'Found it!' exclaimed Dave in a sufficiently raised voice to attract Drake's attention. He came over, coffee mug in hand.

'Here it is,' said Dave. 'He goes back down Watergate Street where they came from. He is on the other side of the Street, though.'

'OK,' said Drake. Now we know he walked that far back, but did he go to The Centre for Industrial Design?'

Dave hammered away on his keyboard, and a video started to play. It was from the camera over the door of the Vice-Chancellor's office. Dave spooled it forward, but no other figure appeared in the next quarter of an hour.

'Where did he go?' asked a puzzled Drake. 'This is not what I expected.'

'Perhaps he walked straight on at that crossroads,' said Dave. 'If so, he would have gone further up Watergate Street towards the Chester Cross.'

'Martin, I need you,' shouted Drake. 'We must find more cameras. Look further up Watergate Street from Nicholas Street towards The Cross. If you can find any cameras, follow the usual pattern. I have a new theory, which may hang on what you can find.'

25

The following morning, Martin and Grace set off for Watergate Street to search for more security or traffic cameras. Perhaps the "golfer" had walked that way after talking and walking with Professor Kuiper on his way to the Water Tower Gardens. Grace was driving, and Martin was navigating. He directed her to a convenient car park off Nicholas Street, and they walked the short distance to the junction with Watergate Street.

Grace was beginning to wonder if Martin was still interested in their relationship. He had been friendly and considerate since he returned from Hong Kong. Drake had deliberately put them to work together on several tasks, but that had not seemed to be an appropriate time or place to deal with personal and social matters. However, as they walked, Martin suddenly broke the silence.

'Is it worth me asking if you would like dinner to talk things over one evening?' he asked.

'That sounds like a good idea,' said Grace, trying to hide her surprise.

'Excellent,' said Martin. 'We'll compare diaries later, and then I'll arrange something. Here we are at Watergate Street. You look at the left side of the street, and I'll take the right-hand side.'

Now only too well aware that some cameras could be surprisingly difficult to spot, they deliberately sauntered and studied the buildings.

'There we are. I see one at last,' said Grace as they reached The Cross at the end of Watergate Street. 'Look up there on that building.'

'Thank goodness for that,' said Martin. He took a photograph to show to Dave and Steve, who would be responsible for following it up and getting any available video. Martin and Grace turned and walked back the way they had come. Just before reaching Nicholas Street, Martin pointed to the left.

'Look,' he said, 'This is Weaver Street. 'He could have turned down here. Let's look for cameras in case.'

Martin and Grace followed their set procedure but reached the end of Weaver Street without success.

Drake called Dave and Constable Steve Redvers over to his chair.

'I have a job for you. I'm afraid it is probably rather tedious. We now know the University camera over the Vice-Chancellor's office door looks towards the building where The Centre for Industrial Design is. The demolition job on their computers may not have been on impulse. It could have been planned. In this case, someone likely went to look at the place first. We will initially examine the whole week before the fateful Tuesday. I want you to go back over video footage. I guess you should look at daylight hours first.'

'What are we looking for?' asked Steve.

'That's the problem. It is hard to say. Maybe a person or people who are looking up at the building. Perhaps they walk past it more than once. Make a note of anyone who comes there on more than one occasion. Dave, please pick out the relevant video, and then we can all look at it to see what we might find. It's probably a long shot, but worth trying.'

As soon as they returned, Grace and Martin reported back to Dave. Martin showed him the photos he took of the camera near The Cross on Watergate Street.

'OK,' said Drake. 'You need to imagine our "golfer" walked across the road and along Watergate Street right up to The Cross. So, look for him at that approximate time on any video you can obtain.'

"OK,' said Dave. 'I can do that. Steve is reviewing the video I have extracted from the camera, looking at The Centre for Industrial Design.'

'Martin, we need to see Aletta again. For one thing, she needs to clear up the confusion of her visit to the unit at Broughton by the airport. Call her now and make sure she is there, then go and collect her. I think the formality of an interview here will impress upon her the need to talk to us seriously.'

Everyone set about their tasks. Drake prowled around his case boards.

Martin entered the case room.

'I've got Aletta van Leyden in interview room one,' he reported. 'She is grumpy about the whole business. She seems to think she's above it all.'

'Good,' said Drake. 'That won't do any harm. Come on, Grace. Let's go and see what she has to say.'

Drake and Grace entered the interview room. Aletta was sitting at the table in the centre of the room. She looked daggers at Drake.

'Good afternoon, Dr van Leyden,' he said. 'Thank you for coming to speak to us.'

'I didn't come,' she replied. 'I was brought. Why have you dragged me over here?'

'We haven't dragged you. You have come of your own free will.'

'So, I can go now then? I am busy. This is a nuisance.'

'You can go if you wish, but since we feel the need to talk to you about a murder investigation, you can either come willingly, or I can arrest you. It is your choice. One piece of advice. It is generally more helpful to both parties if this is done without an arrest.'

'I have been brought a mug of coffee. I need a glass of water.'

'It's just behind you,' said Grace, standing up, going around the table and bringing a bottle of water and a glass. Drake waited while Aletta poured some water and took a sip.

'There are a couple of things we would like to talk about. Firstly, we are trying to understand the position of Max Hamilton. We understand that his appointment was not made permanent. Walt has spoken about it but has suggested you might know more than he does.'

'Max can be prickly at times, and he seemed to irritate Professor Kuiper,' replied Aletta. 'It was a great shame. He is a brilliant chap. He had some ideas that were worth following up on. He suggested approaching one of our problems in a new and different way. Professor Kuiper thought otherwise. If Professor Kuiper had a weakness, it was that maybe, at times, he was too focused. He was so determined to push through our approach that he couldn't see the merit in Max's suggestions. I would have him back in an instant. The Vice-Chancellor has given me the post to refill. We might reappoint him. I understand he has discussed his ideas with our major competitor, Virtual Virtue.'

'Thank you,' said Drake. 'That is helpful. It brings us to the second topic we wanted to talk to you about. We understand you have met with Gundula of Virtual Virtue. Tell us what you have discussed?'

'Who has told you about that?' demanded Aletta.

'That is not important,' replied Drake. 'When we spoke to you first, you described them as competitors. I gather you have changed your mind about that.'

'Not necessarily.'

'I understand you have been to the science park out by the airport to discuss moving there.'

'We are short of space as it is. It was a possibility I had to explore. That's all.'

'Was Professor Kuiper in favour of moving there?'

'Professor Kuiper is dead.'

'But you met with Gundula and went to the science park before he died.'

'No, it was after.'

'Our information is that it was before he died.'

'Your information is wrong.'

'I suppose we could check again with the director of the science park,' said Drake.

'It's not important. Professor Kiuper is no longer here. We must find the way forward now.'

'I think it is important,' said Drake. 'If it was before he died, then it changes your relationship with him. I understand that you were exploring a merger with VV before he died. You both saw him as the obstacle to getting further with a merger.'

'I don't see why any of this is important,' snapped Aletta.

'It is important that we can trust what you say to us. It appears that you knew about all this before he died. You certainly knew about it when you spoke to us previously. Then you described VV as competitors rather than potential partners in a merger.'

'They may remain competitors,' said Aletta. 'We are only at the exploration stage.'

'What does the Vice-Chancellor know about this?'

'I don't see why that is any business of yours.' Aletta seemed to be losing her patience. Drake was not going to give up.

'I can always speak to the Vice-Chancellor,' said Drake. 'He wants me to keep him informed about our investigation.'

'I have seen him. We have discussed it. He is enthusiastic about a merger. There is an overlap in our work. We could be both more effective and more efficient by merging.'

'Would there be room here for you both?' asked Drake.

'He will find us some more space. Another benefit to him is removing one of our competitors and strengthening our work.'

Drake looked at Grace and nodded. She guessed he wanted to lower the temperature.

'If this merger went ahead, would you consider taking Max Hamilton on again?'

'Yes, certainly.'

'I can see the attraction in this merger,' said Grace. 'Are you in favour of it then?'

'Yes, if everything can be arranged,' replied Aletta.

'But we understand that Professor Kuiper was not in favour. How would you have proceeded if he was still alive?'

'I would have persuaded him,' replied Aletta.

'But we understand he refused to be persuaded,' said Grace.

Aletta sat silently, drinking her water. Drake held up a hand. He wanted to be the sterner one in this conversation.

'So, he became the obstacle. From what we have discovered about him and what you must know, persuading him was unlikely.'

Aletta remained silent. Drake allowed the situation to drift for a while. Then he spoke again.

'So, you had the motivation to get him out of the way.'

'If you are trying to suggest I murdered him, that is absurd.' For the first time, Aletta raised her voice.

'I'm not suggesting anything,' said Drake. 'I'm just articulating the facts.' Again, Aletta remained silent.

'Perhaps Max Hamilton would also have a motive for getting Professor Kuiper out of the way?'

'On the face of it, I suppose so,' replied Aletta. 'I have no reason to believe it would drive him to murder.'

'Perhaps he might have had another argument with Professor Kuiper that accidentally turned nasty.' Aletta sat silently. Drake could see she was not going to comment further.

'So, was this merger so important that you thought it was no longer appropriate for Professor Kuiper to remain as director?'

'The situation doesn't arise,' snapped Aletta. She looked at her watch.

'I need to be back at the Centre now for a commitment.'

Drake nodded to Grace.

'Dr van Leyden, I will take you back,' she said.

As Grace drove, Dr Aletta van Leyden remained silently looking through the window. Grace pulled up outside The Centre for Industrial Design. Grace's passenger left the car and slammed the door behind her. It seemed she was rather cross, thought Grace. Her mind was already on another idea. She turned up the road along the side of the building the Centre was in. Sure enough, as she had thought, it was Weaver Street. She drove along it and came to a sharp left turn. She came to another street, going off to her right, and turned up it. She was on Commonhall Street, where Sophia Hamilton had lived. She wondered if it was possible that their "golfer" had gone to visit her. If so, what was the connection?

Grace got back to the station. The case room was silent, with everyone working on their respective tasks. Dave came in and reported that the new camera near The Cross did not show the "golfer" had walked that way. Suddenly, Martin let out a yell and punched the air.

'Come and look at this on my computer,' he said. Gradually, all the others gathered around, including Drake, who was inevitably last. Steve Redvers moved to the side to let him have a good view. Martin's screen was blank.

'Now then,' he said dramatically. 'I've just had an email in response to my posters at the golf clubs. It's very short and precise. Look!' he punched the keyboard. Up came an email that most could hardly read. Martin magnified it, and there was a collective gasp. The email read, "It is Max Hamilton." There was a general cheer and some clapping of hands.

'So,' said Drake, straightening his back. 'Thanks to Martin, we know it was Max Hamilton who chased after Professor Kuiper that Tuesday evening. He gave up talking to him and returned the way they had come. Martin, Grace and Dave could find no evidence of him in the rest of Watergate Street. Thanks to Grace, we now wonder if he turned down Weaver Street and into Commonhall Street. This could make sense. He was going to see his sister Sophia, who lived there. Then what happened? We don't know yet. The answer to that question might get us somewhere. Did he find his sister, or had she already gone to Professor Kuiper's house in Whipcord Lane, where we eventually found her dead?'

26

Constable Steve Redvers sat at the computer Dave had set up for him. He had a lengthy and possibly tiresome task. He was watching the videos that Dave had put on the computer. They were all from the camera over the door of the Vice-Chancellor's office on Nicholas Street. It pointed at the building across the road that housed The Centre for Industrial Design. There seemed to be an endless supply of files. Steve decided to start on the fateful Tuesday. They now knew that Professor Willem Kuiper departed from the Centre late in the evening. On his way home, he was joined by a man. One was the man the team had been calling "the golfer" due to his sporting apparel. They were now sure it was Max Hamilton. The other person was so far unknown. Drake wanted to know whether any suspicious activity connected with the Centre could be seen.

Steve began watching the camera file for the early morning of that Tuesday. There seemed to be little activity until it came to the rush hour. Then the level of traffic increased several times over. Few people were walking along the pavement during the early hours. As with traffic, there was a marked increase in pedestrian movements during the rush hour. Mostly, people were walking in a determined fashion and not hanging around. Steve guessed that if anyone had been up to something suspicious, they would not be walking around at a busy time. He was right. He saw nothing out of the ordinary. The whole of that day revealed nothing of interest.

Steve stood up and stretched his back. This task was tedious, but it demanded considerable concentration. Steve had been sitting staring at the screen too long. He walked around the case room and made a coffee before returning to his task. The Monday videos followed the pattern set by those on Tuesday. Again, he saw nothing worth recording.

The Sunday was different. This was extremely quiet and had no discernable rush hour. There was a slight increase in vehicles, but fewer people on foot. This street was not in the historic centre of town, nor near the river or the City Walls where tourists might be seen. He watched the time advance in the top left corner of his screen. He could speed up the replay a little.

Then suddenly, a man came into view and appeared to stop. Steve spooled back and ran the video at the standard speed. It was a tall fellow in unremarkable clothing. He walked from left to right along the whole length of the building, where the Centre for Industrial Design occupied the upper floors. He went out of Steve's view. Steve was about to increase the replay speed again when someone came in the opposite direction. Steve watched him for a few seconds. Could it be the same man returning? Now Steve noticed that he walked with a slight limp. Steve spooled back to the first time the man came into view. Yes. He limped a little. Steve thought he was favouring his left leg. Now Steve watched until he saw the replay of the man returning. He stopped in full view of the camera and appeared to look around. Perhaps he was worried about other people seeing him. He then took some photographs with his phone. He stepped back away from the building and looked at the upper floors. Then he reversed direction again and finally disappeared from view. Steve spooled forwards. Nothing else happened for maybe five minutes, according to the camera clock. Then there he was again. He returned from the right, walked across the screen and disappeared. Steve made a note of the time when the man first appeared. It was 11:23. He searched up and down the video but could find no further sight of the limping man. Eventually, Dave came over to see how Steve was getting on.

'I think I might have found something,' said Steve. 'Can you extract a section of this camera video and put it in a separate file?'

'Of course,' replied Dave. Steve showed him the section, and he did a cut-and-paste job in his view editing app. Steve wandered across to Martin, who was trying to enlarge pictures of the man they now believed to be Max Hamilton.

'Come and look at what I've found,' said Steve.

'Aha,' said Martin. 'Some progress, maybe?'

'Possibly,' said Steve. 'I'd like another opinion.'

Steve and Martin stood looking at the screen while Dave played the clip of the limping man.

'I think this is worth showing to Drake,' said Martin. 'My own opinion is that you've found something. You say it is on the Sunday before the murder?'

'Yes. Otherwise, it is a quiet day,' replied Steve.

'Makes sense,' said Martin. 'Go when there are few potential witnesses around.'

Martin called Drake over to see the video clip.

'That certainly looks suspicious,' said Drake. 'It isn't a building I would choose to take one photograph of, never mind several.'

'You know,' said Steve. 'I have a strong suspicion I know who this man is. Can you zoom in on him, Dave?'

Dave obliged.

'I can't go far,' said Dave. 'It's the resolution of the camera that is the restricting factor. It starts to get blurred quite quickly.

'It's the limp,' said Martin. 'I might be wrong. I certainly can't be sure. I think it might be a character called Patrick Milligan.'

'I guess he's Irish,' grunted Drake.

'Yes, and he talks rather quickly if I remember correctly. He can be difficult to understand at times.'

'He's an old customer, is he?' asked Drake.

'He's certainly from a good while ago. He wasn't strictly a customer. We had our suspicions. He sailed pretty close to the wind quite frequently. He's the local gumshoe.'

'Really? I don't remember him,' said Steve.

'Could well be before your time in plain clothes,' said Martin. 'It was when I was still a constable.'

'So, he's a private eye,' said Drake. 'Why did you need to see him?'

'It's coming back to me now,' replied Martin. 'He was associated with another local. I can't remember who it was at the moment. My memory is that there was something odd about his name. This other fellow was a hatchet man. He would undertake any nasty business you wanted done.'

'Really,' said Drake. 'Well, now I wonder what we have stumbled on here. Well done, Steve. Excellent work. Martin, can you get this Patrick Milligan to come and talk to us?'

'I'll check the records and see if we still have a contact for him. If I remember correctly, he was not usually cooperative. His claims were often like those of the press. His sources and clients were professional secrets. All that sort of thing.'

'OK,' said Drake. 'This could be important. Please find the contact address for him. I will get a search warrant, and you and Steve can look around his house while we interview him in the station.'

Martin sifted through some old files on his computer and soon had Patrick Milligan's address in Blacon. He passed it on to Drake, who applied for the search warrant.

The following morning, everyone was assembled in the case room when Drake arrived.

'Martin, I want you to take Steve to Blacon. Grace, you follow in another vehicle. If Patrick Milligan is at home, Grace will bring him here. If he refuses to come willingly, then arrest him. We can't mess around over this. Martin, you and Steve can then search the house for any information you can find on who he might be working for. Dave, you go with them in case any work on a computer is required. Collect Jimmy, the locksmith, on your way. If the place is empty, try a damage-free entry first. Is everyone clear?'

'Can I suggest a slight alteration?' asked Martin.

'Go ahead,' said Drake.

'I don't think it is a good idea for Grace to drive him alone. He is known to have a hatchet man who works with him and does all the dirty work. I remember now that he used a false name. We eventually found out it was Patrick's brother, Cormac. They both sail pretty close to the wind. I think Grace needs some support. He could easily get violent or up to some nonsense or other.'

'OK, understood,' said Drake. 'What do you suggest?'

'I suggest we take Constable Katie Lamb. I will then return with Grace. Once we've got him secure here, I can return to Blacon. It isn't far from here. Then you and Grace could do the interviewing.'

'Agreed,' said Drake. 'Let's go.'

Everyone except Drake set off on their various tasks. Drake thought Martin was being especially protective of Grace. His plan to put them together again was working.

27

Half an hour later, two unmarked cars arrived on a road lined with postwar semi-detached houses. Martin and Grace were in the front car, while Constables Steve Redvers and Katie Lamb were in the rear vehicle with Dave, the technician. Martin smiled at Grace and spoke into his phone.

'Are you ready, Steve?'

'Yep.'

'OK,' said Martin. 'I've got the warrant ready.'

'OK, Steve, you and Katie go first. Grace and I will be right behind you. Dave and Jimmy, wait in the car until we give a signal. Let's go.'

The line of four police officers left their respective cars, and Steve opened the front gate. He strode up the short path and hammered on the front door. To everyone's surprise, it opened almost immediately. A man wearing pyjamas and an open dressing gown appeared in the doorway.

'Police, Patrick Milligan?' demanded Steve, showing his ID.

'Nope, he's out. What's the problem?'

'No problem. We want to ask him a few questions,' said Steve.

'Upstairs. I heard a noise,' snapped Martin. Steve pushed his way through the door and dashed up the staircase. On instinct, he shoved open the rear bedroom door just in time to see a hand disappearing from the bottom of an open window. When he reached the window, the escaper was down in the garden, limping to the rear fence.

'Back garden!' yelled Steve. Grace was already on her way down the hall and into the garden. She saw the man climb the tall fence. She chased across the lawn as the man disappeared. Grace climbed up. She had her right hand over the top. As she struggled to get up, the man pulled her hand off the fence, and she fell right in front of Martin, who was following. Grace yelled with pain and clutched her left shoulder. Martin rolled her gently onto her back and called out for help. Steve came to his aid. They sat Grace up. Her face was white as she tried to speak.

'Stupid me,' she groaned. Her head flopped against Martin, who was now kneeling beside her with his right hand supporting her. He suddenly felt more pressure on his hand, and Grace's head fell forward. She had fainted.

Half an hour later, Martin rushed into the Accident and Emergency Department at the Countess of Chester Hospital. He had left Grace in the car right outside the entrance. She was now conscious, reclining in the front seat, feeling silly but trying to look brave.

'Police officer injured in the line of duty. I think dislocated shoulder.' Martin was conveying a sense of urgency to the reception desk. Two nurses were dispatched with a stretcher, and Grace was soon on her way to a treatment room. Waiting patients were simultaneously concerned for Grace and annoyed that their access to treatment still seemed hours away.

'That's the secret,' said one to his neighbour. 'We need to join the police force.'

About three hours later, Martin checked his watch. He called Grace's phone, and she answered.

'Hi Martin.'

'Are you finished there yet?'

'Just waiting for some medication. Powerful painkillers, I think.'

'OK. Stay there and take it easy. I will come over and collect you. You might like to know. It was, as we suspected, Patrick Milligan. He couldn't run with his limp, and he fell on some stone steps at the back of the garden and banged his head. He is being checked out for concussion in the same hospital. Steve is there with him. Drake sends his best wishes for a speedy recovery and tells you to take leave for as long as you need.'

Steve sat in the front room of Patrick Milligan's house. Sat opposite, wearing handcuffs, was Cormac Milligan, who had opened the door. Katie Lamb was in the back room, rifling through a desk diary. She was steadily working backwards from the present. It didn't seem as if Patrick Milligan was particularly busy. Then she saw the letters "DB." They cropped up repeatedly. Katie called Steve, who met her in the hall and stood by the door holding back Cormac Milligan.

'Who or what do you think "DB" means? There are several references here a couple of weeks before Kuiper's murder.'

'No idea,' said Steve. 'let's take him and the diary back to show Drake.'

Martin pulled up outside Grace's house in Christleton. Grace collapsed in laughter as she tried and failed to open the car door. Martin came around to the passenger side and let her out. She was wearing a sling. It would be her permanent companion for the next month. It was doing a great job. Her arm was completely immobile. She rotated in the now open door and dropped her feet onto the pavement.

'We'll have to use Drake's beloved Range Rover for you,' laughed Martin. 'Let me know when you feel like going out. I will arrange something for us.'

Grace smiled and nodded. She remembered how attentive Martin had been when she was in hospital once before. She thought he had matured significantly during his time in Hong Kong.

'That would be lovely,' she said. 'Right now, I feel tired. I might even go to bed.'

The following day, Drake was standing at his case boards. He scanned through Patrick Milligan's diary. He grunted several times before becoming aware that Martin was standing behind him.

'OK, let's go and interview the rogue.'

Martin joined Drake to interview Patrick Milligan. He still had a bandage on his head and looked sorry for himself.

'Why were you so anxious to avoid us?' asked Drake.

'Police represent trouble,' replied Milligan. 'It causes difficulties for me in my work.'

'You know avoiding police is a misdemeanour,' said Drake. Milligan sat in silence. 'You have also injured yourself and caused an injury to a police officer. We take a serious view of this.'

'No comment,' said Milligan.

'We have evidence that you behaved suspiciously on a Sunday morning several weeks ago. What were you up to?'

'No idea what you mean,' said Milligan.

'We have a video of you outside a building in Nicholas Street that houses the Deva University Centre for Industrial Design.'

'Oh, that! I was surveying it. There is a possibility we might take some space that is up for rent there.'

'You didn't survey it,' said Drake. 'You walked up and down and around it.'

'Yes, surveyed it.'

'I have here your diary that we collected from your house. It makes several references to someone who appears to be your client. You use the initials "DB" on several occasions. Who is DB?'

'No comment.'

'Does the name Damien Bewick sound familiar?' demanded Drake. 'What did Damien Bewick want you to do?'

'No comment.'

'Mr Milligan,' said Drake impatiently. 'Do you understand that we are questioning you in connection with a murder?'

'No way! I haven't killed anyone, ever.'

'But what you were doing may well leave you vulnerable to a charge of aiding and abetting a murder. That could carry a ten-year prison sentence.'

'I don't believe he wanted to murder anyone.'

'A murder has been committed. This is a serious situation. What did Damien Bewick want you to do?'

'OK, OK. He wanted me to uncover everything I could about someone called Willem Kuiper. I think he's Dutch. He's a professor or something. Damien said he had done the dirty on him in some deal. He wanted to know about anything that he could pin on Kuiper.'

'So, what was going to happen if you discovered anything?'

'I was just reporting back to Damien Bewick.'

'What had you discovered about Professor Kuiper?'

'Nothing of consequence.'

'Perhaps you arranged to murder him?'

'It was never murder. I don't do murder.'

'But your brother Cormac might?'

'Never discussed it. You can't pin this on me.'

'Perhaps you were going to blackmail him?' asked Drake.

'Not me. Not my style.'

'But your brother Cormac deals in nastiness of that kind. He has previous.'

'Look, we haven't done anything wrong. You couldn't bring a case. You don't have any evidence because there isn't any.'

28

The whole team was assembled except for Grace, who was still at home nursing a painful shoulder. Drake was looking at his beloved case boards. The team members started to chat about the events of the previous day. Drake came across to address them.

'We now have two strands of investigation that need pursuing further. One concerns the Milligan brothers and Damien Bewick. Is one of them responsible for the murder of Professor Kuiper? Katie and Steve, please try to bring Bewick in for questioning.'

Katie and Steve nodded.

'The second strand concerns Max Hamilton. He has a motive, having been made unemployed, and we also know he has a prickly personality and a short temper. Is he responsible? Possibly, he had an argument that turned violent. We know he followed Professor Kuiper part of the way home. He seemed to be talking to him and gesturing wildly, but then we saw him return and lost track of him on Watergate Street. Is it possible that he collected a car from somewhere? He might have been able to catch up with Professor Kuiper. It is also possible he went to visit his sister. None of this is conclusive yet. We need to interview both men. Martin, will you get his address, please? You could either try the University Human Resources Department or the golf club. Then, if you can, bring him in. We may also search his house for anything that might help us.'

'I've got some results that might be interesting,' said Dave. 'It's taken me a long time, partly doing other things, and partly trying to establish the email and password that Professor Kuiper used to back up his data in the cloud. I've finally done it. Many folders and files are encoded, and so far, I haven't been able to unlock them. However, from the names of folders and files, it mainly looks like personal information. There is one folder that I can read, but I don't understand. The folder is labelled "DB." It has a file called "factories" containing a list of odd-sounding names.'

'Brilliant,' said Drake. 'I might understand this. The folder could be about Damien Bewick. It looks like Professor Kuiper was investigating him. We know that he gets clothing made for his shops in Indonesia. The local shop manager told Grace about it. Perhaps these are the places where they are made. I wonder why this was important to him. See if you can track these places down to actual locations.'

Constables Katie Lamb and Steve Redvers drove to the address of Damien Bewick in Curzon Park.

'The house looks empty,' said Katie as Steve pulled up at the entrance to the gravel driveway.

'Well, we should try it and see what happens. There isn't a car in the drive, so I suspect you are right.' They tried ringing the bell and hammering on the door without success. A next-door neighbour looked over the dividing fence.

'Have you any idea if your neighbour is away?' asked Katie.

'It's OK. I always take parcels in for him,' said the neighbour. 'He is away a lot.'

'No, we're not delivering. We are police,' said Katie, holding out her ID. 'It's nothing to worry about. We want to speak to him. We think he may be able to help us with an investigation.'

'He's probably away overseas. He went off yesterday with a suitcase. We chatted briefly. I've no idea where he went.'

'OK, thank you,' said Katie.

Constables Katie Lamb and Steve Redvers pulled up outside the shop, which Grace had discovered was owned by Damien Bewick. They went in, and an assistant came up to them straight away. The shop looked empty.

'We are the police. Are you the manager?' asked Katie. She held out her ID.

'Yes. How can I help you?'

'We are looking for the shop owner, Mr Damien Bewick. Do you know where he is, please?'

'I certainly do. He has gone to Indonesia, where our suppliers are. You can see our stock is getting low, and they are late delivering.'

'How long will he be there?'

'I've no idea. He goes often, and he's usually away for several weeks.'

'Do you happen to know the name of the suppliers?'

'We have several. The main one is called Kuta Garments. I see it on some boxes that arrive now and then.'

'Thank you,' said Steve, as they left to return empty-handed to the case room.

Steve and Katie arrived in the case room to find Martin had been equally unsuccessful in hunting down Max Hunter.

'At least you have some result,' said Martin. 'You have found the name of this factory in Indonesia, and it appears on that list Dave dug out of Professor Kuiper's cloud files. As for Max Hunter, there is no sign of him. His neighbours say it is unusual. They have no idea where he is.'

Drake joined the conversation.

'That does it,' he said. 'I need to go to Bali. There are just too many clues pointing in that direction. Katie, arrange for me to fly as soon as possible. Perhaps you might call Nimade, get her to suggest a suitable hotel and book me into it.'

'How long for?'

'Oh, try for a week and ask them if I can stay longer if necessary.'

An alert bystander might have noticed Grace and Martin nodding and smiling at each other. They had a secret wager about how long it would be before Drake found it necessary to go to Bali.

The following day, Drake clambered into the Range Rover. Katie was driving him to Manchester airport.

'Good morning, Katie,' he said. 'Thank you for being so efficient and making all these arrangements.'

'No problem. I'm sorry I couldn't find direct flights from anywhere in the UK. I could have booked you onto a flight to Amsterdam and then to Bali. The historical Dutch connection with the place gives them enough business to sustain a direct flight. But when I checked with Martin, he thought you would prefer to go via Singapore.'

'Absolutely,' said Drake. 'That flight has become quite familiar. They always look after me well. At my age, nine hours of time difference plays havoc with the body and brain. On Singapore Airlines, I know I can get plenty of rest and good meals.'

Drake arrived at terminal two at Manchester Airport with plenty of time to spare. Flight SQ301 was not due to leave for a couple of hours. He was used to all the airport rituals of checking in and security. Once, they used to drive him mad, but now, he knew the best way through them. He was soon sat with a reviving cup of coffee in the lounge, waiting for the boarding call.

Drake thought he was familiar with all the technology on board his flight, but he had not reckoned with an airline that liked to be up to date. Things had changed. The controls on the seat were different. He had studied them carefully on his previous flight. For a while, he found himself collapsing back or violently lurching forwards. A patient and helpful stewardess came to his rescue and taught him the essentials. It all seemed so simple when explained. Drake remained puzzled. The instructions in his flight magazine managed to make it unutterably complex. Drake reflected on how, with modern technology, it often turns out that a human, especially a Singaporean stewardess, is vastly superior to a computer or a manual.

He wrestled with the entertainment system as he tried to find music he liked. Thankfully, his helpful assistant returned with champagne and sorted him out again. He chose a disc of some calming and delightful Chopin piano pieces. It just remained for him to plug in the sound-deadening headphones. On a previous flight, he had searched for the socket everywhere on his control panel. He was rather smug as he plugged them in on a panel behind his head. He was soon sipping and idly watching the clouds steadily passing his window while he listened to the most amazing pianist. He checked his screen. It was Vladimir Ashkenazy.

At last, he was calm and relaxed. He pulled out his notebook and an iPad that Dave had set up for him with photographs of all the case boards and details of the case. Up here he could look at them in peace. There were no incoming phone calls, texts, emails, and other annoying interruptions. Drake had one of his hunches that, somehow, what appeared to be separate strands of this investigation were interrelated. His trip to Bali was based on this hunch. The whole business had its roots in Bali, and it was his job during this visit to connect things that currently seemed unconnected. He had only recently come to appreciate long-haul flying as an ideal environment for reflection. He had to admit that he had made little progress, but his mind was now fully prepared to attempt some resolution.

Drake started to walk through Singapore Changi Airport before having worked out what he had to do. He stopped at one of those electronic screens full of scrolling flight information. His connecting flight to Bali was due to take off soon. He couldn't remember how long. He stared at the screen until he saw it. Flight SQ938, bound for Denpasar Airport in Bali. It was leaving from Terminal 2, and he was in Terminal 3. He reached the end of one of the lengthy legs that span out from the main buildings in each terminal. He could hop on one of those driverless trains that connect them. It was a slightly shaky but thankfully short journey. He spent a few minutes muddling around in a bookshop. He found a curious book about snow in Bali. It seemed such a ridiculous idea that he picked it up to look at it. Then he checked his watch. He needed to get to his next flight. He hurriedly bought the book and set off again down another airport leg to find his gate. His next flight would take less than three hours. It was a good deal shorter than the fourteen hours from Manchester. The time differences around the globe confused his brain as much as his body. He had left Manchester mid-morning the day before, and it should still be not long after midnight. But it was breakfast time. He had missed half his usual night and had a full day to get through. He might take a nap on the way to Bali.

The taxi pulled into the front of the Oberoi Hotel in a part of Denpasar known as Kuta. It had been a thankfully short drive. He was looking forward to finding his room and resting. The hotel was a splendid example of what Nimade had taught him about Balinese architecture. There were many pavilions set in beautiful verdant landscape. The whole effect was one of peacefulness. He was already glad that Nimade had recommended this hotel to Katie. She had done an immaculate job arranging his trip. He would congratulate and thank her when he returned.

He dropped his bags in what the receptionist called his lanai as she gave him the key. He needed to look the word up. His iPad immediately connected to the hotel's Wi-Fi. Apparently, "lanai" was a Hawaiian name for a semi-enclosed terrace. He was delighted with the room and piece of private outdoor space. It made sense in terms of what Nimade had told him about Balinese domestic architecture. This would do nicely.

He stretched his legs around part of the garden and eventually found himself back at the reception building. Nimade had told Katie that he could arrange a driver and guide there. She had explained that getting around Bali by yourself on your first visit was not a sensible option. The driver and guide would get him everywhere he wanted to go. They knew their way around and had tricks to get them into otherwise inaccessible places. They would also protect him from the insistent sellers of trashy rubbish that frequented all the tourist areas.

He arranged to meet his driver and guide after breakfast. They had the confusingly similar single names that Nimade had described. His driver was called Made, and his guide was Wayan. They would take him anywhere he wanted in a four-by-four vehicle. It all sounded ideal. As Drake began his way back through the garden to his lanai, he checked his watch. It made little sense. He reckoned that his body and brain were somewhere over the Middle East. They would catch up with him after a good sleep, and he would be ready for his trip with Wayan and Made.

29

Drake woke with the sun streaming through the window onto his private patio. He had forgotten to close the night curtains. He looked at his watch. Now, it made sense. It was half past seven. He knew the solar routine in this part of the world. The sunrise would have taken no more than half an hour. Twelve hours later, the sunset would be equally short. He opened the patio door and was met with the combination of sights, sounds and aromas that only Far East tropical countries can offer. His patio allowed him to be outdoors but sheltered from the more public garden. He knew from Nimade's tuition that Balinese design was carefully arranged to achieve privacy in this way.

The birds were singing in the trees that climbed over a high wall. A rustling sound from above told him that one of the local macaques was scrambling higher up in the tree. Luckily, he had been sufficiently alert last night to hang a card on the door handle detailing his breakfast request. There it was, laid out, on a circular table with his seat pulled back and draped with a napkin. He dressed and snacked on a breakfast of muffins and local fruits. Somehow, his digestive system was not ready for a cooked course. He felt at home in this part of the world. Inwardly, he knew he could not live here. He would miss the seasons too much, but it was a delightful place to visit.

Drake walked through the manicured garden to the narrow beach, took off his shoes and plodded along on the high-water marks. The combination of gentle waves and the singing birds was magical. He never ceased to be entranced by this part of the world. He wished he had discovered it earlier when he was young enough to explore more fully. Of course, he would then have had Cynthia with him. He told himself not to get depressed. He must enjoy the present.

He strolled back inland and arrived at a raised terrace. It was an outdoor restaurant surrounding what looked like a performance area. He saw a waiter setting cutlery on a table and asked him what was on that evening.

'We have a local gamelan orchestra coming tonight,' said the waiter. 'I can reserve a table for you right at the front for dinner. You can dine while you watch the performance.'

'Thank you,' said Drake. 'That would be excellent.'

He was prepared for the day ahead. He gathered his phone, notebook and a small shoulder bag. He had remembered to bring the obligatory tiny folding umbrella. He was near the equator, of course. Even on a sunny day, a torrential but usually brief tropical storm could brew in no time. He strolled through the garden with its frangipani trees and hibiscus shrubs. A couple of cheeky mynah birds argued on the path, almost under his feet. Such was the malice of their dispute that they hardly seemed to notice his approach.

Wayan was already waiting for him in the reception area. He was dressed in a flowing upper garment and a full-length sarong. He bowed and set off around a pond covered in water lilies with a pair of tree frogs croaking on adjacent leaves. The vehicle that was to take him to see Nimade's shop, Bali Style, was waiting with Made already at the wheel.

'Where would you like us to take you?' asked Wayan.

'I want to go to a shop in Ubud called Bali Style,' said Drake. 'I will have to look at my notebook for the address.'

'Yes, of course, no need. We know it well. We often take tourists there. It is on the main street.' Wayan held the door open as Drake slid onto the rear seat. It was just the right height for his long legs, and he hardly had to duck to bring his head inside. Wayan shut the door behind him. His sarong swished gently as he climbed into the front passenger seat. He spoke in their language, and his driver, Made, nodded. They were on their way.

'I don't want to pry,' said Wayan, turning to face him. 'We always like to know a little about our passengers so we can take them the best way. Are you here on business or a holiday?'

'I am supposed to be here on business,' said Drake, 'but I have such an interest in your design and architecture that, where possible, I would love to see more of it.'

'Are you by any chance an architect yourself?' asked Wayan, smiling. He spoke with a soft, lilting voice that enchanted Drake.

'No. I wish. My wife was an architect. She passed away not long ago, and I am trying my best to learn about what she did.'

'Ah, I am so sorry to hear you have lost your wife,' said Wayan. 'We can make a short diversion and show you one of our most beautiful historic buildings.'

'That would be lovely,' said Drake. He was so delighted by Wayan's attention to detail and desire to serve his passenger that he thought he should make some small talk.

'I understand that you must be the firstborn in your family,' he said.

Wayan laughed and nodded.

'You understand about Balinese names. How do you know this?'

'Nimade, who owns Bali Style, has taught me.'

'Ah, yes. Of course, we know Nimade. She always makes our passengers feel at home.'

This comment surprised Drake, and his brain gave him a jolt. If, as he expected, Nimade was at the shop, his real reason for visiting Bali would not be a secret for long. Drake felt so at ease with Wayan that he decided to own up. He need not have worried. Wayan gave him the opportunity.

'Please do not feel I am interfering,' he said. 'What is your business here?'

'I am in the legal professions,' said Drake, sounding grander than he meant to. 'I am a policeman.'

'Ah,' said Wayan. 'In which case, the building we are about to visit will be even more interesting to you. I will explain when we get there. For now, I will let you rest and watch through the

window. Please ask me any questions you want. I am here to help.'
With that, Wayan turned to Made, and they spoke with soft tones that suited their language well. Drake watched as buildings gradually gave way to open countryside. He could see the fields were cultivated in tiers as they grew up the gentle hillsides. The occasional wooden structure was to be found in these fields.

'What are the structures in the fields for?' he asked.

'They provide shelter from the midday sun for the workers in the rice fields,' said Wayan. 'We call them "Pondoks." They are handmade by rice workers.' Drake jotted this new word in his notebook and noticed several kites in the sky. He had read somewhere that Balinese children frequently made and flew kites. It was all a world away from the north of England.

Eventually, they began to find themselves in a more built-up area. After a few turns, Made stopped the four-by-four.

'We have only a short walk,' said Wayan. Drake slid out of the vehicle and followed him. He noticed that, to walk any distance, Wayan had to gather his sarong and lift it slightly at his front. He gestured with his free hand.

'Look to your right. This is one of our most treasured historic buildings.'

Drake turned, and the sight that met his stare was extraordinary. A large rectangular open-sided building was sitting on a raised platform in the middle of a small lake full of lilies and koi carp. The hipped overhanging roof was supported by four ornate, round columns across the ends and five down the sides. The whole sat on a tiered set of walls made from panels of lattice stonework separated by stubby columns supporting a variety of sculptured figures. The water in the surrounding lake was so still that it made a perfect reflection.

'If you wish, we can go up the steps into the building,' said Wayan.

'Yes, please,' replied a stunned Drake.

They ascended a flight of steps at one end that connected the building to the land surrounding the lake. The sloping ceilings under the roof were full of glorious paintings.

'How old is this?' asked Drake.

'We don't know for sure, but several hundreds of years,' replied Wayan.

'What was it for?'

'That is the reason I thought you would find it interesting. It was a pavilion in which judicial hearings were held.'

Drake let this information sink in, and then he spoke, voice slightly cracked.

'How clever is that?' he exclaimed. 'We have a saying that "justice must not only be done but must be seen to be done." This building exemplifies that more remarkably than anywhere I have seen. It is secure and defensible. Yet onlookers get a clear view of what is going on inside.'

Drake took out a handkerchief and dabbed his eyes.

'How fitting that you have shown me this. It somehow brings the careers of myself and my wife together. How I wish she were here to see it. She would have loved it as I do. Please, what is it called?'

'Sometimes it is known as the Klungkung Palace, after the historical name of this part of Bali. It was the King's court. It is also known as Kerta Gosa. If you are ready, we will finish our journey to Ubud.'

Drake smiled and nodded. He must turn his attention to the Kuiper case. It was hard to tear himself away from this charming place.

30

Drake sat in the rear seat of the four-by-four. He did not remember ever being so moved by a building before. What a treasure it was. The climate is so kind to old buildings, he thought. It is in excellent condition even though it is open to anyone to walk in. There was no sign of damage or graffiti. This society values its history. They were out in the country again. To his right, he saw an extraordinary landscape.

'Where are we?' he asked Wayan.

'We are on the foothills of our sacred mountain, Mount Agung. It is a volcano that is still alive. Our ancestors believed some of their gods lived there and kept it quiet for them to live nearby. It has erupted in a minor way quite recently. We must drive around it to get to Ubud.'

The rolling hills rose above them, with rice fields covering their slopes. The natural irrigation systems created tiers of landscape marking out the contours. Drake could see the occasional Pondok. He was absorbed by the constantly changing geometry of this landscape. The combination of natural and human-generated forms was just perfect. Soon, they were surrounded by mainly old and low-rise buildings.

'We are in Ubud,' said Wayan. 'Many artists and craftspeople live and work here. There are many galleries and art shops. You can buy sculptures and elaborate traditional wooden carvings. It is a popular spot on the tourist trail. There are several nice hotels so you can stay and enjoy everything Ubud offers. We are now driving along Jalan Raya Ubud. Jalan means street in our language. This is the main street. It goes right through Ubud from east to west.'

'That is interesting,' said Drake. 'I was in Malaysia a while back and their word meaning street was the same.'

'Yes,' said Wayan. 'You will find many similarities. They speak Bahasa Malaysia and we speak Bahasa Indonesia. They are two dialects of the same basic language. Bali Style is a beautiful complex of buildings. We are nearly there.'

This was a busy street with cars, vans and dozens of motorbikes and scooters. The buildings on both sides of the street were mostly one or two floors high. As far as Drake could see, there were restaurants, fashion shops, and art galleries. Suddenly, the car stopped. Drake looked to his left. He saw a collection of pavilions with what looked like thatched roofs. There were no signs. It was all discreet. This was a place that did not need adverts and signs. Much of the property seemed open to the outside. There was a massive tree growing out of a central courtyard.

'Is that by any chance a banyan tree?' Drake asked Wayan.

'Yes, very good. It is old. It plays an important part in our culture. The banyan is an integral part of the "Pura Dalem." It is a temple and cemetery for the dead. There is one in every Balinese village. The banyan tree represents the eternal cycle of death and rebirth. It protects the spirits after death. Nimade is lucky to have such a tree. It brings good fortune.'

As Drake made his way forward, guided by Wayan, he discovered more conventional spaces behind the open pavilions. As he expected from Nimade's description, you could buy things for your gardens and outdoor spaces as much as interior rooms. There was sculpture everywhere. Drake had been fascinated by Nimade's new shop in Chester, but this place was on a grander scale. Potential customers drifted around silently. They looked and touched objects in an almost loving fashion.

Suddenly, there was Nimade. She was dressed in the traditional Balinese clothes that Drake had first seen in her home near the Shot Tower in Chester. Here, she looked different. She was confident and happy. She was at home. She greeted Wayan like a long-lost friend. They bowed slightly to each other.

'You have brought me more customers,' she said. Then she saw Drake's head towering above the smaller Balinese folk.

'Oh, my goodness. Hello, Detective Chief Inspector,' she cried with delight. Drake's anonymity was blown away, and he was put off guard. He felt eyes on him from all around. He felt perhaps some people even moved away from him. Nimade came forward and beckoned him into an office. At least, that was what Drake thought, but it was furnished delightfully. This was no back office. It was a place to receive customers and entertain them. Presumably, business would follow. Drake was in a more foreign world than he had expected. Everything was strange. The surroundings, the culture, the climate. His great height was even more apparent here. People seemed in awe of him.

'I'm sorry,' said Nimade. 'I was clumsy. In Bali, we do not trust our police. Corruption is rife. They are as likely to bribe you as assist you. We don't normally talk about it. I should not have greeted you so formally. I have fallen into British habits.'

'Perhaps it would be better to call me Drake.'

'Yes, of course. First some tea, then you must let me show you around. This shop is the heart of our business. We trade here with the locals and also with tourists. We supply our European shops from here.'

Nimade took Drake around. The shop was mainly a series of room and garden settings showing off all the Bali Style products. They were not arranged by product type but in a way that customers could imagine in their homes. Drake thought his living room in Chester could be furnished this way. Everything was made of natural materials. There were bright colours but also many objects in neutral browns and fawns. They produced a relaxing but stunning effect. There were a few exceptions to this. Drake was attracted to a section showing the ornamental Kris daggers. He remembered he had seen one in the Chester shop.

'These mostly appeal to our local customers,' murmured Nimade. 'I know they look fierce, but they have cultural value and are often used for rituals. Almost all Balinese families follow these traditions.'

Drake was about to move on when Nimade stopped him. 'I must tell you something,' she said. 'I am not sure if it might be important. According to Laurence, one of our Kris in Chester has gone missing. I hadn't noticed it. We normally show two of them. Laurence replaces them from the store on the rare occasion we sell one. He said that he saw one in the shop. He wanted to replace the missing one but found only one more in the store. He thought we had three. He said he would pack two more for our next consignment to Chester. I'm not sure he is right that one is missing, but just in case, I thought I should tell you.' Drake tried to appear indifferent.

'Thank you,' he said. 'I'm not sure whether this is important, but I will keep it in mind.' They moved on to other displays. Drake was drawn to one that showed dozens of puppets.

'These are what we call Wayang Kulit,' said Nimade. 'They are used for traditional shadow performances. The main part is made from water buffalo and goat hide and mounted on a horn handle. The best ones, like these, are made from young female buffalo parchment, cured for up to ten years. The carving and punching of the hide are responsible for the character's image and shadows. A mallet is used to tap special tools to punch the holes through the rawhide. Making the sticks from the horn is a skilled process involving sawing, heating, hand-moulding, and sanding. When the materials are ready, the artist attaches the handle. It is precisely moulded at the ends of the horn. It goes around the figure and is secured with thread. A large character may take months to produce. Each character may have several puppets used in different parts of the story. You must try to see a performance.'

'All your products are charming,' said Drake. 'When I was at your shop in Chester, Laurence Bailey spoke about the need to have special areas where you pack all the goods for transport.'

'Yes, we have one here, but it is only used for local customers. We have a warehouse in Kuta near the port and airport, where Laurence does all his ingenious work. That is for goods which are to be freighted abroad. He is arriving tomorrow. Perhaps I could get him to show you around there. It is interesting. We never get any breakages because Laurence is so clever and careful.'

'Thank you,' said Drake. 'I find the whole process intriguing.'

'Yes, Willem found it fascinating too. He couldn't believe the care that Laurence took with packing. He visited the warehouse a couple of times. Laurence said he'd never had such an interested visitor before. He looked at the costs and what we charge. He wanted to increase our profit margins. Willem was always concerned with the financial side of things. Thank goodness I have Laurence to deal with it all now.'

31

Drake returned from his trip to Ubud in time to shower and prepare for his front-of-house position at the hotel's outdoor restaurant. He had been promised a gamelan performance and all the instruments were already in place. He could see drums and gongs ranging from small to large. Other instruments looked like xylophones but seemed to be made from wood. This promised to be a glorious sound. Soon, the musicians appeared dressed in traditional costumes and took their places. They began playing the most beguiling music Drake had ever heard. They were all playing with sheet music. Somehow, it managed to represent this wonderful island.

Drake noticed smiles and nods from the musicians to each other. It looked as if they enjoyed it as much as he did. He thought it must be wonderful to make such music with other people. Occasionally his flute teacher would play a duet with him, and he loved that, but this was on a different scale. Watching them, he noticed that the musicians were arranged in an arc. It left the centre of the stage area empty, and Drake was about to discover why.

A series of female dancers appeared from behind the musicians. They moved with such delicacy and care that Drake could not take his eyes off the performance. Eventually, one dancer moved to the front and began circling motions with her arms that seemed to originate at the shoulders and end with her fingers. He looked around at all the absorbed audience. He could not remember ever seeing so many people watching someone's fingertips. There was soon a procession of other dancers, some playing human parts and others dressed as animals. Some creatures were aggressive and alarming but were eventually subdued and sent packing by the gentler figures. Drake guessed there must be a story, but he had no idea what it was. The waiter delivering his dinner dutifully tried to explain, but Drake thought it better not to try to understand it.

Drake turned again to see the expressions on the faces of his fellow diners. Every single one appeared transfixed. That was all except for one. A man leaning against a tree with hands in his pockets. Drake felt he had been watching the audience rather than the performance. He made a sudden movement of his head to see the dancers. Drake's brain was sending out alarm signals. The man was watching him. He turned back to his meal. He would look again in a few minutes. Now was not the time to stare back. After a few delicious mouthfuls, his waiter came to ask if he was enjoying his meal. Drake smiled, nodded, and looked past the waiter to see the man who had been staring at him. He was not there.

Drake continued his meal and watched the performance, but now his mind was elsewhere. His brain was trying to tell him something. Drake's memory of people's names was embarrassingly poor. He also knew that he never forgot a face. He had sometimes wondered how he did this. Cynthia frequently commented about it. He remembered her once saying that his memory for faces had infinite capacity and near-perfect reliability.

Her mind was full of places, particularly buildings. She could visit somewhere and later draw it from memory in a manner so accurate that Drake found this ability uncanny. In turn, she was amazed by his recall of faces. He did this without effort or conscious analysis. He did not study noses, ears, eyes, or mouths. It was just the integrated whole that his brain stored. His lack of ability in sketching left him hopelessly unable to draw these faces, but when confronted with one, he would recall it, usually immediately. On a few occasions, he had to think hard about where he had seen the face before and who it belonged to. This was one of those occasions.

He watched and listened to the charming performance, but his brain worked away in the background. Then it came to him. He had seen the face before, and it was that same day. He reconstructed the event. Two men arrived on scooters and sat talking to a third man standing by them. It was when his guide got out of the four-by-four vehicle to take him into Nimade's wonderful shop, Bali Style.

His memory of what the shop looked like was only sketchy. He remembered that it seemed made of pavilions with thatched roofs. How many, he could not remember reliably. But this face, he was sure about. It was one of the men on scooters. Why would the same man appear now at his hotel, and why was he not sitting watching the show but leaning against a tree, looking casual with hands in pockets? But Drake was sure this man was watching him.

The only other interpretation was that he was wrong. Perhaps his memory was playing tricks. He was not as good at remembering Asian faces, particularly Chinese ones, so maybe that was the explanation. Drake momentarily closed his eyes to concentrate. He had to back himself. The logical conclusion was that this was no coincidence. The man was watching him. What, Drake asked himself, was so interesting about his activities? He thought of excusing himself to his waiter and trying to follow the man. He soon decided better of that idea. If the stranger had followed Drake, he would appear again.

The following morning, Drake woke and turned on his phone. There was an alert for a text arriving. It was from Laurence Bailey. He was coming across from Ubud to the warehouse and would pick Drake up on his way at ten. It was still early, but Drake wanted to hear the tropical dawn chorus. He knew from past visits that sunrise took only half an hour and started about seven. He dressed and walked out into the garden. Birds were already singing. Again, there was what he thought might be a macaque in one of the trees. His guidebook had told him that a long-tailed species lived on the island, and this one certainly had a lengthy tail.

He ate a breakfast of fruits and Danish pastries. He sipped a reviving cup of coffee. He was ready for the day ahead. He returned to his lanai to look again at his guidebook until it was time for Laurence to collect him.

As Drake's watch reached 9:50, he set off through the gardens to the reception area. He arrived early and watched the brilliantly coloured koi carp in the pond. Spot on time, a large white van pulled up in front of him. He instinctively moved out into the open so Laurence could see him.

'I'm sorry,' said Laurence, holding out his hand. 'I'm moving some large items today. We prefer to use the whole floor area of the shop for retail, so we have little storage space there. Our warehouse here acts as that storage, and as items get sold, I need to replenish. Today is one of those occasions. I hope that you don't mind being collected in the van.'

Drake climbed up into the cab of the van. In truth, it was easier than he expected. The cab was luxuriously appointed, and he soon sat comfortably in a leather seat that welcomed him in. The journey was short. Laurence pulled up in front of the largest building he had seen since coming to Bali. It was in a district that looked like an industrial quarter.

'This area is attractive for people who trade overseas,' said Laurence, 'We are only a short drive away from both Benoa port and Denpasar airport, so there are many warehouses. Good carriers are just around the corner. I have one who takes slightly longer to deliver, but he guarantees a day of delivery. I like to be there on the same day or at least the day after to unpack.'

Laurence got out and disappeared. He arrived to help Drake down to ground level. He pulled out a large ring of jangling keys and unlocked a human-sized door. It formed part of a larger door, which Drake estimated would allow the van to enter. Drake stepped carefully over the threshold and found himself in a gigantic void. There were crates and boxes of all sizes covering the floor. Laurence took him through this storage area to a part of the warehouse where the floor was clear.

'This is our packing area,' explained Laurence. He pointed to a deep rack of shelving. Drake's eyes wandered around. There were empty cardboard boxes folded flat of every imaginable size and shape. Along the bottom shelf were unfolded versions of each type of box.

'The first job when packing is to choose the right sized box or container,' explained Laurence. 'I can test this out with the boxes on the bottom shelf and then pull a folded version down from the shelves above. Beyond here, there are more substantial crates. The process is essentially the same but just on a larger scale.' Laurence walked past the crates to reveal a small forklift truck.

'Of course, once things are in a crate, we need this to move them. There is a door large enough to get everything through. If we need it, a delivery lorry can leave a shipping container there, and we can load it up. We rarely need a full container, but it does happen.'

Drake scanned the shelves above the cardboard boxes. There were all kinds of things stored there. There were rolls of that clear plastic with air bubbles all over. Drake guessed it was used to pad out space around objects inside the boxes. There were other rolls of much larger bubbles. There were bags of those thin strings of paper used for wrapping. There were some rolls of sticky tape. Then came a whole shelf of what looked like black plastic sheets.

Laurence saw him looking slightly puzzled.

'You are studying all our packing materials,' he said.

'Yes,' replied Drake. 'The bubble wrap stuff is to be expected, as are the curly strings of brown paper. But what are the black plastic sheets for?'

'Oh, we often get delicate flat objects to pack. A good example would be the Wayang Kulit shadow puppets you probably saw in our shop. We sometimes need something semi-rigid or even rigid to avoid damage.'

Drake nodded and continued his exploration. He walked around a crate with one side open, ready for packing. Then he saw a row of grey metal objects more like office machines. There was a computer printer, a photocopying machine and something he could not quite place.

'That's a semi-portable X-ray machine,' explained Laurence.

'Really,' said Drake, 'why would you need that?'

'It's an essential piece of kit,' explained Laurence. 'At Benoa Port and Denpasar Airport, the security people scan with X-ray machines. If their machine shows something they cannot identify or for some reason looks suspicious, the whole thing may be put on one side to be opened. If we are not there when that happens and they cannot open it, the goods miss their slot on a ship or plane. We eventually get called back, but it is often too late. It used to happen all the time. So, to avoid this, we have our scanner. If anything doesn't look right, we repack it. This clever little beast eliminates most of that hassle.'

There was a short row of what Drake assumed were safes. Two had large dials, and a third had a substantial keyhole.

'We put any extreme valuables in here,' explained Laurence. I am the only one who has the keys and codes. It keeps me feeling things are OK when I'm not here.'

Drake followed Laurence around another crate. There was a smaller pile of packages.

'These are all ready to go to Chester,' said Laurence.

'So how long does that take?' asked Drake.

'These are going air freight. The carrier guarantees they will be delivered in five days,' replied Laurence. 'This means I know when I must be in Europe to unpack. I will be over there the next day. Now have a look at these beauties.' He walked around the pile of crates and parcels. There, in all their glory, were gamelan instruments. Each was carefully laid out in its own space, almost like a museum.

'Every village has a gamelan,' said Laurence. 'I don't pretend to understand it all. They say it is not an orchestra but a single instrument that takes thirty people to play.' Laurence laughed.

'Through all Nimade's contacts, we have become known in the arts and crafts industries here. We have several customers who make gamelans. They sometimes need transport. They are precious and delicate, so we are called upon to manufacture custom-made cases. It's an odd business. Each gamelan is tuned in its unique way. It's not like a Western orchestra tuned to an internationally agreed set of scales. If a group goes to play anywhere, they must take their instruments. They cannot borrow from others. The well-thought of gamelans are in demand now, so this happens frequently. It's a nice little side-line for us.'

'Yes, there was a performance at the Oberoi last evening,' said Drake. 'It was beautiful. What a fascinating world you inhabit. Thank you for all your trouble introducing me to it. Nimade told me that Professor Kuiper came and looked around.'

'Yes, like you, he was interested.'

'Why do you think that was?' asked Drake.

'Oh, I think he was looking for efficiencies we could make. He was a hard taskmaster. He always wanted to reduce our costs and increase our profit.'

'Did he suggest any savings?'

'Thankfully, I heard no more from him, so I guess not. I don't run a sloppy business here.'

'When did he come?' asked Drake.

'Not long ago. A month or two, maybe. I didn't keep a diary note. He arrived unexpectedly. I'm sure that was his intention. He wanted to catch us out, but there was nothing for him to see.'

32

Drake woke at dawn having slept well. The previous evening, he had experienced that curious phenomenon of jet lag catching up with him. He had felt like this before. The first day or two in a new time zone, he felt OK. He seemed to work well. After that, his brain finally got fed up with running on the adrenalin that flooded his body on arrival. Quite suddenly, the time difference would catch him out. He had been forced to miss his evening meal and retire. He had just collapsed into bed.

Now, he was well-rested and ready for another day. He ate the breakfast laid out for him on his terrace and walked through the gardens. He was keen to see if there would be another performance that evening. The waiter told him it would be Wayang Kulit, which he had already learned was shadow puppetry. He booked a table. When he got to the entrance, Wayan and Made had arrived in the four-by-four.

'Where do you want to go today?' asked Wayan.

'A clothing factory in Kuta.'

Wayan looked crestfallen.

'This will not be beautiful,' he warned. 'You must be working again.'

Drake smiled, nodded, and passed Wayan the address of Kuta Garment.

'Only a short drive,' said Wayan, passing the address to Made. They set off out of the hotel grounds. Drake looked around to find his follower or a scooter. He saw neither. Perhaps they were getting better at following incognito, or maybe they were waiting out of sight.

Wayan was right. This was not a journey any tourist would take. They drove along a series of roads, some narrow, some wider. There was even a road where two vehicles passing in opposite directions had to stop and creep past each other. It happened to them three times, and then they only made progress thanks to the skill of their driver, Made, who seemed to know to the millimetre how wide the four-by-four was. The buildings were varied along these roads. Drake thought you would probably call them streets. Some buildings were little more than traditional shacks. Others were boring, two-storey modern blocks. Now and then, there would be a section of trees and bushes. Drake assumed that, in this climate, a plot would soon get overgrown if left for any time. Then, they were on streets with shops, bars, and what looked like offices. Suddenly, Made pulled up. Drake looked to his left and right. He could not see why they had stopped.

Made spoke to Wayan in a language Drake had come to know as Bahasa Indonesia. Indonesia has the fourth largest population, so this must be one of the most widely spoken languages. Drake entertained this remarkable thought. Only a few days ago, he had never heard of it. How ignorant we British are, he thought. Then Wayan turned and spoke in English.

'We are here.'

'Where?' asked Drake.

'This is the address of the Kuta Garment factory,' replied Wayan.

Looking to his left, Drake only saw clothes hanging outside what he assumed was a dress shop. Wayan shrugged his shoulders. Drake decided to get out and investigate.

'I will come with you,' said Wayan. 'They may not speak English here.'

Drake and Wayan entered the shop, and a woman came up and spoke in Bahasa. Drake was glad Wayan had accompanied him. Wayan spoke back to her.

'She said she would go and see someone,' said Wayan as the woman disappeared into the rear of the shop. 'I think the factory is at the back. I told her this seemed more like a shop. They sell rejects and spares here at the front on the street.'

The woman returned and spoke to Wayan again.

'She says the factory is closed today.'

It seemed odd that a busy factory would be closed in the middle of the week. Then, he caught sight of a man standing at the back of the shop. It was his follower, the man on the scooter who was at the gamelan performance. He was dressed differently, but Drake knew it was him. This fellow was not going to let him into the factory. A woman came struggling past, laden with heavy bags and clothes draped over each shoulder. Drake watched as she reached his observer. He opened a door in the rear wall of the shop. Suddenly, they could hear the noise of machines. The woman disappeared, and the door shut. All was quiet again. Drake's follower stood and crossed his arms almost in a stance of defiance. He was no longer trying to conceal his presence. Drake decided to cut his losses.

'Let's go back to the hotel,' said Drake to Wayan. 'I need to think about what to do next. We'll have some lunch.' Wayan nodded and took Drake to the street where Made was waiting with the four-by-four. Made had turned on the air-con, and Drake was glad to get in the cool air. The atmosphere in this confined street was oppressive. He was sweating profusely. The driver, Made, navigated their route through the narrow streets to the hotel.

'Can you find somewhere to have some lunch?' Drake asked Wayan.

'Of course,' he replied. 'Do you want us to come and collect you again?'

'Yes, please. I'm sure there will be something else to do,' replied Drake. He walked back through the reception area and across the garden. He stopped to watch two men setting up for the evening performance. They had a large white screen erected in the middle of the performance area. Behind and to one side, there was a large lamp. It looked as if it would be a live flame. To the other side were four of the xylophone-like instruments he had seen in the gamelan. Drake was intrigued. He spoke to one of the men.

'Do you speak English?'

'Yes.'

'Are you setting up a gamelan for this evening's performance?' asked Drake.

'It is called a gender gamelan. We use it to accompany Wayang Kulit. You can see we only have four instruments. There are two pairs. The second pair are tuned an octave above the first. The second one in each pair is tuned just a fraction higher than the first. This is what creates the characteristic shimmering sound.'

'I have been fascinated by the puppets themselves,' said Drake. 'They are beautifully decorated, but they are used to create shadows. Why paint them?'

'We love them and want them to be beautiful. Also, people can sit behind the screen and the Dalang, who is the puppeteer. This means people can choose between the magic of the shadows or being able to see the beauty of the craftsmanship and the skill of the Dalang. My colleague is putting out chairs now.'

'What a wonderful idea,' said Drake. 'So, two people can watch the same performance from opposite sides and have different experiences. I never thought of that. Thank you.'

Drake's tutor smiled, bowed and continued his work. Drake headed to the restaurant to find some lunch and think things over.

33

Drake sat eating lunch. He never tired of the fresh fruit that was available in tropical countries. It all tasted so different from home. He had never thought about it before. For a while, he wondered how long it took to harvest fruit in Bali, pack it, fly it halfway across the world and then get it delivered to a supermarket. Presumably, all this contributed to the loss of flavour in his usual fruit. He finished his meal and put his napkin on the table. Just then, he sensed his brain was trying to tell him something. It was something to do with his morning's work. It had to do with watching the Wayang Kulit performance from the front or the back. That was it! His brain had resurrected an old idea he had used often when stuck. Try seeing the situation from the opposite side, he thought. The Kuta Garment was a shady and dodgy operation, though Drake could not quite understand the details. The factory and Damien Bewick didn't want him to see things they were hiding. His mind raced around this notion as he walked back to his lanai. Then, he got it.

He took out his phone and connected it to the hotel's Wi-Fi. He googled Kuta Garment. Sure enough, nothing completely satisfying the search appeared. There were many websites with Kuta in the name and many Balinese garment establishments. What if he found a garment factory in Bali that was operating legally and openly? Could he then see what was wrong with Kuta Garment?

He performed his general search and found half a dozen garment factories in Bali. Most were in the wider area of Denpasar. One was called The Bali Ethical Factory. He would visit and see what he could learn by looking from the other side. Rather pleased with himself, he set off to find Wayan and Made with their four-by-four. They were dutifully waiting at the hotel entrance.

Made knew how to get to this factory and set off immediately. This was a more pleasant drive through leafy suburbs. It took less than twenty minutes, even in quite busy traffic. As before, Wayan agreed to come in with him. They entered a small reception area and pressed a bell for attention. A smartly dressed man arrived.

'How can I help you?' he asked.

'I'm looking to understand how an ethical factory works here,' said Drake. 'I have found one that seems unethical, and I want to see the difference.'

'Of course. I can explain. Can I first ask if you are Australian?'

Drake laughed. In Bali, that was the default assumption about someone speaking English and wearing Western dress.

'No,' replied Drake, deciding to be open. 'I am British. I am a member of an English police force, and we are investigating garment factories that might be selling to shops in our country. My name is Drake.'

'Let me find my boss to talk to you.' He disappeared, and Drake and Wayan waited patiently. A tall, blond man wearing Western clothes came out to see them.

'It is wonderful to hear what you are doing. My name is Oliver. I am Australian. I own this business together with my Balinese partner. There is a lot of bureaucracy here. Opening a new foreign-owned business is difficult. Maybe that saves Bali from worse exploitation. Indonesia, especially Bali, run a low-wage economy. They see this as the way forward for their current stage of development. However, they set national and provincial minimum wages. These have just gone up again, as they do most years. We pay our staff significantly above the minimum wage. They have sick pay, maternity leave and paid holidays. We offer a healthcare scheme for them. We operate in an energy-efficient and sustainable environment.' Oliver cleared his throat.

'We have staff who work here in the factory, and we also have domestic home workers. Some people, especially with young families, prefer to work on machines at home. We lend them money to buy machines. We deliver materials and collect clothes if they wish at a small price, or they can arrange this for themselves.

They use an app on their phones to get instructions. We have a fully computerised management system. Our costs are greater than some of our less ethical competitors. We wish overseas retail buyers would take that into account. We have a list of loyal customers who do. They are mainly from Europe and the United States. Because of our low-wage economy, our costs are still extremely competitive.'

'Thank you,' said Drake. 'That is most helpful. We are investigating a company that seems secretive and probably could not match your ethical standards.'

'Could I ask who they are?'

'Kuta Garment,' replied Drake, wondering slightly if he was getting out on a limb.

'A few staff have come to us from there,' replied Oliver. 'I need to be careful what I say. They are the worst we have heard of. We think they are British-owned and seek to exploit Bali for their benefit. They use mainly homeworkers, who we suspect are not on the books. They pay below the minimum wage because these poor people are not registered. They are badly treated and dismissed if they complain. We suspect they only declare a small number of workers and present themselves as a retail outfit. We think they have friends in high places. Unfortunately, in Bali, not all our police and regulators are honest. If you are prepared to pay a bribe, you can do anything. It is unfair competition, but my partner and I have clear consciences. I hope I have helped you.'

'You have indeed,' said Drake. 'My thanks for your time.'

As they walked back to Made in the four-by-four, Wayan spoke.

'I thought that might be the situation,' he said. 'Most Balinese people are hard-working and honest. Unscrupulous employers can exploit us.'

'I have come to love your country,' said Drake. 'I will see what I can do back home. I wish I could help. I must think carefully about my next move in this tricky investigation.'

34

The following evening, Drake was on flight SQ945 from Denpasar Airport in Bali to Changi Airport in Singapore. It was a mid-evening flight, which suited him fine. His flight back to Manchester from Singapore departed in the early hours of the following morning. This meant he had been able to visit more sights in Bali under the care of Wayan and Made. Their charges were ridiculously cheap, so he gave them a large tip. They seemed happy, but Drake felt uneasy. The Indonesian Rupiah had suffered so much that the exchange rate was some twenty thousand Rupiah to the pound. He was more than a little frightened by handing over what seemed like a lot of money. In Rupiahs, it was remarkably little.

He reflected on his trip. His initial hotel and flight booking had given him two free days. He wanted to absorb as much as he could of the local architecture. Wayan was delighted to take him to some extraordinary temples with multi-layered roofs. He was constantly astonished by the degree of craftsmanship and innovation that went into Balinese traditional architecture. Wayan got Made to take him to a gallery selling local artists' work. Drake was fascinated by a carved mask of a terrifying creature. Wayan said if he hung it just inside his front door it would frighten away evil spirits. Drake was so amused by the idea that he bought it. It was a magical island, and he wished that he might be able to return someday.

Now, he could turn his mind to the investigation of the murder of Professor Kuiper. Drake now knew that he had been to Bali and explored every aspect of the business that he was running with Nimade. Kuiper must have had a driving motivation and an inquiring mind. Drake sensed that Laurence Bailey was not too pleased with Kuiper's visit to the warehouse. Nimade had fallen out of love with him. His drive and extreme intelligence may have made him difficult to like. Even his close colleague Aletta was not mourning his loss but moving on to create a new company with their old rivals. Likeable or not, it was Drake's duty to uncover the truth about Kuiper's murder.

It was now clear that Damien Bewick was running a shoddy and dodgy business in Bali. He was working on the assumption that Bewick owned Kuta Garment and had set one of his henchmen to follow Drake and make sure he did not get too close to the truth about the business. If so, how had he known Drake was in Bali? Perhaps his shop manager in Chester had told him about her visits from Grace. Bewick probably had some bribed contacts at Denpasar Airport who kept a lookout. Had Professor Kuiper uncovered something about Bewick's real business?

Oliver told Drake how problematic it was to open a new foreign-owned business in Bali. Perhaps that was why Damien Bewick was keen to buy Nimade's business. He was not interested in what Nimade was doing but wanted another Balinese company. That was probably to do with his financial operations. There was yet another person Kuiper had fallen out with, probably for good reason. Nimade certainly disliked the man intensely. Despite Drake's efforts in Bali, this investigation still seemed to have too many unconnected strands. It left him pondering on where to go next. They needed to get hold of Damien Bewick and interview the man. Perhaps that would lead to some further development. Drake reviewed his notes, which reminded him of the potentially significant news of the missing Kris dagger from the Chester Bali Style shop. At this stage, Drake had no idea whether this was true and, if so, what it meant for the investigation.

Grace had been struggling with her shoulder. She felt much better in herself. But having to keep her left arm in a sling was a nuisance. She could not drive, so she could not get back to work. She felt she was letting everyone down. She could write and type one-handed. She was glad that it had not been her right shoulder that had dislocated. She was also grateful to Martin, who had kept bringing her the things she needed. He bought a supply of ready meals. One evening, they ate together. She was becoming a little embarrassed about her previous caution over their relationship. Yesterday, Martin asked her if she felt well enough to go out for a meal. She needed no second invitation. She was desperate to get out of her house. So now she was sitting in her front room waiting for him to arrive. She had put on her latest new dress that she had bought from LK Bennett in the Grosvenor Centre. She was probably overdressed, but she could not face the effort involved in changing.

The doorbell rang ending her dithering. It was Martin.

'What a beautiful dress,' he exclaimed as she opened the door.

'You don't think I'm overdressed?' asked Grace.

'No. You look fantastic even with your sling.' They both laughed. Grace picked up her bag and hooped it over her immobile left hand.

'We are going somewhere special,' said Martin. 'I hope I've done the right thing, and you will enjoy the evening out.'

The journey into town from Christleton was unusually traffic-free, and they made good progress. Martin soon had them on the central ring road and turned down Nicholas Street.'

'Oh, my goodness,' said Grace as they passed the Vice-Chancellor's office to their right and The Centre for Industrial Design to their left. 'You're taking us on a tour of key locations in the Professor Kuiper case.'

'Only to get where we are going,' laughed Martin. 'Don't worry, we are not working this evening.' Grace sat quietly as Martin slowed and suddenly turned to his right into a small car park. It was then that Grace saw where they were.

'It's The Architect Restaurant!' she exclaimed.

'I hope you remember,' said Martin. 'I brought you here when I misguidedly announced my departure to Hong Kong two years ago. Our relationship went downhill from that point on. It was my fault. I thought this would be an excellent place to start again.' Martin stopped the car and looked across at Grace nervously. She laughed.

'What a clever idea,' she said. 'I do remember that it was a lovely meal.' Their laughter freed them from caution, and Grace put her right hand on Martin's knee.

'Let's give it a go,' she said.

They ordered their meals and chatted happily and inconsequentially. Martin was having braised beef, and Grace ordered spiced sea trout. As expected, both were delicious. The waiter cleared their plates and left them with the pudding menu. It was then that a young woman approached the table. She was a stranger. They both looked up to see what she wanted.

'Excuse me,' she said. 'I am sorry to disturb your meal. You do not know me. My name is Beatrix de Jong. I am a research student at Deva University. I work at the Blindsight Unit in The Centre for Industrial Design. I saw you when you came to see us about the awful business concerning Professor Kuiper. I have worried ever since about whether I should talk to you. I had decided not to. Then I saw you here today and changed my mind.' She drew breath. Martin got up and pulled out the spare seat to the side of the table, and she sat down.

'Please tell us what is concerning you,' said Martin.

'It is about this very place. I often come here for a drink with two colleagues after work. It is nearby, friendly, and pleasant. Some time ago, we were here when I saw three people I knew. They were sitting just about where we are now. They were eating a meal but were also deep in conversation. It struck me at the time as unusual. Since the awful thing that happened to Professor Kuiper, I have wondered if it was relevant.'

'Don't worry any more,' said Grace. 'We will decide if it is relevant. Go ahead and tell us what you saw. Who were these three people.'

'The first was Dr Aletta van Leyden. I came to Chester from The Netherlands with her. She created a scholarship for me. I work closely with her and am grateful to her.' Beatrix paused and gripped the table.

'You said there were three people,' said Grace. 'Who were the other two?'

'The second was someone I know as Gudula. She runs an outfit called VV in Delft. They are effectively competitors. I knew that Professor Kuiper was antagonistic to them, so to see her here talking to Aletta was a puzzling surprise. The third person was Max Hamilton. He used to work here but did not have his contract confirmed. The rumours are that he fell out with Professor Kuiper. It seemed even more odd to see him talking with Aletta.'

'Was this before Professor Kuiper died or since?' asked Grace.

'It was before. I am sure of that. It was perhaps a week or so before.' Grace looked at Martin.

'Have you any idea what they were talking about?' he asked.

'None at all. I couldn't hear their conversation. We decided to leave before they saw us as it could have been embarrassing.'

'Do you think this may have something to do with Professor Kuiper's murder?' asked Martin.

'I have no idea about that. It would be a dreadful thought. There have been some rumours in the Centre that Aletta was upset that Max Hamilton's contract was not confirmed. There are also rumours that Aletta may have begun to disagree with Professor Kuiper about the future of Blindsight. I don't know what to think.'

'Thank you for coming to talk to us,' said Grace. 'Is there anything else you would like to say.' Beatrix shook her head, muttered thanks, and returned to her table. Grace and Martin watched her join two others, and all three left immediately.

'Well, well,' said Martin. 'What do we make of that?'

'We knew that Aletta had met with Gudula. However, she swore that it was since Professor Kuiper was murdered. That now seems not to be true. She has been hiding it from us for some reason.'

'Surely one or more of these three conspirators couldn't be responsible for killing Professor Kuiper?' said Martin.

'We also know that Max Hamilton was following Professor Kuiper that evening and appeared to be arguing with him,' replied Grace. 'Was he asked to try and persuade Professor Kuiper to merge with VV?'

'We know that he is reputed to have a bad temper,' said Martin. 'Could they have argued, and the death occurred by accident?'

'Do we believe he would pull out a knife?' asked Grace.

'Whatever we think, the first thing we must do is to bring Drake up to date with this as soon as he returns.'

35

Drake was early into the case room the following morning. He had spent the day of his return writing notes and shuffling the photographs of his case boards. He had given up on his jet lag early in the evening and woke early feeling fit to go to work. He was now ready to edit the material on these boards. As he worked on this task, he became absorbed by the amount of new information there was. Gradually, staff would enter and greet him but then deliberately decided not to interrupt his work even though they all wanted to know what, if anything, he had discovered. He looked at his watch and was surprised that Martin had not arrived. He knew Grace ought to be home recovering from her injury, but where was Martin?

'Does anyone know where Martin is,' he asked.

Nobody had any information. Drake returned to his task just as the door opened. To everyone's amusement, Martin was holding it open for Grace. There was an immediate round of applause. Steve Redvers dashed across to pull her chair back for her to sit on. Others came over and patted her on the back.

'Are you sure you can come to work?' asked Steve.

'I'm ready to get out and try,' said Grace. 'I can't yet drive, so Martin has offered to pick me up.' There was another round of applause. Drake came around his case boards with a grin on his face.

'Wonderful to see you,' he said. 'You are injured, and I am jet-lagged, but we will both do our best.' There was more laughter and clapping. Steve went over to set the coffee machine to its task, and soon, Drake joined them all with his cup cooling. He began to tell them all about his trip to Bali. First, he could not resist passing his phone around, showing pictures of Balinese architecture. There was some laughter. Drake's recent obsession with architecture repeatedly amused the team.

Deep down, Grace wished she had gone. It all seemed so charming. Drake spoke about his visits to the Bali Style shop and warehouse. Grace and Martin said they were not surprised by his report about the dodgy factory owned by Damien Bewick. Drake described how Nimade had told him about the missing Kris dagger from the Chester Shop. There was a collective intake of breath, and everyone looked at their neighbour.

'I wonder how we might connect what you have discovered with some news we have,' said Martin. Drake and the others listened to the events at The Architect the previous evening. Several jaws dropped. Drake sat silently, trying to take it all in. Everyone else waited for him to speak.

'We now need to interview Max Hamilton as a matter of urgency. I put it as our top priority.'

'We have tried several times to meet up with him,' said Martin. 'He seems not to be at home. His neighbour thinks he might be abroad. He told us that Max Hamilton had been travelling frequently. To date, we only have distant video images of him. They would not be too helpful in calling for the public to be on the watch for him. But I have obtained a good portrait photograph of him from the golf club.' Martin pulled a photograph from his file and passed it across the table to Drake.

Drake appeared to study the picture for some time, looking puzzled. Eventually, he spoke.

'My brain is telling me that I know this face. I can't for the life of me think how and when I might have seen him. OK, Martin, go ahead with a press release and a call to the public for information on him.'

The team dispersed and got back to their tasks. Half an hour later, Drake walked across the room to the central table and called everyone to attention.

'I've finally worked out where and when I have seen this Max Hamilton before,' he said. He turned to Dave. 'Do you remember, Dave, when we entered the VV offices in Delft to talk with

Gudula, a man was stood at the back? He quickly disappeared when Gudula started to talk to us.'

'Only vaguely, I'm afraid,' said Dave.

'I'm now certain it was Max Hamilton,' said Drake. 'I am not surprised that Aletta is working hard to resolve the future of Blindsight now that Kuiper is gone. She expressed her enthusiasm for Max Hamilton when she talked to us. She has admitted talking to Gudula and argued that this is the right thing to do for the future. We now discover that these discussions were going on, presumably behind Kuiper's back while he was still alive. We had some suggestions about this from the director of the technology park by the airport. I need to speak to the Vice-Chancellor.'

36

Grace said she felt able to accompany Drake to see the Vice-Chancellor. She was flattered that he felt so strongly that he needed her alongside him. Constable Katie Lamb had come along to drive the Range Rover. They went down Nicholas Street, turned into the lower part of Watergate Street and left into the minor road running along the rear of the Georgian Terrace that housed the Vice-Chancellor's office. Katie turned into the dedicated parking area. Katie remained in the vehicle while Drake and Grace rang the bell and were welcomed inside. Sally, the Vice-Chancellor's assistant, guided them upstairs and into his office. 'He is returning from a meeting elsewhere,' she said. 'He will be with you shortly.' Drake helped Grace across the room to sit at the round table. Drake flipped through the pictures of his case boards on his phone.

'Good morning, good morning,' said the Vice-Chancellor as he strode into the room. He was wearing a black gown with gold trimmings that Grace admired. Drake winked at her. Sally followed the Vice-Chancellor into his office trying to catch up with him. He slipped the academic dress off his shoulders and she got there just in time to catch it. She then had to dash over to the desk to gather his mortar board where he tossed it. She took it back out to her outer office.

'Just been chairing University Senate,' said The Vice-Chancellor. 'The trouble with academics is that they love the sound of their voice. It's an asset when you stand before a lecture theatre full of students, but it can be a pain in the Senate. I'm sorry it has over-run.' He pulled out the chair set aside for him with its high back and arms.

'Now I understand you want to give me a report on progress with the Kuiper business.'

'Yes, certainly,' said Drake. 'We would also like to ask you some questions that arise from our recent work.'

'Go ahead, go ahead.'

'I'm sorry to tell you that the case has turned out to be rather complicated. We are still pursuing a series of strands of the investigation. It turns out that Professor Kuiper was a complex figure involved with many in both his professional and personal lives.'

'I'm not surprised to hear it,' said the Vice-Chancellor. 'He was a clever character. Many people revolve around figures like him. I made a great appointment. It is a real blow to my plans that we have lost him.'

Drake went on to describe the investigation. He told about Kuiper's background, including Nimade and the Bali Style shops. He mentioned the university angle, with some description of the personnel in the Blindsight Unit at The Centre for Industrial Design. Then he came up to date.

'In our latest investigations, Vice-Chancellor, we have discovered that Dr Aletta van Leyden is working with a Dutch woman called Gudula, who runs an outfit in Delft that effectively competes with Blindsight. We understand she may have discussed this with you.'

'Yes, she's a bright woman. Kuiper did well to bring her here. She understands that for the foreseeable future, she must take the lead. I have told her that I will support her for now, but I reserve my position on whether we need to bring in a replacement for Kuiper.'

'In particular, Vice-Chancellor, we understand that she believes the best way forward is to expand.'

'I have accepted her argument that Blindsight needs to grow,' replied the Vice-Chancellor. Drake nodded and continued.

'How will Blindsight expand with all its computers out of action?' asked Drake.

'Good question. Dr Van Leyden told me Kuiper thought he'd got a good deal. Unfortunately, he bought out-of-date computers. She wanted to replace them all and asked if they could have a special grant. I said no. I already gave Kuiper the money to buy the computers they have. If they want them replaced, it will be a cost on their departmental equipment grant. They get a substantial one.'

'But surely all their computers were put out of action in the break-in,' quizzed Drake. 'What about insurance? I can say the police would write you a letter confirming the damage.'

'The university has so much equipment that a total insurance policy would be prohibitively expensive. We don't insure. We take the risk. The Centre must use its funds or raise other funds. They have had a good share of resources so far.'

'I see,' said Drake. 'Dr van Leyden has concluded that the best way to achieve the desired growth is to merge with their competitors, a Dutch company called VV. That company is in financial difficulties but has highly qualified and respected staff. They work in similar fields.'

'Correct,' said the Vice-Chancellor.

'Critical to our investigation is exactly when this idea was first developed. We have evidence that Dr Aletta van Leyden came to see you to discuss this before Professor Kuiper died. Is that correct?'

'Yes, she came once. It was out of the blue. I had no idea about it. She asked if she could come in confidence. I said yes. I was anxious to know what was afoot. That was when she accused Kuiper of buying the wrong equipment.'

'Can you tell us what she said?' asked Drake.

'It was a lengthy discussion. I had to put off my next appointment. Sally was not pleased.' He roared with laughter. Drake tried hard to smile. For the life of him, he couldn't see the joke.

'She told me that she admired Professor Kuiper enormously and was grateful to him for setting up Blindsight and bringing her here, but she had become anxious that he was not thinking ahead. I was worried by that, but I was also impressed with her foresight. I told her to develop her plans and come back and see me again. Then I will decide what to do.'

'Thank you,' said Drake. 'In our talks with Dr van Leyden, she initially told us that she only came to see you after Professor Kuiper was killed. That isn't true, is it?'

'No, it's not. Why did she say that?'

'Perhaps she did not want us to know that she saw Professor Kuiper as an obstacle to progress. We know her plans also involve a man called Max Hamilton. He was employed at Blindsight but then did not have his contract confirmed when his provisional period elapsed.'

'Yes, she told me that was one of Kuiper's blind spots. She said that he couldn't see how clever Hamilton was and got rid of him. I didn't know all that, of course.'

'I can also tell you that we are dealing with another death. It is that of Max Hamilton's sister, and she died at Professor Kuiper's house in suspicious circumstances.'

'Good gracious,' said the Vice-Chancellor. Grace thought it was the first time she had seen him look flustered.

'On the night Professor Kuiper died, Max Hamilton was seen arguing with him. We also know that the Dutch woman, Gudula, is extremely anxious about the financial demise of VV. These are all ambitious people.'

'I like ambitious people,' said the Vice-Chancellor. Grace smiled to herself. He had resumed his pompous self. 'So, tell me, Drake. Who do you suspect was Kuiper's murderer?'

'We have a list of people who, at this stage, we cannot eliminate,' replied Drake. 'It is important that we speak to Max Hamilton. Do you have any information about his whereabouts?'

'None at all. I've never met the man. I hope this isn't going to damage the University.'

'I'm afraid we cannot consider that,' said Drake gruffly. 'We are sorry to take up your time. It has been helpful to us. We hope to make more progress soon.'

37

The following morning, Drake was unusually late. The rest of the team waited for him to give some direction. They were in a collective turmoil, each putting forward theories. None seemed entirely convincing. They seemed to be at an impasse. Then Drake rattled the door as the team members looked at each other, wondering who would open it. Then they heard the key in the lock. Drake had found his keys. He came in wearing that face. Grace had seen it before. He had spent the night turning a problem over in his mind. He had a direction for them. When he spoke, they were no wiser and looked at each other in confusion.

'Dave,' said Drake. 'Get hold of Damien Bewick and check the dates that he was away in Bali. Go to his house and check if his security camera is working. If so, I want you to bring recordings back and review them. Examine the whole period he says he was away in Bali. I think the camera points at the driveway and out into the road. Identify any vehicles that pull up, either in the drive or on the road.' Dave set off, and Drake then turned to the others.

'Today, we are taking a break from our current investigations,' said Drake. 'We have a different fish to fry. I've just called Nimade. She confirmed that the Chester Bali Style shop on Pepper Street received a delivery from Bali yesterday. I was already fairly sure of this as Laurence Bailey showed me the pile of goods due to come over, and he said it would arrive yesterday. I told Nimade they were not to open it until we arrived.'

'What are we expecting?' asked Martin. 'Has this got anything to do with our existing lines of investigation?'

'I can't say,' replied Drake. 'But we need to go through several steps before we worry about that. I've gone out on a bit of a limb on this. I will explain later, but nothing must get out of this room. We cannot do anything until help arrives. I've called Greater

Manchester police to help us and an old contact in London. My London contact has insisted on my suspicions remaining confidential to his officers. I understand why. I hope we both come up with the goods. I need my morning cup of coffee.'

Drake went to the coffee machine and started making coffee for the team. Steve went across and took over from him. Drake took the first cup and settled down with his Times crossword. His favourite chair was soon creaking annoyingly as he rocked it insistently. Gradually, one by one, the team found jobs to do.

Drake's phone suddenly demanded an answer. He picked it up and spoke quietly, pointlessly nodding at the invisible caller. He spoke intermittently until the call came to an end.

'Right,' said Drake. 'Martin and Grace, go to the Bali Style shop on Pepper Street. Nimade should be there with her assistant. Close the shop and wait for further instructions from me. Katie, you and Steve are to wait until my contacts from The National Crime Agency arrive soon. Then you will drive us all to the shop.'

Martin and Grace arrived at Bali Style. Nimade's assistant was at the rear and came forward.

'Welcome to Bali Style,' she said in halting English. 'How I can help you?'

'We need to speak with Nimade,' said Grace.

'Not possible,' said the assistant. 'She now set off for the airport. She going to Bali.'

'Is she driving there herself?' asked Martin.

'She go in taxi. Very nice driver, we use a lot.'

'Do you have his number?' asked Grace.

'I look for you.' The beautifully dressed assistant seemed to glide across the shop as her long skirt drifted just above the floor. Then, quite suddenly, the shop door opened and in came Nimade.

'I forgot my second cabin bag,' she said to the assistant. 'It has my iPad that I need to do some work on the plane.' The assistant disappeared into the back of the shop, and Nimade turned around and spoke to Grace.

'I'm so sorry to interrupt you,' she said. 'My assistant will be…Oh, no, sorry. I know you. You came with Chief Inspector Drake to my apartment. Is there another problem?'

'It's not so much a problem as a development,' said Grace enigmatically. This was not deception but her uncertainty about the events that would unfold. Martin was speaking on his phone to Drake. He closed it and turned to Nimade.

'I'm afraid Drake told me we need you to stay here.'

'Why?' demanded Nimade. 'I will miss my plane.' Martin shrugged his shoulders.

'Drake will be here in a few minutes,' said Martin. 'I expect that he will explain then.' For the first time, Nimade looked flustered. 'Please put up your closed sign and lock the door,' demanded Martin. Nimade nodded to her assistant, who promptly did as Martin had instructed. Just as the assistant came back, the shop door rattled.

'I am losing customers,' said Nimade.

'No, It's Drake,' said Grace. The door was duly unlocked and in came Drake with Steve Redvers, Katie Lamb, and two strangers.

'These two gentlemen are from The National Crime Agency,' said Drake officiously. 'They are to be known as Smith and Jones,' he added, pointing at each in turn. They were carrying what looked like briefcases but they rattled. Drake took them to the rear of the shop and showed them into the loading and unpacking bay next to the shop. They entered, and he closed the door. Drake's phone rang, and he answered it quietly, shielding his mouth with his hand. As he talked, Nimade pulled out her phone and tried to make a call. Grace stopped her.

'I need to check that you can make a call,' she said. Nimade looked shocked and distressed. Drake finished his call and nodded to Grace to allow Nimade's call. It was brief. Afterwards, Grace pointed to a couple of the beautiful bamboo chairs. Nimade and her assistant dutifully sat in them. Nimade opened her cabin bag and took out an iPad. Grace sat nearby and kept an eye on them.

It was about ten minutes later when Drake's phone rang again. He listened for a while and then spoke.

'OK,' he said and closed his phone. He turned to Martin and beckoned Grace over.

'So far,' he said, 'things are proceeding as I hoped and expected. I need you to take Nimade and her assistant back to the station. Make sure they are securely but comfortably detained. Katie, you will drive me back to the station and return to help Steve. You must then assist Smith and Jones as they require. Eventually, they will also need to be brought back to the station. At that point, the whole of the Bali Style shop is to be securely locked. You can use the keys that Nimade's assistant has. She will not need them for the time being.'

About two hours after Drake arrived in the case room, his phone chirped cheerfully. Unusually for Drake, it was sitting on his desk in the open. He picked it up instantly.

'Excellent,' he said. 'OK, return here as agreed, and thank you for all this help.'

Drake sat with his newspaper, rocking his chair contentedly. Martin and Grace remained puzzled, though Grace thought she was getting an idea of what was happening. It was clear that Drake had no intention of coming clean at this point. He was ruthlessly enforcing the security he had demanded earlier.

An hour later, Drake's phone rang. It was Sergeant Tom Denson from the reception desk.

'I have two officers from Great Manchester Police here,' he said. 'They have a secured individual with them.'

'The individual needs to be put in an interview room and kept secured until I arrive,' said Drake. 'Show the two officers up to the case room.'

Grace and Martin looked up from their work quizzically as two officers with badges of the Greater Manchester Police entered. Drake sat them down and made coffee. Grace made more cups for Drake, Martin, and herself.

'Thank you again for such excellent policing,' said Drake. 'You are welcome to stay. All should become clear soon.' The police officers nodded their thanks and sipped at their coffees. Almost immediately, Constable Katie Lamb came into the case room with the officers from The National Crime Agency, known to all as Smith and Jones. One nodded at Drake, and a brief smile flashed across his face.

Drake found chairs for them and beckoned everyone to the table in the centre of the room.

'Our two colleagues from the National Crime Agency have done some vital work for us. Perhaps one of you would like to tell us the results.'

The officer called Smith cleared his throat and began.

'A consignment has just arrived at the Bali Style shop. It was dispatched from Denpasar Airport in Bali. Everything was locked but we have special tools for this situation. He held his briefcase up and placed it on the table. We have made a preliminary search. A more thorough search will be required. We suspect there is much more to be found. However, we have uncovered some packages that were cunningly concealed, and we performed what is known as the Scott Test. The fluid duly turned blue. The packages contain cocaine.'

The officers from Greater Manchester Police nodded their heads and smiled knowingly. Then Drake spoke.

'Our colleagues from Manchester have brought us the person responsible for the dispatch. It is, of course, Nimade's right-hand man, Laurence Bailey. He has just flown in from Bali and was arrested at Manchester Airport by our friends from the Greater Manchester Police.

38

'How on earth did you work all that out?' demanded Martin. Drake laughed.

'I went out on a bit of a limb to tell the truth,' he said.

'We've all seen the limbs you go out on before,' smiled Grace.

'On this occasion, I was rather constrained,' said Drake. 'I needed my old friends at the National Crime Agency, and they demanded complete security. That still applies. They are working with their colleagues in the Netherlands and following up loose ends here. They hope to get some more people before they have finished. They are rather pleased, however, to get someone as high up the food chain as Laurence Bailey. A problem we all have is knowing which parts of the police force in Bali can be trusted. It's not straightforward.'

'So how did you uncover it all?' asked Martin.

'The usual thing,' said Drake in a throwaway manner. 'I kept looking at the case boards and thinking, what if. But I was also lucky.'

'In what way lucky?' asked Grace.

'I picked up this book at the airport in Singapore. It looked very odd and caught my attention. It is called "Snowing in Bali." I had no idea what it meant, and it seemed so absurd that I picked it up. Then I had to rush for my plane and forgot all about it. When I unpacked it at home, I started to read it. Of course, the snow it refers to is slang for cocaine. Bali is the most beautiful and magical place I have ever been to. Sadly, this is countered by a dark side. It turns out to be an ideal place to run drugs. They are mostly imported from South America. Then they are sold in Bali to a sizeable drug market there, but more importantly, they go to Australia and Europe, especially The Netherlands and England.'

Drake paused, coughed, and mopped his brow.

'It suddenly occurred to me that our friend Laurence Bailey had an ideal setup. He was regularly packing up large consignments and dispatching them to excellent locations for the distribution not of beautiful Balinese furniture but of drugs. He kept all the packing and unpacking to himself. The packing in Bali was done in a warehouse in Kuta well away from Nimade's Bali Style shop in Ubud. The unpacking was done in separate accommodations in Delft and Chester. He gave perfectly plausible reasons for this. He needed space that was cheap and did not take up the retail floor area. Then he told me he used a carrier that might take slightly longer than others but would guarantee a delivery date. He didn't want it all hanging around when he wasn't there. He always flew in the day after delivery.'

'I suppose he thought he was safe from detection,' said Grace.

'When I visited the warehouse in Bali, I saw several items he explained away. Putting them all together and doing some research, this became suspicious. He had sheets of almost black, slightly textured material. They looked like plastic, but I am sure we will find they are carbon fibre.' Drake looked around at some puzzled faces.

'Carbon is transparent to X-rays. The machines in security would not see it. Using this device, you can insert a dummy floor in a parcel or object and hide the drugs behind it. He also had rolls of tinfoil. He wanted that to be picked up by metal detectors. It could be used to wrap around drugs to make them look like different objects. He had an X-ray machine. He even gave me the reason for this. It was logical. He wanted to ensure that his consignments did not look suspicious under X-rays. He said this was to ensure no hold-ups caused by security who would want him to open the parcels.'

Drake collapsed into his favourite chair as if exhausted by all this explanation.

'Do you think Nimade is involved?' asked Martin.

'Good question. On the whole, I think not. His process hid everything from her.'

'Well, that's great,' said Grace. 'We've solved a crime we didn't know had happened, but what about the ones we started with?'

'Ah,' said Drake. 'Excellent question. We may have to wait a little longer to answer that.'

'So,' said Martin, 'can you explain what we've been doing today?'

'Of course,' replied Drake. 'Luckily, almost by chance, when I was at the Bali Style warehouse in Kuta, I saw a stack of parcels and crates all on their own. Laurence said it was the next consignment to go to the Chester shop. He was boasting about having a good deal with the shippers. It guaranteed the day of arrival, and he always came over on the same day or the day after. Later, I saw this was evidence of his secrecy about the shipments. So, once I had worked out what was happening, we were ready to go. None of us could unpack a shipment of carefully disguised items and find what we needed. So, our friends from The National Crime Agency came into play. They also know their corresponding outfit in The Netherlands and the key people who are not corrupt in Bali. They were delighted but wanted to spread the net more widely. They needed secrecy at this end. Once I knew Laurence Bailey's plane had landed, I told Nimade enough to get her to phone him. The Greater Manchester police were following him, and his car turned at the next motorway junction and returned to the airport.'

'Ah, I see, very clever,' said Grace.

'I knew he would not want to return to Bali. If he was caught there, he could face the firing squad. Our NCA colleagues are sure his drugs arrive in Bali from South America. One possibility is Ecuador, and the other likely origin is Columbia. Ecuador is not a safe place these days, so we guessed, as it turned out correctly. He bought a one-way ticket to Bogata via New York. Our Manchester colleagues are used to intercepting villains at Manchester Airport. When I flew out, I noticed several officers at a convenient pinch point after security. According to my sources, anyone doing what Laurence Bailey did will have some local police in his pay. But he would have planned his escape route early on. His game is likely to end in trouble eventually. You know the rest.'

'You don't think Nimade is involved then?' asked Grace. 'I do hope you are right; I quite like her.'

'Correct, but I agreed that the NCA people should handle that.'

'So,' said Martin. 'As Grace says, we have solved a crime we didn't even know had happened.'

39

The following day, Martin and Steve finally found Max Hamilton at home and brought him in for questioning.

'He's in interview room one,' said Martin proudly. 'I think he looks nervous.'

'He can wait while I get a cup of coffee for Grace and myself,' said Drake. The machine duly hissed and squeaked its way through the task, so Grace and Drake were quickly on their way.

'Good afternoon, Mr Hamilton,' said Drake. 'We have been wanting to speak to you for some time. You seem to be away a great deal.'

'I'm busy doing things,' replied Max Hamilton, 'and I'm busy now. I resent being arrested like this.'

'That is not correct, Mr Hamilton,' said Drake. 'We have not arrested you. Rather, you have come of your free will to help us with our investigations.'

'So, I am free to go then?' asked Max Hamilton.

'We would much rather you stayed to help us by answering some questions.'

'I'm afraid I am too busy right now,' said Max Hamilton, standing up.

'Of course,' said Drake sharply, 'we could always arrest you if you prefer.'

Max Hamilton sagged back down into his chair.

'The first question we have is where you were on the evening when Professor Kuiper was murdered.'

'I can't remember. I don't keep a diary, and I can't remember what day that was. I wasn't involved.'

Grace opened her calendar and laid it on the table. She pointed to it with her good hand. 'It was this Tuesday,' she said.

'I'm sorry, but I still can't remember,' replied Max Hamilton.

'Perhaps we can help to jog your memory,' said Drake calmly. 'We think it might have been a day when you played golf. You were probably not so busy that day.'

'How do you know I was playing golf?'

'I think it is time we stopped playing this game,' said Drake. 'We have evidence that you were in the city that evening, wearing your golfing clothes.'

Max Hamilton suddenly looked rattled.

'I might have been in town that day,' he said. 'I needed to go and see my sister. She was probably already dead. I was too late. I haven't even been asked to identify her.'

'We know that now,' snapped Drake. 'So, did you drive to your sister's house?'

'Yes, I suppose I did.'

'Where did you park your car?'

'It is difficult near her house. I usually park further down Weaver Street. I used to park there when I worked at the university.'

'So did you see your sister?'

'No, her house was locked, and I don't have a key. I assumed she was out.'

'You said you needed to see her. What did you mean by that?'

'I got a disturbing text from her. I thought she was having another incident. She has not always been well recently.'

'In what way has she been ill? What are these incidents you are referring to?'

'She has tried to commit suicide a couple of times. Thankfully, she didn't make it. I found her and got her to the hospital.'

'What time was it when you visited her home?'

'I can't say exactly. It was late in the evening when I picked up the text. I played golf and spent some time after in the bar at the club. It's a noisy place. I didn't hear the text arrive.'

'So, what did you do when you couldn't get into your sister's house?'

Max Hamilton started to look more flustered. His bravado had disappeared, and Drake thought he was worried about what else was coming. Eventually, he spoke carefully.

'I went somewhere else where I thought she might be.'

'Where was that exactly?' asked Drake.

'I went to Willem Kuiper's house. I couldn't get in.'

'Why did you go there?'

'She worked for him at the university for a while. They also had a relationship, which they kept quiet. Of course, I knew about it. I think it was a stormy affair, and he dumped her. She was in a state. I assume you now know she went to his house, probably intending to try to rescue their relationship. It seems that she was probably drunk and overdid her painkillers. In the end, she died alone and in distress. I was not even informed of her death nor asked to identify her.'

'I am sorry about the lack of information,' said Drake. 'We did not know who she was for some time and then did not know her relations. Her doctor identified her.' Max Hamilton grunted a grudging acknowledgement. Drake continued.

'So, you blame Professor Kuiper for her death?'

'If she hadn't met him, she would still be alive.'

'So, you were angry with him?'

'Yes, but I have been angry with him for some time. He arranged for me to be dismissed. If you are trying to blame me for his death, you are quite mistaken.'

'What did you do next that evening?'

'I dashed back to the Blindsight Unit. I guessed he would still be at work. I half thought she might have gone there to see him.'

'So, what happened then?'

'It was all locked up. I went home.'

Drake maintained a long silence. He knew that Max Hamilton now appreciated they were at the crux of the matter in the interrogation. He was nervous. Eventually, Drake spoke again.

'We have evidence that contradicts your last statement, Mr Hamilton. Would you like to reconsider your last answer?' Max Hamilton's hand on the table was shaking noticeably.

'I have no reason to alter it,' he replied nervously.

'Mr Hamilton, you recall you said you had just come from the golf club. You were wearing your golf clothes. That would have made you stand out. We have evidence that you did not go straight home. What did you do?'

Max Hamilton looked shaken. He sat thinking for a while. Drake guessed he was beginning to face up to the situation, but he was not fully there yet. Drake was going to have to push him further.

'I drove home. I have no idea what this other so-called evidence is.'

'I had hoped,' said Drake, 'that you would be honest with us without me having to lay it all out for you. You were caught on video meeting with Professor Kuiper.'

'OK, yes, that is true. I went back to the Blindsight Centre, and it was locked. Then, I caught sight of someone walking down Nicholas Street. It was late. I thought it might be him, so I chased after him. He said he had no idea where my sister was. That is all.'

'But it is not all, Mr Hamilton. There are several video cameras around those streets.'

Max Hamilton remained silent, so Drake had no alternative but to take it to the next step.

'You caught up with Professor Kuiper and walked alongside him for some distance, apparently arguing with him violently.'

'That is true, but I got nowhere with him as usual. I left him and went back to my car and drove home.'

'Mr Hamilton, I suggest you got in your car to catch up with him. Perhaps you had a weapon in your car.'

'No, that is not true.'

'You threatened him. Perhaps you did not mean to kill him. You are known to have a bad temper. Perhaps it got out of control.'

'No. That is not true.'

'Do you have a key to The Centre for Industrial Design?'

'Yes.'

'Shouldn't you have returned that when you left?'

'I was never asked to.'

'So, did you use that key on that evening? Did you return to the Centre and conduct a rampage of destruction and vandalism?'

'No. Why would I want to do that?'

'Mr Hamilton, are you involved in a movement to redesign the future of Blindsight.'

'I have nothing to do with Blindsight now.'

'You have, however, had meetings with Dr Aletta van Leyden and Gudula from VV in Delft. We even saw you in the VV building when we visited. Is that the case?'

'This has nothing to do with Kuiper's death. I admit now that he has gone, I have been invited to return and work there again.'

'But these meetings began before his death, didn't they? Professor Kuiper was seen as an obstacle to the future. You were recruited because of your hatred for Professor Kuiper. You were useful to Dr van Leyden and Gudula.'

'Nonsense. I was involved because Aletta thought I was unjustly dismissed and that my work was valuable.'

'Do you deny this was what you argued with Professor Kuiper about?'

'It might have been mentioned, but I was concerned about the welfare of my sister.'

'Do you deny you caused all the damage in the Blindsight Unit in The Centre for Industrial Design?'

'I certainly deny that. Why would I want to cause damage to a unit that I was being recruited to return to?'

'As far as we know, you are the last person who saw him alive. I am arresting you in connection with this investigation. You may, of course, apply for police bail, which you will be granted. You must remain at your home and not leave the city and certainly not leave the country.'

40

Dave crossed the case room looking for Drake, who was standing staring at his case boards. Dave knew not to interrupt a process that he could not understand but knew it was often successful in generating a breakthrough. Drake turned and smiled.

'I have some news,' said Dave. He held out a sheet of paper covered in photographs of fingerprints.

'When you formally arrested Max Hamilton, we performed the usual procedures and fingerprinted him. His fingerprints match a set found on the hammer recovered from the Centre for Industrial Design.'

'Do they now?' exclaimed Drake. 'We must put that information to him and see what reaction we get. Ask Steve to bring Max Hamilton in for questioning again, please.' Drake picked up his cooling coffee and wandered to where Martin was working.

'How are we getting on in the search for Damien Bewick?' he asked.

'There's still no sign of him at home, but I guessed he will use the same flights as you did. If he is returning from Bali, we will intercept him at Manchester Airport. I've managed to contact someone in Singapore from the airline. Initially, they were reluctant to discuss their passenger lists. However, I finally managed to contact a helpful lady. She is checking for us to see if he is booked on any flights from Bali or Singapore. Hopefully, I'll get an answer pretty soon.'

Drake grunted and patted Martin on the back. As he turned away, Martin's computer issued a cheerful ping.

'Hang on,' said Martin. 'This might be the email I'm waiting for.' He tapped away on his computer as Drake turned and hovered in anticipation.

'Yes. It is, and we have a result. He is booked in business class on SQ52 tonight.' Martin screwed up his face as he worked out the consequence. 'He should arrive first thing in the morning. Do you want us to intercept him at the airport?'

'Let's send someone to track him rather than intercept,' said Drake. 'I don't want to start by being heavy. Have someone follow him. If he drives his car, we can pick him up at home. If he doesn't go there, we will be following him.'

'OK, got all that,' said Martin. 'I'll send a couple of cars to Manchester airport. It shouldn't be too difficult. We have his registration number from when Grace tracked him some time ago.'

Two hours later, Constable Steve Redvers came into the case room. Drake looked up at him, and he nodded.

'Max Hamilton is in interview room one,' said Steve. 'He is angry, but I think it's more nerves. He is worried.'

Drake smiled. 'He's never happy that one,' he said. 'Come on, Grace, do you fancy joining a session with Max Hamilton?' Grace pushed herself out of her chair with her good right arm.

'I'm ready and willing,' she laughed. The two of them went down the corridor to the interview room.

'Why have I been brought here again?' demanded Max Hamilton.

'We want another chat with you,' replied Drake, lowering himself onto the chair across the table. 'Last time we met, you denied causing all that damage in the Centre for Industrial Design.'

'Correct. I had nothing whatever to do with it. I have heard about it from Aletta. It's dreadful.'

'So, you wouldn't know how the damage was done?' asked Drake.

'Yes, she told me that it was with the big hammer from the workshop.'

'Do you still deny that you caused all the damage using that hammer?'

'Absolutely.'

'So, what were your fingerprints doing on the hammer?' demanded Drake.

Max Hamilton laughed.

'Ah, that is why you're suspicious,' he said. 'That hammer hardly ever gets used. It hangs on a hook in the workshop. I borrowed it to free a rusty bolt under my car.'

'When was this?' demanded Drake.

'I can't remember exactly. It was quite a while back.'

'That is interesting,' said Drake. 'I guess we can check this?'

'Not sure how you could,' replied Max Hamilton.

'Detective Sergeant Grace Hepple will get you a drink,' said Drake. 'I will be back to continue this conversation shortly.'

Drake walked as quickly as his dodgy hip would allow back to the case room.

'Steve. Are you around?' he shouted.

Steve Redvers appeared from behind the case boards.'

'Yes. What can I do?'

'Somewhere in the notes you have of this case, you should have the telephone number of Frank Richards. He is a technician at the Blindsight Unit at the university. Get him on the phone for me, please.' Drake sat in his chair, rocking back and forth until his phone rang. He picked it up immediately.

'Hello.'

'Hello, Chief Inspector, Frank Richards here.'

'Hello, Frank. You remember when we first came to the unit to look at all the damage, I spotted your big hammer on the floor, and we took it away as possible evidence.'

'Of course.'

'We have someone we suspect as causing the damage, but he claims to have borrowed the hammer some time ago. Can you confirm that?'

'No, I can't. I don't think anyone has used it for ages. We don't normally need heavy engineering tools here. I am just checking back in my record of loans to confirm this.' Drake could hear

Frank leafing through his record books. 'No record of it being borrowed, sorry.'

'OK, thanks,' said Drake.

'Hang on a minute, though,' said Frank. 'I remember now it went missing for several days then mysteriously reappeared. I was busy then, so I paid little attention to it. I never followed it up. Then, later, Max Hamilton came in and said he took it. Sorry, I'd forgotten that. Does that help?'

'When was this?' asked Drake.

'Sorry. Because I didn't note a record in the book, I can't trace it. It must have been several weeks ago.'

'I see,' said Drake. 'Thanks for your help. Sorry to interrupt you.'

'No problem. I hope you find the rascal who did all the damage. We are hoping to get some replacements soon. It has held work up quite seriously.'

Drake returned to the interview room. Max was drinking the tea Grace had brought.

'I've checked with Frank Richards, the technician,' said Drake as he sat down. 'He has no record but thinks you took it for several days.'

'That's because I came in late one evening and took it,' replied Max Hamilton.

'When did you return it?' asked Drake.

'I've no idea. I don't remember that sort of thing. I'm sure I said thank you to Frank. But he seemed busy at the time. Perhaps he didn't take it in.'

Back in the case room, Drake turned to Grace.

'Frank Richards said it was taken without a record being made and returned equally casually a while later. He thinks it might have been Max Hamilton who took it. It was several weeks ago. What do you think?'

'It all sounds plausible,' replied Grace. 'But it doesn't prove he didn't cause all the damage. Admittedly, he has a reasonably well-checked explanation. Taken together with his reasoning that he thinks he has a future at Blindsight, I'm inclined to believe him.'

'OK, I agree,' said Drake. 'He seems to have a terrible temper, and I am still not convinced he didn't do it. Get Steve to take him home and read him the bail conditions again. Let's leave it now and concentrate on Damien Bewick when he arrives.'

41

The following morning, Drake arrived in the case room to find Martin monitoring the progress of tracking Damien Bewick.

'I'm just talking to Steve,' said Martin. 'He is in one car, and Katie is in another. They are at Manchester Airport. The plane arrived early, and the last time Steve spoke, they were waiting to establish contact. Hang on, Steve is just talking again. I'll put him on speaker.'

'Hi Steve, I've got Drake here, so I'm putting you on speaker.'

'Good morning,' said Steve's voice. 'It looks like they are coming through from baggage collection now. Katie is outside in her car to give us flexibility. We've got a third car with a constable from the uniform branch. We will perform the proper following procedure.'

'Excellent, well done so far,' said Drake.

'Yes, this is him pushing his case and cabin bag. I have picked him out for sure. OK. He is going out of the front doors. He isn't going in the direction of the taxi rank. I think he's heading into the multi-storey car park. No, correct that. He is standing outside, looking around. Someone has just pulled up in front. They are loading his cases into the boot. I'll go to my car, which is perfectly positioned to follow. I cheated on the parking.'

Drake and Martin laughed, perhaps more to relieve the tension than because anything was amusing. For a while, there was nothing from Steve. Then he came back on.

'I've just given our other cars the registration. It's a black Mercedes saloon.' There was another protracted silence. Drake began looking at his watch. He was not sure why. He had not checked the time earlier, so it was not helping him much. Then Steve spoke again.

'We are out on the spur back to the motorway. I assume he is being brought home and will call you again to confirm or inform you of any change.'

Drake made two cups of coffee and brought them to Martin's desk. Steve reported again.

'We are headed exactly how I would have gone to get back to Chester. We're now on the M56 heading for Chester. I'll let Katie overtake and follow him for a while.'

'Well done again,' said Drake. He and Martin sipped their coffees.

'Martin, what will we do if he arrives home?' asked Drake.

'We have another constable from the uniform branch sitting there. In plain clothes, of course. He will apprehend him, and Steve can bring him in.' Drake went to have yet another prowl around his case boards, and Martin dealt with some emails. Martin and Grace smiled at each other. Grace slid her sling off while she thought nobody was looking. Martin saw it and growled at her. She grinned sheepishly and pushed her left arm back in. Drake noticed all this and thought to himself that the relationship appeared to be going well.

One and a half hours later, Steve arrived in the case room looking rather pleased with himself.

'All present and correct,' he said. 'The target is sitting in the interview room.'

'Come on, Grace,' said Drake. 'You know I always like you there to play nice cop for me.' He waited for Grace to pick up a notebook and follow him.

'Good morning, Mr Bewick,' said Drake as he entered. 'I'm Detective Chief Inspector Drake. This is Detective Sergeant Hepple. We want to talk to you about an investigation. We believe you might be able to help us.'

'I'm tired and need some sleep,' said Damien Bewick. 'I've just flown in from Bali.'

'I understand,' said Drake. 'I've not long ago done the same thing. It takes it out of you.'

'Do you mean you have just been to Bali?'

'Yes.'

'Why did you go there? Was it a holiday?' asked a puzzled Damien Bewick. Drake chose to ignore the question.

'We have invited you here to see if you can help us with an investigation,' said Drake.

'We understand that you run a couple of businesses. One is second-hand cars, and the other is a chain of clothes shops. Is that correct?'

'Yes.'

'Where do you source the clothes?' asked Drake.

'Mostly from Indonesia. They make them at very competitive rates so we can supply them to our customers at good prices.'

'You said you had just returned from Bali. Is that specifically the part of Indonesia you mean?'

'Mostly. I have sourced items from Java, but at the moment, it is mainly Bali.'

'Do you have a clothes manufacturing business there?'

'Yes, but I may also commission others to supply when we are under high demand.'

'What is your business in Bali called?' asked Drake.

'It is Kuta Garment,' replied Damien Bewick.

'I can understand that your business would produce clothes at competitive prices,' said Drake. 'As I understand it, Indonesia operates a low-wage economy, and in Bali, they set minimum wage levels. Is that correct?'

'It is, yes. It is all well-regulated.'

'Is Kuta Garment effectively a factory then?' asked Drake.

'Yes, but it doesn't operate like most UK factories. Most of the employees over there are what are called home workers. They have their machines in their house. It is a popular system in Bali.'

'This has advantages for you, too?' asked Drake.

'Not particularly. It requires more management to supply all the fabric and materials and collect and check all the clothes.'

'But these workers do not have to be paid the minimum wage. Is that right?'

'Not really. They have to be declared and accounted for.'

'But you can find ways around that, I imagine.'

'I'm not sure what you are driving at here,' snapped Damien Bewick. 'Are you trying to suggest that we break the law?'

'Do you?'

'Certainly not.'

'We understand that you bought a business from Willem Kuiper recently. Is that correct?'

'Yes, Design East. It has been a bit of a nightmare.'

'In what way?' asked Drake.

'There was a lot of confusion over what assets I was buying and the staff who would transfer with the ownership.'

'Surely, the products that Design East were selling were rather different. I have visited the shop in Bali. I think it is called Bali Style now. It sells Bali-crafted objects. You sell cheap Western clothes. Why did you want this business?'

'We needed to expand. It was handy to have a ready-made business in Bali.'

'Starting a new business in Bali is difficult, isn't it?' asked Drake.

'Yes. There is a terrible amount of bureaucracy.'

'So. You were in a dispute with Professor Kuiper over your deal?'

'Yes. Where is this leading?' asked Damien Bewick.

'Usually, that depends upon the answers we get,' snapped Drake. Grace was surprised by his sharpness, but she trusted his methods. Drake sat silent, waiting for another response. It came from an anxious-looking Bewick.

'I understand that you are investigating what you believe is a murder. Is that's right?'

'We are investigating the death of Professor Willem Kuiper. I haven't said it was murder.'

'Why are you questioning me then?'

'We are questioning everyone who has had recent dealing with him. You would expect that.' Bewick sat, alternatively looking around the room and directly at Drake in what Grace thought was an aggressive manner. She was beginning to understand why Nimade didn't like working with him. This time, it was Drake who spoke.

'You have had recent dealing with him. We understand you were in dispute.'

'Yes. He made false promises about the deal.'

'What were they?'

'Pretty significant things.'

'Such as?'

'Well, he assured me the major staff were anxious to stay in post. That wasn't true. He also misled me about which retail outlets would be in the deal.'

'Surely,' said Drake. 'These kinds of things would be in the contract, wouldn't they?'

'We both decided not to give loads of money to lawyers, so it was a more personal business. Now, I know that lawyers might save you money. I wouldn't do it again. You have to trust people. It doesn't work if they're not trustworthy.'

'So how did you get it sorted out then?' asked Drake.

'I didn't. What particularly gave me grief was the shop in Bali. He sold me a company in Bali, but he had another company that owned the assets. It was deliberately misleading.'

'So, the two of you had quite an argument when you discovered this?'

'I see what you are driving at. I thought as much. You want to pin his murder on me.'

'We don't pin anything on anyone,' snapped Drake. 'We try to discover the truth.'

'So, you don't believe me?' Drake remained silent. Grace wondered where he was going next.

'When was the last time you saw Professor Kuiper?' he asked.

'Oh, I can't remember things like that.'

'Surely, you must have some idea. Take your time. Sergeant Hepple has a calendar. That might help.' Damien Bewick shook his head.

'Nope. Doesn't help.'

'What about this Tuesday?' said Drake, pointing to the calendar.'

'I get your tricks. I can see through them,' said Bewick. 'I'm not falling for that. I can't remember, and that's all there is to it.'

'Perhaps you might have a diary at home,' said Drake.

'I don't keep a diary. I'm not Samuel Pepys.'

'Perhaps your appointments might be on your phone?' tried Drake.

'You're not mucking around with my phone. I'm not playing that game,' snapped Bewick.

'Perhaps you don't understand, Mr Bewick. This is a police investigation of a serious crime. We are not playing a game. We believe you might be one of the last people to see Professor Bewick alive. We need answers to my questions. Obstructing a police investigation is a crime. I am terminating this interview now. I am arresting you in connection with the murder of Professor Willem Kuiper. You may return to your home on bail. You must not leave without notifying us. Detective Sergeant Hepple will give you instructions.'

Drake arrived back in the case room.

'I've arrested Bewick,' he said.

'So, we've arrested two people who are not connected,' said Martin. 'What do we do now?'

'I've got a feeling something will turn up,' replied Drake enigmatically.

42

Drake strode over to his case boards. Martin had never seen him walk so quickly. Something was up.

'OK, Martin,' he said.

'Has that search warrant come through for Damien Bewick's house.'

'Just arrived,' replied Martin.

'Right then, execute it immediately. Get as many officers as possible who know what they're doing and get over there. I want you to be in place when he arrives. I don't want a forced entry at this point. Let me know when you're all in position, and I'll release him.'

'What if he refuses to stay any longer?' asked Martin.

'I'll arrest him for obstructing the police,' replied Drake. 'I'm afraid you're going to find him awkward. He can watch and help with your search if he wants to. If he plays silly buggers with you, arrest him, and we'll have him back in the station. Right now, I can't decide whether he is trying to hide something or being a bloody nuisance. Once we've searched, I'll decide how to tackle him.'

Constable Katie Lamb fetched the Range Rover around to the front of the station and waited for Drake. He was not long coming. He had that look about him that his team had learned to spot. He thought they were at some crunch point. She pulled into the gravel drive of Damien Bewick's house, and Drake clambered out of the car. Detective Inspector Martin Henshaw was there to meet him.

'He's refused to hand over his phone. He tried to stop some of our search team from opening various cupboards. He's generally behaving as if he has something to hide.'

'I'm not sure,' said Drake slowly. 'You could be right, but equally, he could be flipping awkward. I can't make up my mind.'

'Well. I arrested him,' said Martin. 'It was impossible to continue. We had to restrain him on several occasions.'

'Do you need him here?' asked Drake.

'Not really,' said Martin. 'We might be better off if he was not around.'

'Right,' said Drake. 'Get someone to take him to the station. Put him in an interview room and tell Sergeant Tom Denson to look after him. That might sober him up a bit. We will let him review his position.'

The search team kept asking Drake what they were looking for.

'Anything interesting,' he replied unhelpfully. Most of the team looked puzzled, but they all kept working. Drake explored the house, examining things as he went. Everything in the house looked as if it was expensive. There was gold plating on bathroom and kitchen fittings. The kitchen worktops all looked like genuine marble. Drake guessed that most of the light fittings would be costly. The living room furniture was partly fitted and partly freestanding. The room had the widest television that Drake had seen in a private house. It was fed by a satellite disk system as well as disc readers. Several reclining leather chairs were facing it.

There was a sunken area with multiple-seat sofas surrounding a glass coffee table. On one side was a bar fully stocked with spirits, beers, and a range of wines in a cooler. At the back of the room was a set of folding doors that could be opened to reveal a large dining room with a huge table. Drake estimated that it could seat a dozen people comfortably.

Drake felt unimpressed by the house. He struggled to put his finger on why. A good deal of money had been spent. He had seen no evidence of a hobby or even a pastime. There were several motoring magazines on the glass coffee table. Drake concluded that it just did not feel like a home. It was not lived in. It was all wonderfully well-appointed. It reminded Drake of a business class seat on one of the top airlines. It felt about as homely. A place to pause but not a place to live. He concluded that Damien Bewick spent little time here. The search team were bustling around, opening doors and cupboards. Drake guessed the house had never previously seen so much human activity. He went back into the shiny kitchen. He opened the doors of the built-in oven and microwave. On the counter was a large air fryer. You could cook a Christmas dinner for a whole family in it. On the outside of the vast American-style built-in fridge were several magnets. They held notes that seemed to be for a cleaner, a gardener, and a more general assistant. They had instructions written in almost indecipherable script. The house had a small staff. Drake doubted they were well looked after.

It was then Drake stopped and pulled himself up. Was he in danger of jumping to judgements about the house and owner? They certainly painted the picture of a well-off but probably lonely individual who had little in the way of education or social skills. Drake pondered this situation. His reverie was suddenly interrupted by the sergeant heading up the search team.

'We've gone over the whole house,' he said. 'Nothing looks in any way suspicious. It reminds me of one of those demonstrator houses on a housing estate up for sale.'

'That's very good,' replied Drake. 'I know what you mean. You put it nicely. Yes, a demonstrator house. Not a home. What about outside? Have you looked around?'

'We've searched the garage. It wasn't locked. You couldn't get a car in there. It's full of mostly empty packing crates. We wondered if he was about to move.'

'More likely they are left over from him moving in,' grunted Drake. 'What about the garden?'

The sergeant groaned. 'We can look around, but there's not much to see.'

'Give it go,' said Drake.

'OK,' said the sergeant. 'We'll start with the outhouse. It's an extension of the garage. It's like a garden shed. I noticed a ride-on mower and lots of garden tools.'

Drake had made another tour of the house, looking for clues about the owner. By and large, they just were not there. He didn't seem to have managed to leave his stamp on the place. Drake had done all he could and was about to leave when the sergeant directing the search appeared.

'I think you had better come and see this, Sir,' he said emphatically. 'It's in the outhouse cum garden shed at the back.' Drake nodded and followed him through the kitchen and into the back garden. It was a dull and uninspired sort of area. It was mainly grass, surrounded by high fences, with a couple of trees. Drake stood looking around. He noticed the sergeant had reached the door to the outhouse.

'Like the garage,' he said. 'It wasn't locked. This chap is not very security conscious. Everything is left open. Look at this huge ride-on mower. It must have cost a bob or too.'

'Perhaps he has so much money, things like that don't worry him,' said Drake. 'In any event, he is not a homemaker. What is it you want to show me?'

The sergeant pointed at a pile of white sheets. The sort used by a painter. He could see what looked like some clothes below. They were all placed on the top of a pile of wooden seed boxes. The sergeant pulled on his blue rubber gloves and gently lifted the pile of sheets to reveal a man's tweed jacket. He waited while Drake took this in.

'It's the next bit that's most interesting,' said the sergeant. Then, with a deliberate sense of drama, he lifted the jacket.

Drake grunted immediately and crouched over. There, lying on what looked like some old overalls, was a dagger. It was about thirty centimetres long overall. It had a wavy blade, and the hilt appeared to be a figurine. Drake immediately thought of the ones for sale in Bali Style. Then he remembered Nimade saying that Laurence Bailey had told her that one had gone missing. Drake could not resist the obvious conclusion.

'We uncovered it straight away,' said the sergeant. 'We haven't touched it. I assumed you would want to see it in situ before we lifted it with gloves into an evidence bag.'

'Absolutely!' Exclaimed Drake. 'You've done the right thing. Get it photographed properly,' he said as he pulled out his iPhone and took several snaps. 'We need to get it back for forensics to examine in detail.' Drake stared at Martin. 'This changes everything,' he said. 'Or does it?' He added as an infuriating afterthought.

43

Drake called Martin and Grace over to his case boards. He seemed in a serious mood, and they wondered what was coming.

'I've been thinking,' he said. 'I need to get more brains working on this. We need to remember there are three events in this investigation. First, of course, the murder of Professor Willem Kuiper. Second, the death of Sophia Hamilton, and third, the damage done to The Centre for Industrial Design. All three appeared to occur on or about the same day. We know precisely when Professor Kuiper was murdered. We have his phone call to the emergency services. We know when the damage was done to The Centre and the Blindsight Unit. We are not yet sure when Sophia died, nor do we know whether she was murdered or committed suicide. All three may be related. Because of timing, that seems likely. But they could also be three events only coincidentally at roughly the same time.' Drake paused and looked into the distance. Everyone else kept quiet. Suddenly, he spoke again.

'I have been testing the idea that they are separate events. I don't think we have given enough attention to that possibility. We have, understandably, given little attention to the vandalism in The Centre for Industrial Design. The smashing of the computers in the Blindsight Unit could be random vandalism, but I suspect it is not. If it is not, perhaps it was done by someone with a grudge against Professor Willem Kuiper. We have two clear candidates. First, there is Damien Bewick, who doesn't deny having a spat or two with Kuiper. Second, there is Max Hamilton. He has a double reason. Firstly, he was angry about the way his sister was treated. Secondly, he also resents not being reappointed to the Blindsight Unit.' Drake paused to see what reaction he was getting. It was Grace who spoke first.

'I suspect Max the more,' she said. 'We know from the camera videos that he argued with Kuiper that night and returned to his car parked near the unit. We have a suspicion that he may have driven back to assault Kuiper, but at least as likely he may have gone into Blindsight and smashed the computers.'

'The trouble with the latter idea,' said Martin. 'Is that we know Aletta van Leyden had recruited him to rejoin Blindsight. Why would he smash the very computers he might be working on?'

'I have a theory about that,' replied Drake, 'but I want to think about it more before I offer it. We also know he was in those golf clothes that night. Why don't the two of you get a search warrant, look for those clothes and see if they have any clues attached to them?'

'Brilliant,' said Grace.

'Let's go,' said Martin.

The administrative work done, and armed with their search warrant, Grace and Martin set off for Max's residence. Grace pressed the doorbell. She and Martin were expecting no answer, but the door opened. Grace held out her ID.

'I don't need that,' said Max Hamilton. 'I know you. You want me to answer more questions?'

'Not exactly,' replied Martin. 'We have the warrant to search your house. You may remain here while we do it, but please stay in one room.' Grace beckoned the two constables who were waiting to assist in the search. Max Hamilton shrugged his shoulders in a resigned sort of way. Without saying a word, he stood to one side to let the little posse through.

Martin put his head around the door into the living room.

'OK,' he said to Max Hamilton, 'perhaps you would like to wait here for now.'

Grace spoke to the constables. 'One of you helps us with the search, and the other stands guard in the living room. See that he doesn't come out. If he does, block his way and call us. Warn him that we will charge him with obstruction if he doesn't stay there.' One constable nodded and stood deliberately across the door. The other officers dispersed. A constable went into the kitchen while Grace and Martin went upstairs. Martin looked in each room in turn.

'I'll take his bedroom,' he said. 'You could check the bathroom and other bedrooms.'

Max Hamilton's bedroom had a double bed under the window into the garden and a built-in wardrobe right across the opposite wall. He opened the wardrobe. It was the most orderly cupboard he had ever seen. Trousers hung in a row on one rail with shirts above. The shirts were grouped in colours. Another rail had jackets and suits. Then, the shelves had jumpers and underwear all very neatly stacked. Martin looked at his iPhone to see the pictures from the videos of Max Hamilton walking with Professor Willem Kuiper. He checked each jumper. None matched the diamond-checkered pattern.

Grace came in and beckoned Martin onto the landing. There was a large wicker basket, like the ones in the Ali Baba story. Grace wore her gloves and lifted the lid. There, sitting all crumpled, was the jumper they were looking for. She gently moved it to one side.

'Those look like the trousers,' she said. 'Bingo,' said Martin. 'We've got them. You would have thought he would have hidden them.'

'I imagine they are here because he intends to send them to the cleaners,' said Grace. 'I don't think he has thought it through very thoroughly.'

'I think we should take the Ali Baba basket as well,' said Martin, picking it up. As they reached the bottom of the stairs, the constable who had searched the kitchen came out with his blue evidence bag.

'On the window ledge in the kitchen are two sets of keys. One set looks like door keys or keys for padlocks. The other set is car keys. They have the manufacturer's logo on the side.'

'Excellent,' said Martin.

Dave, the technician, arrived at The Centre for Industrial Design with a forensic expert. Dave was carrying a heavy-looking blue bag. They soon found Frank, the technician, in his workshop.

'Where are the damaged computers?' asked Dave. Frank pointed behind him to a pile of crumpled metal near the door to the service access.

'The Centre had to continue functioning, so we cleared them away and put them here,' he said.

The forensic expert took out a small penknife and started to peel paint away from one computer case that was badly bent and scratched. Fragments of paint came away from around the badly dented areas without any effort. They were held by sterile tweezers and carefully deposited into evidence bags. More fragments were prized out from each computer in turn. The computers and the evidence bags were numbered with a felt-tip pen.

'Now,' said the forensics expert. 'Have you got the hammer there?'

Dave pulled it out of his bag.

'I can confirm we have done all the tests we need to on this hammer,' said the expert. He started to swing the hammer, wearing his blue gloves. Then he stopped, opened a small blue bag, and took out a white towel.

'OK, Dave,' he said. 'Hold it up against me and let it hang down.' He swung the hammer repeatedly at the computer and caused some more dents in the case. He then took the towel from Dave, carefully rolled it up, and put it back into the blue bag.

'We've done,' he said. 'I can get to work.'

44

Drake was standing by his beloved case boards, scratching his head in the way he has. Then he noticed Dave, the technician, standing waiting to speak to him.

'What is it, Dave.'

'We've got forensics back about the dagger. The handle is completely clean. No fingerprints, no DNA. Nothing at all. It's quite a complicated shape, so investigation has not been easy. But they are sure that they cannot find anything.'

'Bother,' said Drake. 'I was hoping it would at least give us some clues.'

'However, the blade has some small spots of dried blood. They have managed to recover a DNA reading from them. The DNA perfectly matches that of the deceased, Willem Kuiper.'

'That's a little odd,' said Drake. 'You go to the trouble of cleaning the handle but leave the giveaway blood on the blade. I need to think through what that tells us. For now, though, the immediate task is to confront Mr Bewick with the evidence.'

Damien Bewick had been released on Police bail, but Martin had now gone with Steve Redvers to bring him in for questioning. Martin arrived to tell Drake he was in an interview room.

'He's pretty cross about the whole business,' said Martin. 'The fact that we refused to discuss any reasons for this interview made him stroppier. I think he is used to getting his way and telling others what to do. He's not had it this way round before.' Drake laughed.

'In that case, I'll let him stew for a while. Have you brought Grace in this morning?'

'No. She came on her own,' replied Martin. 'She's got fed up with the sling and slung it! I hope she's not doing more damage.'

'Ask her to come and join me, will you? I often think that her presence calms people down. She can also often see an angle I might not think of.'

'Why have I been brought here?' demanded Damien Bewick as Grace and Drake entered the interview room,

'We have some more questions to ask you,' said Drake. 'As you know, we have searched your property. I should warn you that my officers are thorough. I want to make life as simple as possible for you under the circumstances. It would make life easier if you came clean about everything you know. I wonder if you now have anything else to tell us.'

'I've no idea what you are driving at,' snarled Bewick. 'I've already told you that I know nothing about the death of Willem Kuiper. Except that even in death, he is making life difficult. I can no longer get what I deserve from him. It would be a huge battle with lawyers, and they would charge the earth.'

'Mr Bewick,' said Drake. 'I am trying to give you every opportunity to volunteer some answers. I said we have searched your property. This is more than just your house. Does that remind you of anything?'

'This is getting ridiculous,' snapped Bewick. 'I don't have any idea what you are getting at.'

'We searched your outhouse. Or do you call it a shed?'

'I don't call it anything. I never go in there. The gardener uses it to store tools, including the expensive mower I bought.'

'Very well,' said Drake. 'We'll do it the hard way. In your shed, hidden under a pile of sheets, we found an old tweed jacket.'

'Yes. I put it there when I helped the gardener.'

'Under the jacket, we found a dagger. Does that trigger your memory?'

'What?! You mean my gardener put it there? It's probably used for pruning.'

'We are bound to suspect that you put it there,' said Drake. 'It wasn't hanging on a hook or lying on a shelf like all the other tools. It was hidden in a pile of sheets and clothes.'

'Why would she do that?' asked Damien Bewick.

'So, you deny putting it there?' demanded Drake. He nodded to Grace, who went around the central table to show Damien Bewick some photographs of the Kris dagger.'

'We took these photographs,' said Drake, trying to remain patient.

'Blimey,' said Bewick. 'It looks a bit fancy for gardening. I've never seen it before.'

'Mr Bewick, I don't think you understand the seriousness of this situation. We have evidence that strongly suggests this dagger was used to murder Willem Kuiper.'

'You mean my gardener killed him?'

'No, Mr Bewick, we suspect you killed him.'

'Nonsense. Never seen it before.'

'Under the circumstances, I have no alternative but to cancel your police bail. You will remain in custody until we sort this out. Please give Sergeant Hepple the contact details for your gardener.' Grace passed Bewick a notepad and pen. He scribbled, paused for thought and scribbled again. Grace took the notebook back, raised her eyebrows and pushed under Drake's eyes.

'This says Gillian Matthews,' said Drake. 'Your gardener is a woman?'

'She certainly is,' replied Bewick. 'She's very fit!' He gave a sort of sneer that both Drake and Grace thought they were intended to notice.

'Mr Bewick,' said Drake. 'This interview is terminated. Grace, please call Sergeant Denson to accompany Mr Bewick.'

'What? You can't just keep me here!'

'Mr Bewick. We have already arrested you in connection with a serious crime. You must understand that.' With that, Drake stood and left the room. Grace followed Drake back to the case room. Tom Denson was left to supervise Bewick.

'Steve,' said Grace. 'See if you can raise this person. We could go to her home, but if possible, Drake would prefer her to come in. It might make questioning simpler since Bewick is already here. As soon as possible, please.'

Drake and Grace entered the interview room where Gillian Matthews was waiting, sipping tea.

'I am sorry to trouble you,' said Drake. 'We are in the middle of an important investigation and hope you can help us to sort out some details.'

'That's quite thrilling,' said Gillian Matthews. 'I've never been in a police station before.' She sat bolt upright and gave Grace and Drake a wide-eyed stare. Drake had suggested that Grace should start the interview.

'We understand you do gardening for Mr Damien Bewick. Is that correct?'

'Well, yes and no.'

'What does that mean?' asked Grace.

'Oh. It's a bit awkward. I've worked for him for a while now, but I felt it was getting a little inappropriate. So, I was considering terminating the job. The trouble is he pays well, and I need the money. I'm not quite sure what to do.'

'What do you mean by inappropriate?' asked Grace.

'He has a habit of getting too close to you. At first, I thought it was just an insensitive personality. After the last time, I've changed my mind.'

'What happened to cause that?' asked Grace.

'I leave some of my gardening overalls in the outhouse, where the mower is. I put them on when it rains, or I need to kneel. Twice now, he has followed me in and caught me by surprise. I've thought about it and wondered if he thinks I change more clothes than I do, and he wants to catch me by accident on purpose if you like. The last time, he finally tried it on. I'm fairly strong because of my work. I can look after myself. I pushed him away, and he got all apologetic and almost seemed to cry. He left quickly, but I don't trust him now.'

'You say you leave your gardening overalls,' said Grace. 'Is there anything else you leave?'

'No, what do you mean?' Drake took over.

'We have seen your overalls lying under some sheets over a wooden box. What are the sheets for?'

'I use them to collect leaves. Next door has deciduous trees that drop all over the garden. It's a pest.'

'When was the last time you used those sheets?' asked Drake.

'Last autumn, so some time ago. Why?'

'Have you looked under the sheets? Have you seen anything else there?'

'Oh yes, there's his tweed jacket. He tried to help me once. He was pretty useless. I found his presence a little creepy. I thought he was trying to make a pass but didn't know how to do it. He is a wealthy man, so I assume he isn't stupid. He lacks social skills. When we finished, and I took my overalls off, he deliberately covered them with his jacket. It felt like a symbolic gesture of ownership. I find him altogether a weird man. Now you mention it, I noticed something that I thought was a little odd. He told me he was going to London and Indonesia for a long time. He said he had a lot of business to sort out there. So, I waited and timed my visits to coincide with his absence. Perhaps I'm being silly and pathetic, but it seemed like a good idea. The first time I was there was the day after he left, and his jacket was still there over my overalls. I put it back where he left it when I finished. Then when I came again, it wasn't there. I assumed he'd taken it. I thought he was still away. I assumed he had returned early, gone out and needed his jacket. Maybe I got his return date wrong.'

'When was this second visit?' asked Drake.

'I'm sure it was a Thursday a few weeks ago.'

Grace held out her calendar, and Gillian pointed. 'Yes, that Thursday.'

'Two days after the Tuesday we are interested in,' said Grace.

'So, Bewick was still away,' grunted Drake.

'Gillian, can you tell us if you have seen anything else under the sheets and jacket apart from your overalls?'

'No, there's nothing else there.'

'Yes, there is,' said Drake firmly.

'We want to know if you put it there.'

'I can't remember leaving anything there. When I finished with the sheets last autumn, I folded them up. They're on his jacket and my overalls on top of old wooden seed boxes.'

Drake nodded to Grace. She got out the photographs of the Kris dagger and showed them to her.

'This is what my officers found under those sheets and his jacket.' Gillian Matthews put both hands to her face and let out a long puff of air.

'You think he might have been going to attack me?'

'Would he do that?'

'Oh, my goodness. I've wondered if he's one of those, but I never dreamt of this. It just shows. You can never tell. I suppose I must thank you. I've had a lucky escape.'

'I should tell you we have no evidence that he was about to attack you. Our investigations are about another matter. However, I do suggest, for the time being, it might be wise not to visit his house. Thank you. That is all. You have been helpful.'

'What do you think?' asked Drake as they returned to the case room.

'Difficult to know for sure,' said Grace cautiously. 'But I thought she was genuine. I am also not too surprised to hear her suspicions about Bewick.'

'I agree,' said Drake. 'We need to think where we go next.'

'Surely Bewick can't have murdered Prof Kuiper,' said Grace. 'According to Gillian Matthews, he was away at the time.'

'It's not quite that simple,' said Drake. 'At the time of the murder, he could have still been in the UK. Gillian said he told her he was going to London first. It could all have been carefully planned to give him an alibi.'

'What do you suggest?' asked Grace.

'The problem is that there are no fingerprints on the Kris. Could we demonstrate beyond reasonable doubt that Bewick is guilty?' Drake didn't wait for an answer to his question. Grace knew he was thinking aloud and stayed quiet.

'If his barrister put him in the witness box, his bluster could influence the jury. That is a real problem, but his barrister doesn't have to show that somebody else put the dagger there. It's up to us to show Bewick put it there. How can we do that? We need some other evidence.'

'But what if he didn't do it, and we believe the gardener? How did the Kris get there?' asked Grace.

'We have to conclude that it was put there after Kuiper's murder. Although Gillian doesn't express certainty, it seems as if the tweed jacket might have been put there then. It's another mystery.'

45

Dave appeared in the case room with his laptop, looking pleased with himself. 'I've got the forensics report on the Max Hamilton affair,' he said.

'What's the news?' queried Drake.

'It's a long and comprehensive report, but I can give you the main points.' Drake nodded.

'They say that they had already detected tiny samples of paint in the scratches on the surface of the hammer. As we expected, they match the paint on the computer cases. There is dust and flakes on Max Hamilton's jumper. They also match. Finally, they found dust on the towel I held up. That also matches.'

'So, this is evidence that someone wearing the golf sweater used the hammer to smash the computers. Max Hamilton is seen in the videos that evening wearing the sweater and once had the hammer. Excellent,' said Drake.

'Of course, there is a caveat. They cannot prove that the dust and flakes came from the computers or the hammer. They say they can only give evidence that the data is compatible with that conclusion. They have also said they would be happy to testify in court and feel the case is strong.'

'Well done,' said Martin. 'So, it was Max Hamilton. We've solved the crime of vandalism at The Blindsight Centre.'

'Probably,' said Drake enigmatically.

'Yes,' said Grace. 'I still don't understand why he would destroy the place he had been recruited back to.'

'Exactly, Grace. You are quite right to be suspicious.'

'The only explanation I have been able to come up with involves yet another crime. Max argued with Professor Kuiper that evening, presumably before he smashed the place up.'

'So did he go on and murder Kuiper as we have suspected?' Martin was looking puzzled.'

'It's possible but surely unlikely,' said Grace. 'It could be the other way round, given the timing. If he did the destruction first, Kuiper would have been well home and discovered Sophia Hamilton.'

'But he still had to get back to his car and drive round to intercept Kuiper before he left Water Tower Gardens,' said Drake. 'I have another theory that may be a long shot. I don't know how to prove it. We know Max Hamilton had meetings with Aletta van Leyden and Gudula. I remember something odd when Aletta came into the unit to see the destruction,' Drake opened his phone to look at pictures of his case boards. 'Yes, here it is. She said, "What, surely not." It seemed slightly odd, and she looked at her watch. I had forgotten this detail, but it is on the case board. Remember that when we interviewed Frank here, he said he was grateful to be interrupted working on a tedious task. He was filling in an insurance claim for the damaged computers. He told us Aletta had taken out an insurance policy on the computers. What if she, possibly Gudula, and Max Hamilton had hatched a plot to claim back on that policy? They knew they needed new machines. The Vice-Chancellor told her and then us that he didn't insure things, otherwise known as saving money. That's quite common in large companies. Effectively they take the risk and insure themselves. What if Max had agreed to do the job but at a later date once the policy had been in place for a while? Aletta was checking the date and puzzled as to why it had happened so soon.'

'If so, why had Max done it early?' asked Martin.

'We know he has a bad temper. He had a furious argument with Professor Kuiper. It was probably about how his sister was treated. Maybe he even knew or guessed his sister had committed suicide. He just lost it and went and did the job in a huge fit of temper. Perhaps I am too far out on a limb here. We can certainly do him for wanton damage. Whether we, or the insurance company, can prove fraud is another matter.' Drake paused, and there was silence as everyone thought this idea through.

'So, what do we do?' asked Grace eventually.

Drake and Grace entered the interview room where Max Hamilton had been brought. They sat down opposite him, and Drake spoke. There was no nicety. He was firm and terse.

'Mr Hamilton. I am charging you with carrying out substantial wanton damage to a series of computers in The Blindsight unit at The Centre for Industrial Design at Deva University.' Max Hamilton shook his head, but Drake continued regardless. 'We have evidence that the instrument used was the heavy hammer held in the workshop there. Paint dust from the computer cases has been found on the hammer. I also have to tell you that similar fragments have been found on the golf jumper you were seen wearing that evening. Detective Sergeant Hepple will formally charge you and read your rights. You may request a legal representative to be present before this is done. Do you require this?'

Max Hamilton suddenly looked crestfallen. He nodded his head silently.

'Sergeant Hepple will help to arrange that for you. I have other business to deal with. We are still investigating the murder of Professor Willem Kuiper that same evening. We may wish to discuss that with you again later.' Max Hamilton gasped and sat open-mouthed as Drake left the room.

The following morning, Drake was reviewing his case boards and looking frustrated. The technician, Dave, came dashing back in. 'I've got it, but it doesn't work,' he shrieked. 'It has taken a lot of work, and I don't think it helps us. It's probably the start of a lot of new work.'

'Calm down, Dave,' said Grace. 'Tell us what you are talking about.'

'I've been working on the video from Damien Bewick's house. The camera points out from the house and covers the driveway. You can also see the pavement and road. I've got this clip on the day Gillian Matthews told us she visited the premises to do some gardening.'

The team gathered around the big screen as Dave hooked his laptop up. Dave pressed the play button. The picture showed the gravel driveway and a wide opening onto the main road in the housing development known as Curzon Park. A white Ford van appeared from the right, swept quickly into the driveway, and turned across the front of the house, where it stopped. Only the side of its rear portion was still visible. Then it reversed, backed across the main house, and turned towards the garage, where it stopped. Dave pressed the stop button.

'Steve checked the registration of her van with Gillian Matthews, and it matches what we can see as it turns into the drive.'

'Good work, Dave,' said Drake. 'This confirms her first visit on the date she gave us.'

'I have another almost identical clip that comes from two days after the murder of Professor Willem Kuiper.' Dave pressed the play button, and everyone watched the clip.

'So far so good,' grunted Drake. 'This is the evidence we need to confirm the testimony she could give in court if this proves material. She made the two visits to the garden on the days she told us.'

'Now comes a more complex but exciting set of videos,' said Dave. Drake noticed that he puffed out his chest just a little and thought that was a good sign. Dave was coming along nicely since his studies of forensic science. Dave pressed the play button and spoke again.

'The first clip is from two days before Kuiper was killed.' After a short while, a white Mercedes cruised across the shot from right to left. It pulled up across the driveway entrance. The car remained stationary for a while, and the team could see a blur of movement inside by the front passenger seats. Then, a head appeared above the roof. It was bending forward, and an arm came across and pulled up a hood masking the face. The figure walked to the left and around the front of the car.

'Watch this bit,' said Dave.

'Just play that bit again,' said Martin. Dave pressed his controls, and the clip replayed with everyone grunting and nodding. The figure came towards the camera and disappeared to the right.

'He's almost certainly gone around the garage and into the back garden,' said Dave. Everyone watched, but the image was still for a while. Then, the back of the figure appeared to the right and returned to the car.

'Good work,' said Drake as the car set off. It disappeared from view to the left. 'Unfortunately, it is not possible to see the registration plate. There must be millions of white Mercedes like this one.'

'Of course, we can't see anything incriminating except that the figure is trying to conceal his or her identity.' said Dave.

'Excellent,' said Drake. 'He could have collected the tweed jacket. It was concealed under his coat.'

'Exactly,' said Dave proudly. 'Perhaps he even put it on under his coat.' Everyone nodded.

'Keep watching,' said Dave. 'There is another clip from the day after the murder.' After a short time, the car appeared across the screen from right to left. The car parked, and the figure came around. It seemed to go to the back garden again. 'The problem is, again, we don't see the registration plate.'

Martin groaned. 'I see what you mean,' he said. 'Excellent work, but no real information unless we can identify the vehicle.'

'Exactly, said Dave. 'But there's more.'

This time, what appeared to be the same car crossed the screen from left to right. 'Of course, he has turned the car round,' said Dave. 'I went to the site and found the next house also had a camera. It's identical to the one on the Bewick house. It looks as if the two of them might have had them installed together. So here is the video from that camera.' Dave lowered his finger dramatically on the keyboard. The car passed from right to left slowly. Then it re-emerged, backing into the driveway.

'This happens between the two previous clips. He is reversing the car in the next-door house driveway. We can see the registration plate on the back of the car quite clearly,' said Dave.

'Excellent,' said Drake. 'Well done indeed. Have you traced it?'

'That's where it all goes wrong,' groaned Dave. 'It is a hire car from a local firm. I checked with them, and the name of the driver they gave me was Harry Jefferson. So, it's all a dead end. Perhaps it was someone innocently delivering something.'

'But making two similar visits,' said Drake. 'That doesn't seem likely. This is so frustrating. We have all the pieces with your excellent videos. First, we see Gillian Matthews coming. This is when she says the tweed jacket was missing. We presume the driver of the white Mercedes took it away. Then, after the murder, he returns. Presumably, he puts the tweed jacket back where we found it. He must also deposit the Kris and place it over Gillian's overalls. It all seems as if we are frustratingly near to unravelling this, but who is the driver of the white Mercedes?'

46

All was quiet in the case room. Everyone was at work. Drake was prowling around his case boards, alternating between studying them and looking at the pictures of the Kris dagger on his iPhone. Out of the corner of his eye, he saw Grace struggle out of her chair and come across to talk to him.

'Yes, Grace.'

'I've done some thinking about Sophia Hamilton,' she replied. 'We've never really resolved what happened to her.'

'We have no evidence that a crime was committed,' said Drake. 'So, in a sense, our job is done.'

'I have a theory,' said Grace. 'We know she died of an overdose. It was a fatal combination of alcohol and her dangerous tablets of Myloxifin. She was in Professor Kuiper's house, which was locked. He had been at the Blindsight unit until late that evening and was murdered in Water Tower Gardens before he could have reached his home. I don't see any way he could have been involved.'

'Agreed. So, where does that leave us?'

'We know that a man banged on the door of Kuiper's house that evening. A neighbour reported that. Her brother Max has told us that when he picked up her text, he dashed over there after trying her home. He suspected another suicide attempt. He said he couldn't get into Kuiper's house and got no reply. Her neighbour found her set of keys to the house and her car under some bushes between the houses. It is clear from her history of suicide attempts and associated texts to her brother that she was in a poor state of mind. I guess that she went to Kuiper's house and threw away the keys in a symbolic gesture. She hoped he would come and find her. I think it was a cry for help that went wrong. If Kuiper had not been murdered, he would probably have got there in time to save her, but we will never know for sure.'

'That's an excellent analysis, Grace,' said Drake. 'I'm afraid I have rather put her death at the back of my mind. Thank you for thinking about it. Under the circumstances, I expect there will be an inquest. You will be able to present this to the coroner.'

Grace's phone rang and she hobbled back to her desk to answer it.

'It's Tom Denson downstairs,' she said to Drake. 'He's got an uninvited visitor called Justin Makepeace who wants to see you.'

'Really? Now I wonder what he wants. Ask Tom to bring him up.'

A few minutes later, Justin arrived in the case room.

'Welcome to our little home,' said Drake. 'How can we help you?'

'I'm not sure if I should bother you,' said Justin. 'As you know, my home is here in Chester, and I returned today. Then this arrived, and I thought I should bring it straightaway.'

'What is it,' asked Drake.

'Well, as you know, Willem and I have a fair grasp of information technology. Some time ago, Willem set up this app, which is like sending text messages, but it's encrypted. You can also send things to an email address, not a phone number. To make matters even more secure, we used different email addresses from those we normally use. Willem had not used it for some time, and it was a pest logging out and in again with my other address, so I stopped looking at it. The other day, I thought about our meeting in Delft. I decided to check the app. Have a look. This is the message Willem had sent.' He held his phone out for Drake to see.

'I need to talk to you urgently about the Bali operation. Not sure what to do - W,' it read.

'When was this sent?' asked Drake.

'I've looked back, and it is the day before he was murdered. That Monday. The fact that he sent the message this way makes me think he was being careful not to have this intercepted. It's dreadful that I never responded. I feel awful. He died thinking I had deserted him.'

'I understand your feeling,' said Drake. 'However, if it is any help to you, I can say with a strong sense of confidence that he wouldn't have been thinking about that when he was killed. We know from our pathologist that he died extremely quickly. He tried to make a 999 call but never got to finish saying anything.'

'That's awful,' said Justin.

'Thank you for coming so quickly to see us. We do appreciate it,' said Drake. 'At the moment, I cannot say that it helps us as we have no idea what it was about. But as investigations continue, that might become apparent. I hope so.'

Justin left, and Drake sat wondering what Kuiper's message about Bali meant.

Suddenly, Drake grunted and tried to get out of his chair.

'Brilliant work, Dave,' he shouted. 'You've cracked it.' Dave turned to Drake in open-mouthed amazement. Everyone fell silent.

'Have I?'

'I have just had a text from our friends in Manchester. They have checked their notes. Harry Jefferson is the name used by Laurence Bailey to book his flights. He holds a fake Australian passport in that name. The person in the white Mercedes is Laurence Bailey. If you accept Damien Bewick's assertion that he had no idea the dagger was hidden in his shed, then Laurence Bailey would be the obvious candidate to hide it. He had access to the ones at the Bali Style shop and even told Nimade that one was missing. In what he thought was one clever move, he murdered Professor Kuiper and got even with Bewick by setting him up for it. He hated Bewick, who had been messing up his business since the takeover of Nimade's company.'

'But why did he want to kill Professor Kuiper?' asked Martin.

'Justin just told us about Kuiper's message to him. It suggests he suspected something and needed to talk it over with someone. From what I learned in my visit, Kuiper had been there asking questions. Bailey suspected Kuiper had worked out his drug-running racket and was about to spill the beans. He had to make a desperate move. He would either have had to make a run for it or dispose of Kuiper. He chose the latter, and then eventually when I worked it out, he also chose the former and tried to get away to Columbia. Luckily, our friends from Manchester managed to stop him.'

'He's going down for a long time accused of drug running and murder. We had better let Damien Bewick go with our apologies. He's a thoroughly unpleasant fellow. He treats his staff poorly, but he hasn't committed a crime. My only concern at this point is whether we have enough evidence to get a conviction of Laurence Bailey for the murder of Professor Willem Kuiper, which is where all this started. Justin's message is not specific. The video of Bailey's visits to Bewick's house is inconclusive evidence.'

47

Two days later, Dave came in with some good news for the team. The DNA evidence had been investigated. Professor Willem Kuiper's DNA had been found on the left cuff of the tweed jacket. Laurence Bailey's left wrist showed signs of a recent injury. Together with the pathologist's evidence, it presented a pretty strong case that Laurence Bailey had indeed approached Kuiper from behind and put his left hand across his mouth to silence him while stabbing with an upward motion into his heart with his right hand. He had, of course, been wearing Bewick's tweed jacket. He replaced it under the white sheets in Bewick's outhouse.

The matter found by the pathologist, Professor Cooper, in Kuiper's mouth, proved to be from the jacket. Professor Kuiper had bitten into the jacket's left cuff. His bite cut Laurence Bailey's left wrist. Bailey was probably wearing that jacket. It got stained when Bailey dragged Kuiper's lifeless body into the undergrowth.

'I think Bailey tried to get a bit too clever,' said Drake. 'He must have been obsessed by his hatred of Kuiper and Bewick and was desperate to make them both suffer. Now I'm going home to do some much-neglected flute practice.'

Two months later, Sergeant Tom Denson opened the door to the case room.

'I have a visitor for you,' he said, smiling. In walked Nimade.

'Hello and welcome,' said Drake, struggling out of his chair.

'I just wanted to come and thank you all for sorting everything out,' said Nimade.

'No need,' said Drake. 'We just do our job but thank you. I'm sure the team are grateful.' Everyone nodded and murmured thanks.

'I have some news,' said Nimade. 'I opened the locker that Bailey had in the shop in Bali. I found the watch that Willem always used to wear. Willem had not changed his will, so it now belongs to me. Of course, it's the last thing I want. I have put it for sale in an international auction. They say it will fetch a great deal of money. It will help put Bali Style on a sound footing, and I am buying a shop in London. I am so angry that Laurence Bailey fooled me. I have made changes to the way things are done and have appointed his replacement. It will not happen again.'

'That's all good to hear,' said Drake. 'Things have not yet reached a trial. When it does, the watch will prove to be a useful piece of evidence. I expect you will be asked to appear as a witness.'

'There's more news,' said Nimade. 'I heard from a good friend who is a policeman I trust. They have found the phone Bailey kept in Bali. They found information that enabled them to arrest a whole string of his mules.' Drake smiled and spoke quietly.

'From what I have heard about the penalties for drug running in Bali, they will not be treated kindly. More importantly, Laurence Bailey will not see freedom for a long time, perhaps the rest of his life.'

A DEGREE OF DEATH
Bryan Lawson

A member of the Singapore Parliament is found murdered on a footbridge in Chester. A DEGREE OF DEATH is a crime novel about the past sneaking up on the present and making a real mess of things. It is September 2005. Murky oriental history is entangled with events at Deva University in Chester, a brand-new institution doing its best to invent tradition. But do these new ivory towers hide more worldly pursuits? What goes on behind the genteel façades in the historic city of Chester?

DCI Carlton Drake is widely recognised for being as clever as he is tall and clumsy. He resumes duties after a sabbatical, taken for personal reasons, to investigate this diplomatically sensitive case. By contrast, his high-flying young assistant Grace Hepple is stylish but inexperienced. Together they uncover an intriguing mystery.

The investigation takes Drake to Singapore where he discovers that the past is never far from the surface in this modern metropolis. Chinese societies, illegal ivory trading, academic jealousy and raw ambition jostle together to create a confusing and dangerous cocktail.

Readers say: -

"Highly recommended"

"The intricacies of the plot keep you absorbed and the conclusion certainly does not disappoint."

"From an ex-policeman…a good thought-provoking thriller."

"I look forward to the next in the series of this detective duo."

WITHOUT TRACE
Bryan Lawson

Lord Richard MacCracken, a minister for the arts in the British Government, disappears during the interval of a performance at Covent Garden. He seems to have vanished without a trace between the two acts of an opera. The nightmare gets darker when the postman delivers a copy of the Royal Opera House programme. It contains death threats and a set of the victim's bloody fingerprints.

DCI Drake and his assistant DS Grace Hepple are called in to recover Lord MacCracken safely and discover who is holding him. The kidnappers have covered their tracks with a web of deception that leads Drake around the world. The sinister and dramatic crimes he uncovers could have come straight from the operatic stage.

Readers say: -

"I really enjoyed it and found it extremely absorbing."

"Another great edition with exciting adventures and drama."

"The plot twisted and turned as a good detective novel should, leading to an unforeseen conclusion...

"...attention to detail in terms of background information from experts brought in to assist the case is incredible."

FATAL PRACTICE
Bryan Lawson

An internationally famous architect, Sir Julian Porter, fails to turn up to the public launch of a series of new landmark buildings for the UK Government. Detective Chief Inspector Drake and his assistant DS Grace Hepple investigate. They begin their work in the historic city of Chester where Porter's architectural practice is located. Drake soon discovers that Sir Julian seems to have made many enemies. Some strangely mutilated bodies become the focus of the investigation. One is in Chester and another on the Malaysian Island of Penang where the practice has a prestigious housing development on the drawing board.

These two murders appear linked but the question is how? The case leads Drake into dangerous water involving organised crime and a mysterious oriental cult.

Readers say: -
"Have just finished it. I enjoyed all the parts in Penang."

"As well as the intriguing mystery, it transports you to
a fascinating part of the world."

"Just finished reading Fatal Practice – very entertaining. Makes me want to visit Penang one day."

"International intrigue and fascinating architectural insights enhance this clever and twisty mystery…"

THE FLAUTIST
Bryan Lawson

The historic city of Chester has just built a new concert hall thanks to the generosity of an anonymous benefactor. A gala concert is arranged to celebrate the opening and an internationally famous flautist, Evinka Whyte who lives locally, has agreed to play. The concert is, however, marred by a dramatically sinister event.

DCI Drake and his assistant DS Grace Hepple are called in to investigate. They soon discover that Evinka Whyte had a confusing and mysterious private life. This is made more complex by the history of her illustrious but secretive family. Drake travels to Prague, that most historic and musical city where the mystery deepens.

Readers say: -
"In Drake and Hepple we have two detectives who can rival the best."

"The best Drake and Hepple mystery so far."

DANGEROUS KNOWLEDGE
Bryan Lawson

The badly mutilated body of a woman floats down the River Dee in Chester and disturbs evening drinkers at a popular pub on the riverbank. Detective Chief Inspector Drake and his sergeant, Grace Hepple, investigate. Their first problem is that it proves almost impossible to identify the victim, and nobody has reported a missing person.

She is identified as a highly successful painter. Her paintings sell well in Chester and the Far East. It is not long before Drake follows in her dangerous footsteps. Drake and Hepple are soon working on a confusing mystery. They discover a world in which they have no experience. It seems art has a dark side. It is run by ruthless crime syndicates working across at least three continents.

Gradually, the victim's tortured personal life begins to emerge. Drake and Hepple also discover a curious quasi-religious sect. It has had a disastrous effect on the victim's life. But has it also had a hand in her death?

Readers say: -
"A captivating tale of international intrigue. Lawson really invokes a genuine sense of place in his locations, be it the local area around Chester, where the majority of the book is set, or the more exotic trip around the streets and countryside of Hong Kong taken by his main character, the very tall and slightly crotchety DCI Drake. This story draws you in as it delves into the world of high art, fraud, and murder."

"Thought this was a really good plot and moved at a really good pace."

Printed in Great Britain
by Amazon